THE HALLS OF MIDNIGHT

THE BOOKS OF CONJURY, VOLUME THREE

KEVAN DALE

KEVAN **DALE** FICTION

1

VIGILANT

Vigilant. Every moment I could, I watched August Swaine, my master. As he worked. As he ate, spoke, listened. Even as he slept. I noted his every gesture and expression, vigilant for signs of early-stage possession. I studied him, alert for any hint of the *Signis Quinque Vilis*—the Five Vile Signs, a measure of demonic infestation drawn from the tales of human wreckage found in the annals of sorcery. While a demon might possess an ordinary person with some rapidity, insinuating its will over the victim in a matter of hours, days, or weeks, possessing a skilled sorcerer required more subtlety, silently weaving the infernal threads past the sorcerer's defenses and awareness over months, or years.

The signs included *Diabolus est Mora* ('the devil's pause'), short interludes of a trance state, unnoticed by the victim. *Oculi Malignus Spiritus* ('eyes of the fiend'), a rapid shifting of the eyes at irregular intervals. *Fuga Speculo* ('mirror flight'), a notable avoidance of mirrors, a frenzy provoked by the sight of one's reflection. *Sepulcrum Lectus* ('grave bed'), a profound sleep from which it is impossible to awaken the victim, also linked with sleep-avoidance. And finally *Conspicio Homicida* ('murderer's gaze'), momentary flashes of murderous rage that cross the victim's face.

So far, I'd seen—or *thought* I'd seen—*Sepulcrum Lectus* and *Diabolus est Mora*. But did more banal explanations, notably Swaine's punishing work hours and chronic illness, explain them with ease? I'd come by the notion that my master was possessed from Inverressayte, a demon who hadn't taken kindly to being tethered to my will. A lying demon, glad to poison any part of my life that mattered. Yet as fraught a source as the demon was, Swaine's behavior of late veered noticeably from his normal meticulous caution. And so I watched him, keeping track, unwavering in my commitment to seeing no one in my life fall prey to a demon ever again.

As he hesitated to answer Doctor Ephraim Rush's question, his lips pulled to a frown, his gaze vague as he stared off into the center of the public room of the Alderbrook Tavern in a quiet corner of Reading, I counted the seconds to myself. The *devil's pause* could be anywhere from twenty-seconds to five minutes in length.

Thirteen. Fourteen. Fifteen. Six—

"I find it rather curious, indeed," Swaine said, snapping out of his reverie.

"Curious?" Rush asked, leaning forward. "Not *alarming*? *Disturbing*? August, perhaps I'm not adequately conveying the depths of my concerns."

We occupied a narrow table in the corner, next to the hearth, where we might talk without being overheard. The room stretched out away from us, a pair of windows letting in mid-afternoon light that gave a warmth to the dark wood of the floor and other tables, empty save for a traveler by the door devouring half a chicken, washing it down with a tankard of beer. With a tuneless whistle, the tavern keeper replaced the nubs of candles in the holders by the windows.

Swaine straightened the cuffs of his shirt. "Your concern is quite appropriate, Ephraim. We can't have demons stalking the townsfolk throughout the eastern half of the province. And there are methods we might employ without drawing undue attention to ourselves."

"The very talk of such events is enough to give our soon-to-be governor the exact cudgel he craves," Rush said. "Such public furor makes his argument for him. The man will do what he can to fan the flames, even as he decries the perils of the spreading conflagration."

"Lionel Sackville is a fool."

"A fool on the threshold of becoming governor. He won't make our task any easier." Rush folded his hands on the table. "Of course, the incidents with the demons I've outlined are only part of our problem, worrisome as they are. Such intrusions are but a symptom of the true threat we face: unprecedented shifts in planar alignment."

"Yes, yes—*plana noctis subcinctus.*"

"I've measured three within the last six months." Rush showed no sign of letting Swaine's dismissive tone ruffle him. "Furthermore, I've made six planar soundings over the last two months, and have recorded readings of, in order: *primum gradum opacare*; *secundo gradu opacare*; *umbra praesumptum*; *primis tenebris*; *surrexerint umbras*; and just last week, *omnis lux solis*. I trust you grasp the implications."

Swaine glanced at me. I kept my focus on Rush, whose readings used Gustav Koeffler's methodology, ranked according to his *Magnifice de Supermundanae Amplitudinem* (Grand Scale of Planar Amplitude), a system of measuring the degree of penetration of planar influence within our world. The readings Rush presented translated as: 'First Degree of Dusk'; 'Second Degree of Dusk'; 'Second Degree Shadow'; 'Shadow Encroachment'; 'First Darkness'; 'Shadow Rise'; and 'Eclipse of All Light'.

"Koeffler made quite a career of expounding on his scale."

"I have sixty-one years of soundings taken from fifteen stable locations around the colony. And yet in all that time, I've only recorded a single shift that exceeded *primum gradum opacare*. Should I expound on that point, sir?"

Swaine sniffed. "The planes shift, and even Koeffler himself recognized that we're somewhere along the cycle between *grand alignments*. Such readings could well mean nothing."

I was surprised at his response. Rigor, exactitude, precision—had Swaine not drilled those principles into my head every day I'd been in his service? That he so cavalierly dismissed what Rush told him was concerning. I watched his eyes.

"And if you're wrong?" Rush regarded him over his spectacles. "I would be more than happy to share the precise readings with you—perhaps you might point out where I've erred."

"I assume your readings are accurate. My issue is both with Koeffler himself and the rather breathless interpretations of his work that have grown to dominate the discussions of planar theory. The Great Man was hardly as troubled by such fluctuations as his followers now claim. Careful study of his earlier writings reveals that he carried doubts—reasonable doubts, given what he'd found. It was only later, when he'd been fawned over for that area of his work, that his views on the matter grow more expansive and detailed. And who can blame him? He was bringing unprecedented respectability to the magickal sciences. If he wanted to make his reputation more all-encompassing—well, he was only human."

"So we've all been beguiled by one man's vanity, is that it?"

"Vanity makes beggars of kings. Why should magicians be any less susceptible?"

"Indeed," Rush said quietly. "Perhaps also sorcerers?"

"Ephraim, is it not possible that we're thinking of all this the wrong way?"

"You're suggesting there's a better way to think of a looming catastrophe?"

"Catastrophe is one risk—yes. If met boldly, on the other hand—might we think of it as a powerful *disruption*?"

"I don't see how the semantics are relevant."

"They very much are. We may have an opportunity on our hands the likes of which hasn't manifested in the civilized world in centuries. Longer. Should we scurry along in the shadows, doing our best to tamp it all down in secret? Keeping our roles hidden out of what—shame? Fear? Habit?" He tapped his index finger on the table. "Or do we seize the disruption of the planes to demonstrate how we might advance civilization? Convince every honest eye of the value of shrugging off the ignorance and superstition that's driven the practice of the unseen arts underground?"

"I'm not sure the citizens of the Crown will be convinced of much advancement as they flee in terror from the unnamed demons laying waste to their homes and towns."

"Demons can be dealt with."

"Half a dozen, perhaps. Yet what if the planes converge further? If the breach widens? Might one hundred demons be dealt with? One thousand? Forgive me, but I remain unconvinced. My obligation— and one might say *our* obligation, if the practice of the unseen arts indeed carries as much weight as you say—is to protect the citizenry, first and foremost. Furthermore, should there be even a one-percent risk of the worst happening, we *must* treat it as though it were a certainty. The stakes are far too high. We can't afford to be wrong."

Swaine rubbed a hand across his eyes. "No, of course—you're right. I suppose hoping for more in the face of the threat is asking a bit much."

"With Sackville in the governor's seat, yes." Rush straightened. "But my duty hasn't ended yet. I've spent five decades as the Royal Doctor of Magickal Sciences for the Province of Massachusetts Bay, invested with the full authority of the Crown, serving fourteen governors and the general council. Any incident, effect, transmission, execution, or perpetration of magic has fallen solely under my responsibility. Even the faintest hint. The laws of the colony are clear in the matter. My commitment to my duty is even clearer, in my heart, as long as it continues to beat. Should His Majesty or Sackville revoke my office—well, even so I will be hard-pressed to relinquish my duty."

"Of course," Swaine said. "I wouldn't imagine otherwise, Ephraim."

In that moment, I thought the two of them understood each other better than I'd hoped. They were, after all, both gentlemen of profound learning. Both accomplished at the highest level of the unseen arts, serious to their cores about their work. Both recognizing the dangers we faced. As Rush outlined his thinking —driving off or capturing the demons, ceasing any unnecessary magic, careful monitoring of planar intensity, tracking appearances of the demonmere, identifying the witches' seals most in danger of failing—my master nodded along, interjecting here and there with probing questions, fully attuned to Rush's concerns. I saw no hint of the Five Vile Signs, only Swaine bringing to bear his full intellect to the problems at hand. The tightness in my chest loosened.

When Rush finished, Swaine nodded. "Finch here can assist with much of this. Catching lesser demons—which I believe to be the majority of what you've described—is something of a specialty. The seals—well, she's better suited to that than either you or I, as I think we'd both agree. For my part, a detailed survey of the forces in and around Salem seems like the best use of time and expertise."

"And an immediate withdrawal from your efforts there," Rush said.

"Without question. For the best."

As the two men developed their plan, I breathed easier than I had in months, all but certain that together we could drive back the shadows. All but certain Inverressayte had lied to me.

2

GLAMOURS AND WARDS

I f my master had proven unexpectedly agreeable to Doctor Rush's plan, I soon realized, it was only because none of it mattered to him—he was utterly distracted by the sorcerium. The strange building in the midst of Salem entirely consumed his thoughts. Having burst from the soil like the prow of an elaborate, peculiar ship to loom over the abandoned buildings nearby, this mysterious expression of the demonmere proved irresistible to Swaine. To outward appearances, it matched all the features of the plans Swaine and Robert Twelves had devised. Three stories in height, with an octagonal base, a gabled second story, and crowned with a domed observatory beneath a tall spire, the only departure from their plans lay in the dimensions: taller than intended, as though designed for humans fifteen feet in height. As with what we'd already seen of the demonmere, the materials defied precise identification. The stone, slate, and wood wore hues of cinder, iron, soot, and midnight. What glass filled the narrow windows warped the light with subtle imperfections. All bore signs of weathering – centuries' worth – yet the surfaces held no grime, dust, or mold.

Stranger still was the interior, which Swaine wasted no time in exploring. Thirteen rooms and four staircases greeted our first inspection. Our second excursion yielded twelve rooms and three staircases. The third time we entered, we were back to thirteen rooms, yet with five staircases, including one that led deeper into the ground, ending in a chamber with two sinister-looking doors of black wood, exhaling frigid wind from their gaps. The arrangement of the rooms remained generally the same, yet the details shifted—it was as though two separate teams of architects and builders had realized Swaine's initial plans. Even more alarming, when we took a series of measurements, we discovered that the interior dimensions exceeded the exterior dimensions by nearly nine feet in one instance, less than three in another, leading Swaine to conclude that the sorcerium existed in some form of planar dislocation, perhaps even in more than one plane simultaneously.

And even that hadn't kept him out of it.

As we rode back from Reading, he'd remained mostly silent, occasionally commenting on some facet of the sorcerium as he worked through his evolving thinking. By the time we returned to Salem, he'd scratched out two full pages of wagon-jarred notes, seeming to have forgotten everything we'd discussed with Rush. I pulled the wagon to a stop by the stable. Before the rocking of the springs stopped, Swaine climbed down, holding his notes in his mouth. Taking them out and brushing the dust from his breeches, he said, "Let's head down there."

I didn't need to ask which *there* he meant. "But, sir—didn't we agree that we'd leave Salem?"

"Hardly."

"You said we'd withdraw our efforts." I climbed down and unhitched the horse.

"I committed to a detailed survey of the planar manifestations here—which is exactly what I'm doing with the sorcerium." He slid his notes into his coat pocket. "As for withdrawing our other efforts—well, there are no other efforts, so we've already done it."

"I'm not sure that's how Doctor Rush would see it, sir."

"Of course it's not. He has his theories. I have mine. The difference is mine haven't gathered the requisite centuries worth of dust and debate. No watered-down consensus has been reached by a dozen solemn doctors of the magickal sciences. I haven't cross-referenced a dozen bland theories to support my arguments."

After unbuckling the last of the horse's tack, I led the tired beast to the trough, where it gratefully drank.

"So you don't believe the danger is as great as the Doctor says?" I said.

"Danger lurks in everything we do, Finch. Think of it clearly for a moment. The very tools we take for granted and use daily are more than capable of taking our lives, are they not? Fire. Axes. Ropes. Your horse might trample you to death. A morsel of beef might choke off all air—should we stop eating? The higher one goes in the pursuit of achievement, the greater the danger. Magic itself has left burial yards full of mistakes. Sorcery? Why, even more, and even more harrowing paths to said burial yards. Yet we bend the danger of blade and spell to our will—ever mindful of the risks, we conquer it to our own ends. As long as we're eternally vigilant with all of it, we shall have all our digits to show." He spread his fingers. "We walk, talk, breathe. Our sanity remains intact. Our will, our own. I'm afraid Doctor Rush is of a more cautious type. Not to invalidate his concerns, mind you— but there will always be those at the vanguard, and those who follow afterwards when the path has been sufficiently beaten and tended. There is room for all sorts—and probably a need for all sorts. Yet I'm of the former temperament, and he of the latter. Listen, we'll get this problem taken care of, working together as much as we might. In the end, I'm not worried for the citizenry of the province. It will all be fine."

I led the horse into the stable, mindful of Swaine's impatience with such mundane chores. When the horse was settled I followed Swaine down the lane. The sorcerium rose between us and the harbor, drawing my eye. Even the manner in which the afternoon light shone on it betrayed its unnatural origin. The shadows were not quite right. Devouring the light so as to maintain a shifting faintness. Queer angles of wall and window. Doors opening as black, mouthless screams. All of it warning the senses that it wasn't of this world, that it was thrust from the shifting and restless realm that lurked between unseen planes.

The sorcerium stirred such unease in me that I ripped my gaze from it, looking instead at the strait and the ocean beyond. As I followed Swaine, it struck me as implausible that I'd really spent my formative years on the other side of the Atlantic. It might have well been a different life, that of a different person. A story I'd read. I bore no solid evidence of it, after all, save for my memories. I'd been a child, had a family, lived in London—and yet none of it had any more substance than the gauzy handfuls of dreams that floated out of mind upon waking each morning. The water stretched out to the horizon, straight as a blade that cut the heavens in half, a blade that had cut my life in half by way of a storming, wave-tossed, miserable voyage along with poor Silas Wilkes.

Since then, I'd often felt that I was more than one person. Seen and unseen by all who crossed my path. Sometimes an apprentice, other times a mentor. A witch, a sorcerer. Truthful, or deceiving, depending upon the day, or the hour. Dutiful in most matters, deliberately disobedient in others. The ease with which I switched from one face to another was shameful, yet not so shameful that I didn't do it. Were anyone to put the pieces together, they would see me for the fraud I was, I believed—for I was all of these things, which I assumed that in a profound way meant I was none of them.

Swaine startled me from my thoughts as we neared the main doors, a fresh path already marking our comings and goings. "Caution is the key, Finch—and I think I've come up with a strategy. Strange that the ride back from our meeting was more fruitful than the meeting itself." He paused, motioning to the sorcerium now looming over us. "To maximize our safety, I propose a complex arrangement of glamours and wards."

I could practically hear Doctor Rush's retort: *To maximize your safety, don't set as much as a foot inside it—in fact, leave the area as quickly as you can.* I said nothing. Swaine crossed over the threshold, between the two massive doors and into the shaded interior. I followed. Gooseflesh danced along the back of my neck as I passed inside after him.

He took the folded paper from his pocket. "Thirty-seven glamours and wards, to be attached to walls and flooring. Most can be keyed to small iron, silver, or copper ingots. I'll have Twelves devise mounting plates. Fashioned out of brass, I should think."

The entryway ran for half a dozen feet before reaching a set of three descending steps, where the large octagonal space opened. Smooth stone covered the floor. The windows let in a warped view of Salem. What sunlight fell in appeared uneven, thicker and thinner in spots, like sheets of melted wax. Two curving stairways ran along opposite sides of the large space, detailed with intricate ironwork railings bearing a vine motif, unchanged since our last visit.

"It will require painstaking precision," Swaine continued. "The effects will need to overlap, giving us the greatest coverage. Once installed, however, we can entrain them to twins back in at the manse. Securing the various rooms from intrusion, infernal or otherwise. Providing us notice of a breach. Or even a change in dimensions or configuration. It will require maintenance, no doubt, to account for shifts—but if done properly, there won't be a single cubic inch within the sorcerium not layered over twice, or even thrice, with protections."

He headed to the left-hand set of stairs.

"Will glamours work in here, sir?" I asked, following.

"If anything, I'd expect them to be more powerful than designed, given what we've seen so far."

What Swaine referenced were several instances of magic not behaving properly within the walls of the sorcerium. A simple fire spell emitting a wall of flame instead of igniting a wick. Illumination spells proving to be glaring—though in one case, the light manifested as shadow. As a result of these and other unexpected intensities of spells, we'd limited any such attempts. At the top of the stairs, we reached the summoning chambers. Four smaller rooms occupied the corners, while the center of the floor was reserved for the grand summoning chamber: Swaine's masterwork, the heart of the sorcerium.

He waved the paper in his hand. "The breakthrough I'd been looking for."

"Sir?"

"The glamours and wards I've already told you about shall be standard—but of course we wouldn't want that for the work that will go on here." He stepped into the wide space, open on four sides by arches of stone rising into the gloom. A circle of inlaid metal, silver but not quite, ran twenty feet in diameter, filling the floor. An intricate pattern of lines and glyphs subdivided the circle, some scribed into the floor, others inlaid like the border. "The most powerful glamours and wards for this. Nothing less will do if we're to harness the massive planar energies converging on this one point of focus. But at the same time, they need to be flexible—for such energies, as dear Doctor Rush reminded us, are wily, prone to changing in amplitude and intensity without warning. Static glamours won't do. My idea: we will create custom glamours for the grand chamber that can be activated and fine-tuned through a series of dials and levers tapping into as many frequencies as we can identify, allowing for the creation of a massive *countervalence* capable of being tuned exactly as needed."

"Countervalence, sir?"

"Modelled after what is known as a *Graves Countervalence*, to be specific. Benjamin Graves of Hull discovered the principle last century. It involves *diaglamourism*, that is, the tendency of a magicked substance to counter a correlated glamour field by repulsing it. By tuning the various layered glamours involved to a specific set of valences measured in the planar energies, a massive field of magic can be generated – one that can theoretically withstand even the most potent planar disruptions that we might encounter. Or inadvertently cause one. Do you understand?"

"I think so." As with most of what my master said when focused on his work, his logic and ability to skip ahead by three or four orders of ramification left no doubt as to his genius. It was rare to find a person with an original vision; rarer still to find one with the skills, knowledge, and wherewithal to execute such vision. "Might it impact the witches' seals, sir?"

"I see the good Doctor has rubbed off on you, Finch." He paced the inside circumference of the circle, rereading his notes. "And no, I see no reasons why it would. Now, you may well ask if such control over the planar energies in this spot might serve an additional—and far more intriguing—purpose. What say you?"

"Time, sir—as Bostram suggested?"

"Ha, yes—well done, Finch! Time. Such intense levels of energies as are generated by the collision of planes here in the demonmere—of which this is clearly an extension—that with the proper control and calibration—such as with exactly the mechanisms I've described, limiting, guiding, shaping these enormous currents—we might not merely attenuate, but focus. And in doing so, given what we've seen with the temporal displacements of our prior experiments, we'll be able to claim time itself as a commodity—an ingredient at our constant disposal. If we could reduce the time required for a summoning to a tenth—a hundredth—of what we've known... think of it! Spells of complexity that might normally require months of incantation—done in hours. The horizon of what's possible extends well beyond our ken. Who could then argue against such utility to humanity?" He lowered the paper. "All from here, this one point of focus—do you understand?"

"I think so, sir. Yes."

In truth, I paid less attention to my master's theory than his manner, once again measuring his behavior against the signs of possession. His speech was rapid—though I'd seen it so often enough when he'd had too much tea, or too little sleep. Leaping from one idea to the next, in the throes of a breakthrough, it wasn't unusual. Grandiose thoughts? This was August Swaine, after all—his aim stayed true at the apex of achievement, nothing less. His demeanor was perhaps a more intense version of the man I'd come to know since the prior summer, but his eyes were clear, his talk steady, his manner quite in keeping with his natural enthusiasm. Of the Five Vile Signs, I saw none, despite the unease I felt as he strode across the location of the grand summoning chamber, laying out his vision.

"Now," Swaine said. "Supplies. Let's find Twelves, start putting a list together. Mechanisms. Levers. Brass, silver—well, we'll need more of everything. Including coin to pay for it all, eventually."

As I trailed after Swaine, collecting and organizing the growing list of materials he tossed off his tongue, my fears of his possession dwindled further. Yet given that he'd entirely ignored Doctor Rush's warnings as we wandered rather casually through the massive building manifested by and from the demonmere as though it were simply an extension of his workshop—perhaps the fears I'd entertained should have been heeded.

3

THE TIDES OF DREAMS

S waine sent me back to the house in Andover the next morning to fetch a vial of rather expensive realgar crystals —also known as *ruby of arsenic*—he was certain had been misplaced during the move back to Salem. His tone suggested that the oversight rested on my shoulders. I held my tongue: he'd been the one to organize the packing of his workbench, implying at the time there was an optimal way to do so to which he alone knew. Still, I didn't mind the ride westward, for it both gave me time to clear my head and to check in on yet another worry.

In Andover, I skirted the fork that led to the house, diverting instead to a narrower path through a wooded stretch of ridges, low oval hillocks shaded by birch and pine, granite faces wearing splashes of lichen. Warm wind shifted the boughs overhead. A hawk cried out from her perch and flew off in a swoop of brown and white feathers to glide between the trunks. Where the path curved, a cabin sat fifty yards from the shore of a pond whose bronze-green water reflected the far tree line. Faded pine needles littered the slouching roof. The place gave off the impression of slowly sinking back into the earth, as might a boulder or a fallen tree. I was glad to see that smoke rose from the cabin's chimney.

Tying my horse to the hitching post out front, I approached the door and knocked loudly. "Hello? May I come in? It's Katie." Before I could repeat my knock and call out again with higher volume, the door opened. Clara looked out at me, relief washing away a wary narrowing of her eyes.

"Miss Finch," she said. "Thank goodness. I saw the horse and grew frightened. I ran back inside."

She looked healthier than when I'd rescued her from the demonmere. Her cheeks, grown gaunt, had filled back out. Her color looked right, no longer dreadfully pale. Only her eyes remained haunted. And who could blame her? Months alone in the demonmere, lost and terrified. Most peculiar of all, she'd emerged clear of demons and free of lingering planar magic, to all appearances unscathed—save for having lost nearly a decade in age. Nineteen on the night of General John Whitelocke's death, she seemed to be no older than ten years old when I'd found her. Nor was it simply a physical phenomenon, a biological reversal of age; her mind and emotions had regressed, at least appropriate to her physical appearance. I'd begun to think even further than ten, perhaps eight, maybe younger still. Her memories of time prior to the demonmere remained, though they appeared to be filtered through the perceptions of a child. She'd used a pistol, *but pistols were scary*. Francis had become *that man with all the nice words*. Rattlesnakes weren't *really snakes, but naughty lads causing mischief*. And so on.

As for her family proper, I don't think she had one. She certainly didn't have one she wanted to talk about, growing stubborn and silent with an almost comical frown when pressed about the matter. In the absence of any better ideas, I'd watched over her when I could, seeing to it that she was taken care of when I wasn't available. I'd brought her a pair of dresses, which she'd clumsily hemmed—and the rest was up to Ignatius Nagle.

"Is that him? He's been gone a right bit. Not like him." The voice of Bertram's grandfather had the quality of a goose with a head-cold and a waver that coincided with the tremors of his head.

"No, Mr. Nagle," I said, raising my voice to counter his near-deafness. "It's me. Katie Finch."

I stepped past Clara. Ignatius sat on a hard-backed chair cushioned with threadbare blankets by the hearth. His rheumy eyes, pale blue, didn't miss much—though more often than not, his memory did. Still, he stayed cheerful enough, the same trait I saw in Bertram. His white hair hung down to his collar and the whiskers on his face made up, in their unruly plenty, for the scarcity of hair at the top of his head. Blue veins showed clearly on the backs of his hands and his teeth had largely deserted his mouth.

He stared at me for a moment. "Well you're a sight prettier than Bertram, no offense to the lad. Speaking of—have you seen him? He's been gone a right bit. Not like him."

"I'm sure he's fine, Mr. Nagle."

"He's what?"

Louder. "I'm sure he's fine, Mr. Nagle."

"Oh, aye. Smart enough once he gets out of his own way. Helping his sister, in all likelihood. A good lad. Keep them all busy, I say. Keeps them honest." He nodded agreeably.

I cringed, thinking of poor Iris and her children, innocent victims of the demon tormenting me. In the chaotic aftermath of rescuing Clara, I'd scrambled to buy time, to keep the chaos engulfing my life from spilling out into public knowledge. With no better solution presenting itself, I'd taken the bodies of Iris and her children out into the nearby woods, under cover of darkness, burying them in a shallow grave. Hanging a hastily written note at both doors to the tavern announcing the establishment closed for the fortnight while Iris went to see kin, I'd delayed the inevitable. Further, I'd given myself memories that haunted my nights forever after: covering Iris' pale face with shrubs and soil, her arms wrapped around her beloved children. Guilt and despair threatened to break me, but I held on, vengeance my lifeline.

"I'm sure he is," I said.

"Who is?" Ignatius said.

"Bertram. Helping his sister."

"Course he is. Keeps him busy, I say. Keeps him honest." He folded his gnarled hands in his lap. "But you might tell the lad to come round. Not like him to be gone such a bit. Not like him."

"I will, sir. I promise. And thank you for watching over Clara here."

"Who?"

I put my hand on Clara's shoulder. She flinched. "Clara."

"Oh, her," Ignatius said. "It's lovely to have her around. Keeps my blankets folded. Keep the soup warm." He turned to her. "Thank you, Iris."

"He thinks I'm his grand-daughter," Clara whispered. "I tell him I'm not. He forgets."

"I'm going to speak with Clara for a moment, sir," I said, keeping my voice loud.

"Who?"

"Clara. Right here."

"*Clara*, you say? Oh, I see. You're quite welcome here, Clara." He smiled.

To her credit, Clara curtseyed and thanked him, certainly not for the first time. Before we could get caught in any more of Ignatius' backtracking, I took Clara by the hand and led her outside. Birdsong filled the morning in the deep woods all around. "How are you getting on?" I said.

She crossed her thin arms. "He's nice. Even when he repeats himself. Which he does a lot. But I'm frightened. I don't want to sleep."

"You don't want to sleep?"

"The nightmares. Horrible nightmares, every night." She squeezed her eyes shut as though she might keep out the very memory of her dreams. "That I'm back—in there. That if I dream too much, I'll fall back in. Through my dream."

I leaned over, resting my hands on her upper arms. "Listen to me. You're not going to slip back in there—not from a dream."

"But they're terrible."

"I believe you. Terrible dreams are terrible things—but they're just dreams. You're safe. You always wear the pendant I gave you?"

She touched the space between her collarbones, where the pendant rested beneath her dress. "Yes."

"Then you're safe. Nothing is going to hurt you."

"But I want to stay with you. Please. Take me with you. I'll clean. I'll sweep. I can sleep like a mouse curled up by your feet and you won't even know I'm there. Please."

"You're safer here than where I stay—trust me."

"I don't even need to sleep on your bed. I could sleep by the foot of it. I won't make a sound, I promise." Tears quivered in the corners of her eyes. "Please."

I wrapped her in my arms, holding tight. "You're safe. I promise. I won't let anything happen to you." Had I thought the same of Iris and her children? Of Silas Wilkes and the other unfortunate masters? My own family? I may have—but I'd learned the hardest lessons of all at the hands of the demon.

Still, I wasn't a frightened lass anymore.

For another few moments, I held Clara, then pulled back and straightened. "Come—I brought supplies for you."

She wiped her eyes and followed me to my horse. I pulled a sack out of a saddlebag and handed it to her. "Two jars of jam. One of honey. Biscuits. A rasher of bacon. Garden peas. Six sausages. And a fresh nightgown. Maybe some of that can help you stay brave."

"Jam?"

"Blackberry and strawberry. From last fall. They're both delicious."

She hefted the sack, uncertain.

"Remember," I said. "Stay out of sight—but don't worry about your dreams. Sleep as much as you can. Watch over Ignatius. I'll be back soon, with more help. You're doing a lot. You're very strong, Clara. You know how to look after yourself – you've proven it already. You can do this."

"I'll try." Her voice didn't convey confidence.

"You will. We girls shall stick together, won't we? We're stronger than even we think." Maybe I was giving myself just as much encouragement as I was giving her.

"I don't feel strong."

"We don't have to *feel* strong—we just have to *be* strong. We will be, both of us. Promise?"

She looked me in the eye, searching. "I promise."

"Good. I promise, too."

Soon after, I rode out of the deep woods, two more promises to keep.

At the Andover house, I found the vial of realgar crystals still in its stand, a lone sentinel watching over the empty workbench. "Not my fault," I said, relieved. I made a quick tour of the by-then largely empty house, satisfied that we hadn't left anything else important behind. The mice had made the same circuit, I saw, taking a few minutes to sweep up the droppings scattered about. Locking the house behind me, I watered the horse and started back on the ride to Salem.

The heat of the day spoke of the summer to come. On those stretches of road barren of shade, I squinted, feeling the sweat gather on my neck and back. The marshes I passed hummed with insects. A few times, I detoured off the road when I spotted other riders, leading the horse through thickets and stands of woods—soldiers or not, I wanted to minimize any talk of a one-eyed lass out and about on the lanes by herself. Such other travelers grew infrequent as I neared the edges of Salem, where I soon passed the weathered signs forbidding further travel. The lane I took faded to little more than a memory, an overgrown hint of passage winding through warm meadows, tumbled stone walls, silent trees. Noon approached as I neared the manse. Beyond, the dark of the sorcerium mocked the cloudless spring day, the sight of it bringing the tension back to my shoulders and stomach.

By the rusted iron gate leading up to the manse, I slowed the horse, patting his flank. "You did well." I almost missed the revenant seated with its back to the broad gray trunk of a chestnut tree a stone's toss from the gate. Getting a peek at a worn dress, I realized it was the female revenant whom I loathed. No amount of hints or, eventually, actual requests had convinced Swaine to heed my suggestion that we dispose of her. He remained convinced in some infuriating fashion that my unease with the demon or the corpse that contained it was no more than a reflection of my age and gender, the insecurities of a young woman.

"What on earth are you doing here? Back to the house." I touched the key I now wore on a bracelet, the key that gave me basic control over any revenant under Swaine's thrall. She stared at me, her pale eyes unblinking above high cheekbones, narrow chin, pale skin. In the sunlight, her hair revealed hints of copper.

"You're not safe," she croaked.

"Oh, shut up. What are you doing out here? Answer me."

"The shadows have passed over him."

"That's enough out of you. Get up." I motioned. "Back to the manse."

The revenant made a face of profound sorrow. "You've become so used to the shadows that you ignore them. Pretend they're not there. You tell yourself there's nothing wrong—but there is."

I pointed to her. "Get up. Right now."

There was only so long a demon could refuse a clear

command, so the revenant got to her feet. The dress she wore had gone threadbare at the cuffs and hem, the charcoal color faded, a tear at one shoulder. She stood the same height as me. Robert Twelves had recently remarked that we looked like sisters, an observation I found horrifying. I'd had enough on my mind already and didn't take kindly to being compared to a corpse. He'd gone no further with that line of conversation—which was, I suppose, progress in his dealings with the fairer sex.

"You won't find answers until you look in the right places," the revenant whispered. "Look for what he's written."

"What are you on about?"

"You'll see what he has planned for you—his true plan."

"Yes, well that's dire sounding. How will I ever sleep again? Here's an idea: the next time you feel the need to speak yet another lie—don't. In fact, don't speak at all. Starting now. For the next week. Not a single word."

Her mouth—which was about to release another fabrication designed to ignite my paranoia—closed. As useful as the revenants were, and as much of a stroke of genius it had been for Swaine to conceive of his method of binding multitudes of demons, I sometimes wished that he'd never succeeded. It wasn't just the peculiar difficulties of procuring and readying corpses for the process—though that had its own challenges. No, it was that a demon within a human frame had more access to the emotions of an observer than a demon in either its true form, or as a discorporate voice in the ear, a scrawl of writing on a page, or any of the methods of demonic communication that involved mechanics, transposition, or less intimate avenues of contact.

The revenant stared at me with widened eyes, and all of the instincts within me were wrong: she looked sad, she had something important to tell me. It was all a ruse. She wasn't even a *she*. She was an *it*. Those thoughts that sometimes passed my mind— *who had she been in life, had those lips ever kissed a lover, what had she been like as a child, as a babe?*—were not only pointless, they were dangerous. They kept my attention away from the only thing that mattered: this was a demon, and no demon was ever tamed, only bound. The appearance of humanity held a powerful potential to compromise caution.

I waved it along. "Back to the manse. And never stray so far again unless bidden."

She continued to stare at me, but walked. As she stepped aside, something caught my eye. On the ground next to where she'd sat was a book.

"Who told you to—" My words stopped short. It was the *Occultatum Ostium.* "What were you doing with that?"

More miserable frowning. She pointed to her mouth.

I sighed. "Fine. Speak—and I only want to hear answers. You can save the rest. Now why is this here?"

"It rides the tides of dreams," she said.

"I said no riddles." My temper flared, and I wanted to immo-late her with a wall of flame cast from my palms. "Did you take this out of your master's cabinet?"

"It took me."

"You're forbidden."

"It bid me."

I held up a frustrated hand. "Stop. No more. You will answer either *yes* or *no*. One word, and only the *truth*." I grasped the key. "Do you understand?"

"Yes."

"Did you remove this from the cabinet it is kept in?"

"No."

"But it came to you?"

"Yes."

"In the manse?"

"Yes."

"Where you were, beneath the stairs?"

"No."

"But it appeared before you?"

"Yes."

"Did it call you? Alert you to its presence?"

"No."

I waved a hand in dismissal. Did it even matter? The book was strange. The demon was strange. Untangling one from the other mattered less than getting the book back. I needed to tell Swaine. It was his book and his demon—and therefore his problem, not mine. As I stared at the worn book nestled atop tarnished pine needles, I guessed my master wouldn't take such news well. I might receive the blame, though I'd done nothing to earn an ounce of it. Worse, the idea that the world's most infamous book of sorcery might be growing restless in his possession would fester in his mind.

I swung down from the horse and picked up the book, keeping its frayed bindings together. As before, it was a strange weight—heavier than its dimensions would suggest. The magic about it prickled my skin and sent a quiver along my spine.

I pointed at the revenant. "Go, right this instant. Don't stop until you're back beneath the stairs. Now."

She—it, I reminded myself—said, "It shines like a lighthouse over the night sea."

"Go. And silence."

Unable to resist the command any further, the revenant turned and trudged off through the trees, her faded dress moving like a leftover blot of midnight. I examined the cover of the book as her steps faded. It seemed an ancient relic, like the desert pyramids, or wood from the crucifix of Christ. How many hours had my master spent poring over this book? Weeks, months, if it were all added up. *Depths of meaning. Layers and levels. I always find more, you see,* Swaine had remarked.

What would I find if I opened it again?

"No," I said aloud, my voice a small thing.

The urge wrapped around my thoughts, tempting and irresistible. I shook my head as if to clear it, looking instead at the meadow on the other side of the lane where swaths of black-eyed Susans, cardinal flowers, and blue lobelia swayed amongst the tall Indian grass. I glanced back down at the book in my hands. Hadn't it shown me valuable images before? Might it answer the questions about Swaine that gnawed at me? *You won't find answers until you look in the right places. Look for what he's written.* How could that *not* dare me to crack open the covers of the book in the hopes of finding answers?

My fingers almost flipped open the book of their own accord.

"No," I repeated, louder this time. I tucked the book under my arm and walked back to the horse, slipping the book into one of the saddlebags so that I didn't even have to touch it. Resting my hands on the saddle before climbing on, the urge became irresistible: fetch the book back from the saddlebag, step over to the woods where I wouldn't be seen, pore over all the secrets the book might show me.

It rides the tides of dreams. It shines like a lighthouse over the night sea.

All I wanted were clear answers—and all the book offered were answers. I shook my head, banishing the thought. Just behind the overpowering desire to see what the book might show me was another thought to tickle my paranoia: the book had *wanted* me to look in it. The revenant certainly hadn't wandered out on her own to investigate the peculiar blank pages. It hadn't been for Swaine himself to stumble upon, nor for Twelves, for any reason I might fathom. No, it was for me—after all, it'd happened once before. The thought sat uneasily in my mind.

Whatever my misgivings, I decided to bring the book directly to Swaine. However high the flames of his fury might reach, it seemed the safest course of action. Imagine my surprise, then, when he waved me to put the book on his writing desk while he continued to notate a page filled with a hand-drawn diagram of some device or another. "Just leave it there. I'll put it away later."

I paused, not sure he'd heard me. "It's—it's the *Occultatum Ostium*, sir."

"Yes, so you said." He pointed with the quill in his hand. "It will be fine right there." He dipped the nib of the quill in ink, and continued writing.

I placed the book in the spot he'd indicated, glad to have it free of my grip. "But how might a revenant have gotten it, sir?"

"It's hardly a normal book. I'm frankly surprised it hasn't happened before." He held a place open in one book, frowning as he read, then scratched another note onto his diagram. After a minute, he paused, straightening. "Is there anything else?"

"No. No, sir." I was still waiting for the blow to strike. "Only I was thinking of riding into Boston in the morning to see if the proper silver has arrived for the countervalence work."

"That's fine. You might ask after the Hamburg shipment as well."

"Yes, of course."

He rifled through a pile of papers. "And bring back something from one of the bakeries. Tarts, or something suitably delectable. A reward for the work ahead of me."

It had gone far too easily. I eyed the book, then my master. "I'll see if they have the blackberry ones you like."

"Marvelous." He continued with his work, as though I'd vanished from his concentration.

I left the room, more shocked than grateful.

4

UNDESIRED COUNTENANCE

B oston hummed as much as ever, regardless of who occupied the governor's manse. Flags snapped on harbor gusts carrying the scent of low tide. The piers cleared of fishing boats at dawn, the catch returning later, hauled off in woven baskets and tubs. Carriages clattered down the roads, drivers navigating the ruts with rein and crop. Tobacconists, hatters and booksellers all drew in customers, coin flowing in all directions. A lone rider such as myself might have passed unnoticed amidst the bustle—but, even so, I kept myself disguised, using a variant of the magician Chester Trembley's *Undesired Countenance*, wary of the soldiers and constables now under the authority of Lionel Sackville, Earl of Middlesex and the newly appointed Royal Governor. I wore the most muted clothes I owned, gray and faded black, and a battered tricorn that once accompanied one of the corpse deliveries from the previous fall. The spell would bring about discomfort in any casual observer. Whatever they found most unpleasant to observe—any appearance that might trigger shame, guilt, fear, or revulsion—would spring into their hearts as they gazed on me. The effect was noteworthy. Used to being stared at (a one-eyed young woman on horseback drew a fair amount of attention, I may attest), I noted every pair of eyes turn away after a split-second of intense scrutiny.

Yet even with the spell in place, I stayed off the main roads of the city, making my way along the lanes back from the waterfront. Every so often, I stopped and pulled a small glamoured compass out of my pocket. The needle wavered, leading me generally northward, its movements more rapid as I neared the target. Skirting the eastern side of Mill Pond, wrinkling my nose at the mixture of marshy stink, privy waste, and other filth dumped into the brackish waters, I eyed the grist mill atop a small rise. At the foot of the hill was one of the city's rope-walks, a thousand foot long covered path where the ropes needed for ships were assembled and wound. Workers called back and forth as they concentrated on the task, shaded from the sun beneath canvas awning. I checked the compass again, feeling the tug of the spell wanting to drag the small device out of my grip.

They were in the grist mill. Four giant sails, cloth and lattice-work affairs, turned slowly with the wind. I led my horse off to the nearby grazing field and walked through the tall grass to the back of the mill. Shadows of the sails swept over me. A wide door set at the height of a wagon bed opened into a yard marked by wheel and hoof. A fine layer of grain-dust showed footprints and streaks from sacks and boxes dragged across the wooden loading dock. From within came the sound of millstones turning, grinding wheat or corn into flour. I didn't even need to look at the compass to feel its pull through my clothes.

Putting my hands on the wooden dock, I lifted myself up and stepped into the interior. The walls themselves vibrated with the turning of the spur-wheel and the shafts, upright and horizontal, which turned the stones. A miller in a dusty apron looked up from a bin on a scale, shock registering on his face. He staggered back.

"I know they're here," I said. I held up my hand in a calming gesture. "I'm a friend."

The miller gaped, knocking over a trio of wooden hoes as he tried to flee.

Then I remembered. I passed my right hand counter-clockwise before my face, muttering the couplet to release the *Undesired Countenance.* I'm afraid the sundering of the spell did little to set the miller at ease. He turned as pale as the apron he wore.

"God's wounds, Finch—why not just fly in on a fiery broomstick?" came a voice. "You've scared poor Arthur here to death."

Grayson Whitelocke sat on a small barrel off in the corner, his legs stretched out in front of him, a tin cup of steaming tea in his hands. He looked worse for the wear since the last time I'd seen him, but at least he was alive. Bertram Nagle lifted his head from the stack of crates he'd hidden behind. From overhead, Francis Knox clicked his tongue as he lowered the end of the musket pointed at me. He stood on a narrow catwalk that led to the gearing coming in from the mill's sails.

"Don't worry about Arthur," he said. "I almost shot you."

"Good thing you're not a trained officer in the Governor's Own Regiment. Quick reflexes, dead aim, steely eye, all that," Grayson said.

Bertram stood, brushing the grain-dust from his breeches. "I told you she'd find us."

"Every quarter of an hour or so, yes," Grayson said.

"I see you're all getting along about as well as I'd expected," I said.

Grayson shrugged. "Let's just say that if one is to be dragged about the city, this cellar to that, baker to printer to warehouse to grist-mill—these two aren't the ones you want to do it with."

Francis started down the stairs that wound along the inside of the mill. "Next time I'll make sure to have gilded carriages, footmen, roast pheasant, and fine liqueur in all the appropriate quantities, Major Whitelocke, sir. What a dreadful trial this must have been for you, sir."

"Oh, go on," Grayson said. "I never tire of your sarcasm."

"Better than a jail cell is all I'll say," Bertram said. "How did you find us, Katie?"

Grayson held up his hand. "How do you think, Bertram? What are we all wearing, given to us by dear Katie?"

"Oh. The rings."

"Yes, the rings. Well done."

"That's more of a private conversation," I offered, nodding toward Arthur, who remained silent.

"Says the woman who just burst into the mill looking like a frightful hag, only to wave her hand about and transform into a somewhat less frightful young lady," Grayson said.

"He's fine," Francis said. He leaned the musket in the corner by the bottom of the stairs. "He's a good friend."

"She looked like a Regular—a big brute of one, no offense, Major," Bertram said.

"Brutes are our specialty, no offense taken."

"They obviously haven't found you, in any event," I said. "That's good."

"They haven't found us *yet*," Grayson said. He finished off his tea and put the mug aside. "By barest luck, I'll wager."

"It's not luck that I know the city better than they do," Francis said.

"As I was saying," Grayson said.

"Such cheerful optimism has truly sustained us," Francis said. He turned to me. "What about you?"

"I found Clara," I said. "She's fine. Changed, but fine."

"Thank God. I'll hand it to you—you kept your word. Where is she?"

"I'm keeping her safe for the time being. There were some—complications. It's not safe to bring her down here yet. In fact, I want Bertram to come back with me, to help watch over her."

"Me?" Bertram said.

"She's with your grandfather."

He frowned. "I hope he's not boring her with his stories. Over and over. And Clara is who exactly?"

"Another friend of mine," Francis said.

"So a Rattlesnake," Grayson said.

"With my granddad?"

I laid a hand on Bertram's arm. "He's fine. She's not dangerous. No one's looking for her. I promise." I turned to the others. "That said—there are plenty of people looking for you."

"Hence our questionable accommodations," Grayson muttered.

"And I need them to *keep* looking for you," I said.

"Beg pardon?"

"Because if they keep looking for you, they won't be looking for Doctor Rush and me. And we need time. Unobserved. Unbothered. Unseen."

"Go on."

"There are locations across the eastern half of the colony where our unwanted friends from the other side are slipping in—"

"Just ask my late father," Grayson said.

"—that require our attention. Our urgent attention. If we can't close these off, they'll weaken further, letting in more unwanted friends. With some possibility that it spirals entirely out of control."

"How out of control?" Bertram said, his face already wincing.

"Worse than what happened in the jail. Worse than what happened in Salem. Much worse."

"You're frightening Arthur again," Grayson said.

Francis crossed his arms. "Let her finish."

"If I must," Grayson said. "Though surely you don't need it spelled out, no pun intended. You see where all this is headed? *We're* the bait, forgive my bluntness. A distraction. We toddle about, keeping Sackville's men occupied while Miss Finch and Doctor Rush attempt to stop what they haven't been able to so far."

"I can think of plenty of ways to distract them," Francis said.

"And I can think of plenty of ways to get caught—which, I might add, is precisely what you managed to do whilst engaged in your heroic and confident distractions less than a fortnight ago. You do recall your jail cell, don't you?"

"I'm not in a jail cell now."

"Thanks to Finch here." Grayson raised his hands to me. "Do you see what I'm dealing with? The man positively refuses to abandon the wish to have his proclamations written down for posterity, no matter how unmoored to reality they are."

"What does a Whitelocke know about reality?" Francis said.

Grayson spun on Francis. "Says a printer's apprentice who fancies himself Robin Hood."

"Says the pampered son of wealth and political power who didn't personally do much more to grow prosperity beyond spreading coin across the insides of most of the city's taverns," Francis said.

They faced each other with chests out, chins level.

"Nothing wrong with embracing good cheer," Grayson said. "At least I never embraced murder, you hypocritical shit."

"You don't know what you're talking about."

"Tell that to my brother lying dead in his coffin, Rattlesnake."

Bertram raised a hand. "I'm not sure any of those demons care much about any of that, begging your pardons."

"Bertram's right." I stepped between Grayson and Francis, putting a hand on each chest and pushing them apart. Neither one wanted to back off, so I shoved them both back on their heels. "None of that matters."

"Easy for you to say," Grayson said.

"There's no time for blame for anything that happened before," I said. "Think about what happened to your father instead. *That's* what we're facing. All of us. Everyone outside of this mill. Everyone. You're not stupid, Grayson—you see it."

He turned away from me. "Fine. Right as usual, Miss Finch."

Francis nodded. "Never thought I'd hear—"

I turned to him. "And you need to learn to hold your tongue. And your preening."

"Excuse me, but—"

"No. Enough. I kept my promise to you. Clara is safe. You owe me and you're going to do what it takes to keep Sackville's men busy. You and Grayson. Together. He knows how the regulars and officers think. You know how to get about without getting caught —for the most part."

"So you're taking his side," Francis said.

"I'm not taking *anyone's* side. Good Lord. The two of you. Leave it be. I can't think of any other way to do this but to trust you. Both of you. Not that either of you has inspired me to trust you completely—but I'm out of better choices. I've seen what can happen if we can't fix this, and it's worse than you can imagine. This isn't a joke, or a competition, or a theory, or a cause. This is about survival. *All* our survival. Do you understand?"

They both stood there, each refusing to look at each other, like unruly children scolded by their nanny. As if I hadn't enough other worries on my mind.

"Now," I began, bringing my voice back down to a normal volume. I slipped a rough map I'd drawn of the towns surrounding Boston, stretching up to Salem. Across it, I'd marked the area into five sections, numbered. It showed none of the seals—in case they were captured and the map found. "We're going to start up here." I tapped the section numbered '1'. "Therefore, you keep the attention anywhere *but* there. The farther away, the better. We're going to alternate. When we finish with '1', we're going to '5'. Then '2', '4', and saving '3' for last. That's Boston itself—which will be the most difficult. Do you see the pattern?"

Grayson took the map. "Why even Francis here can count all the way to five."

"Stop it," I said. "Everything I said to him applies to you."

"Couldn't help myself."

"Learn to."

Francis leaned over my shoulder, peering at the map. "How long will it take? Each section, I mean."

"I'm not sure. I'll have to find way to get word to you."

"How will you find us?" Francis said.

Grayson held his hand up. "Rings."

"Ah. Of course."

"We're going to start soon," I said. "Within days, I hope. I also need to speak with Mary."

"Whatever for?" Grayson said.

"Because she can keep Sackville distracted in other ways."

"He's married, probably to a nun."

"Not that way. But she can work her magic on the social circuit. Rumors. Insinuations. Chatter. Enough to make him realize that taming Boston isn't the same as whispering in His Majesty's ear. Anything to keep him from getting too comfortable too quickly."

"If anyone can poison a well quickly, it's my sister." Grayson handed the map to Francis. "Word is that Sackville is being sworn in tomorrow morning. I'm sure Mary will be there—he wouldn't have dared clap her in chains. I'm sure she's being watched, but that might be your best chance to speak with her—as long as you replicate that hideous appearance you did when you came here."

I nodded. How was I going to find another excuse to get back to Boston? One problem at a time. "I'll figure something out. As far as the distractions go, only bring in people you trust. *Really* trust. We can't risk anyone turning on us."

"Francis knows people," Grayson said. "As he's reminded us more than once. Believe it or not, so do I. A few, anyways."

"Good," I said. "Be careful. Both of you."

Bertram stared hard at the map, his arms crossed to the point where he appeared to be hugging himself. "Both? What about me, Katie?"

"You're coming with me." I took him by the sleeve. "I've another job for you."

"Is it—not that I—well—"

"Spit it out, lad," Grayson said.

Bertram flushed under the stare of Grayson and Francis both. "Not that I'm afraid of danger—but I'm not quite as fast as these gentlemen—nor as trained, if you see what I'm getting at."

"You ducked behind those crates faster than a rabbit," Grayson said.

"I'm quick at hiding, to be sure."

"It's just as important," I told him, not letting go of his sleeve. "And possibly as dangerous. Or more. I'll tell you all the details as we ride north."

"But—I'm not staying with them?"

"Try to contain your disappointment," Grayson said.

"No. And if we're lucky, their influence hasn't rubbed off on you," I said. I passed by the miller, who'd said nothing as we'd spoken. I patted his arm. "Nice to meet you, Arthur." Before I reached the wide doorway, I paused, turning back to Grayson and Francis. The noise of the grinding of the millstones forced me to raise my voice. "You both owe me. I'm counting on you. Get along. Be nice. Keep the attention away from us."

"Why do I feel as though Bertram is the lucky one?" Grayson said.

Francis tilted his head. "He doesn't look like *he* feels he's the lucky one."

"I'm fairly certain that's just what his face does."

"I think you're right."

"Don't disappoint me, boys," I said. I climbed down from the loading dock and helped Bertram down after me. The wind drove the mill's sails faster now even as the day had grown hotter. Shadows rolled across us with each sail passing before the sun.

"It's not as though I can help what my face does," Bertram said.

"Ignore them." We passed down the hillside toward the grazing field. "Now they only have each other to taunt."

"I suppose there's that. Couple of roosters, no mistaking."

The sounds of Boston trailed us as we started off north.

5

THE ARROW OF TIME

n uneasy feeling of being watched marked my work
inside the sorcerium. As much as I focused on the work
at hand—the installation of the numerous glamours
and wards designed to stabilize the interior—I could never shut
out the touch of malevolence that seeped from the open doorways leading deeper inside. Currents of chilly air rose from the
stone floors and walls, tickling the back of my neck. Subtle shifts
in dimension each time I entered eroded any sense of familiarity
I might otherwise have developed. Swaine felt it, too—though he
didn't seem as bothered by it as I was. Nor was that the only point
of divergence in our experience. The more time Swaine spent
within the sorcerium, the more exhilarated he grew. For me, the
conviction that our work was the very last thing one ought to
pursue in that strange outcrop of the demonmere deepened by
the hour.

I placed a small silver ingot into a bracket set by Robert
Twelves to the wall next to one of the two curving staircases
leading to the second floor. The ingot's twin—already entrained
—rested amongst a neat row of others lined up within the workshop back at the manse. I'd already activated the glamours on

three ingots of copper. Such incantations were at the edge of my abilities, and the oppressive atmosphere of the sorcerium wasn't helping my concentration. I closed my eye and gestured before the silver ingot.

"*Wræte þæt ða hildlatan holt ofgefan, tydre treowlogan tyne ætsomne.*" The air around my outstretched hand grew cold, frost scribing the back of my knuckles and the fine hairs on my arm. "*Lumonna argent galdre bewunden—*"

Before I could get any further, the ingot exploded, sending twisted shards of the bracket and slivers of raw metal into my palm, across my chest, and all over the floor. The reverberation of the explosion echoed off down the stairs and up to the floors above, leaving me stunned, wafting away at a cloud that reeked of gunpowder and sulfur.

"Finch?" Swaine called out from the grand summoning chamber on the second floor.

"I'm fine," I said, the words squeezed between coughs as I inhaled the acrid smoke.

My master appeared at the head of the stairs. "What happened?"

"I was starting the incantation for grounding the charge," I said, referring to the step known as *et super terram*, "when it blew up."

"Silver?"

"Yes, sir."

Swaine barked out a laugh. "I once burned a house to the ground attempting a similar glamour with that temperamental metal. My left ear still rings with a distant note played high on a violin because of it." He came down the stairs. "The magic ignited the impurities in the silver with some violence. I suspect that's what you just had the pleasure of experiencing."

"I'm just thankful I used the privy beforehand, sir."

"Well said. The silver was of the improper purity standard, clearly. It should be *fine*. I'm guessing it's merely *Britannia*."

"Not *sterling*?"

"*Sterling* would have blown your head off." He crouched and inspected the fragments strewn across the floor. "We shall have to speak with Mr. Broone about guaranteeing his standards. Perhaps his suppliers are less reliable than he fancies them."

I ignored his words about the silversmith we bought the ingots from. "Blown my head off? That's rather alarming, sir."

"As it should be. Is your hand all right?"

Three cuts, none deep enough to cause undue concern, trickled blood. Lighter scratches decorated my wrist. The pieces on my chest had merely punctured the fabric of my dress, not the skin beneath, thankfully. "I think so. I was more startled than hurt." I dabbed at the blood with the edge of the canvas apron cinched around my waist.

"How far have you gotten?" he said, standing.

"This was the last one before I can start on the stairwell wards. Those are ready, all the spells and preliminary incantations done. They're lined up on the extra workbench. All I need to do is put them in their brackets and ground the charge. Mr. Twelves already set the brackets."

"Come." Swaine started for the main door to the outside. "Let's see to that hand of yours. We're making faster progress than I'd expected. Still, we can't afford to get careless. We'll have to set up a station designed to better assess the purity of silver—I've had a few ideas knocking about in the back room of my thoughts for some years now. Time to drag them out of storage and put them to use. No one needs to be injured for lack of decent protocol."

"Or decapitated, sir."

"Or that, yes." Swaine led the way out through the door. As I'd learned to expect, leaving the sorcerium entailed a strange moment of disorientation when passing over the threshold. I likened it to coming up from a tumble—a touch of vertigo coupled with a racing heartbeat. Swaine claimed it to be more akin to a lightening of gravity, as though shedding a leaden coat and breeches. Our late supper the night before had revolved around the issue, with Mr. Twelves offering a dream-to-waking analogy. Curious that we all had differing sensations. In my case, perhaps more reasonable, as a witch, yet Swaine and Twelves found no common ground, either.

Outside the main doors, we passed through a collection of construction detritus: saw horses; curls and chips of pine shaved from rafter, joist, or beam; remains of pegs and wedges, cracked and discarded; various tools used by Twelves in creating the modifications Swaine required for the grand summoning chamber.

I retied the braid in my hair, come loose in the explosion, and straightened out my skirts. The day had grown warm, the air thick and humid, more appropriate for early August than late May. By the time we reached the barn, my back was slicked with sweat, my hair too hot on my neck. I was parched. I stepped inside the cool of the barn, glad for the shade. Mr. Twelves hunched over his workbench, his magnifying glasses swung before his right eye as he tinkered with a fine gearing. I headed straight for the bucket of well-water that hung from one beam and dipped the ladle, the cool water running from the corners of my mouth as I guzzled it. I wiped my chin with my sleeve.

"How are you coming along?" Swaine said.

Twelves swung his glass aside. "This gearing will be the death of me."

"Now bite your tongue. First Finch, then you. I can't have such extraordinary assistants dying off on me. That won't do at all."

Twelves and I exchanged a quick glance. Swaine's mood—mercurial most days, leaning toward foul of late as several key ingredients failed to arrive at Winslow & Sons—rarely reached such an expansive good nature.

"Finch. Hand," Swaine said.

"What happened?" Twelves said.

"An unruly ounce of silver misbehaved."

I stepped over to where Swaine stood. "I'll be fine, it's not serious," I said to Twelves.

My master plucked the cork from the neck of a brown bottle at the back of one of the workbenches. With his other hand, he reached for my wrist. "This will hurt immensely."

"No softening the blow, sir?" I said.

"I'd say you've had enough surprises for one hour. Hand."

I let him take my wrist and closed my eye. The liquid he poured on it—a concoction of alcohol, mineral spirits, and a carefully distilled potion of healing—ran into the wounds on my hand like liquid lightning. A tear blurred my eye. I groaned.

"Oh, look at that," Twelves said. "I've seen her cut a splinter out of her finger with a blade, jam her finger between two quarters of maple shifting on the pile, and burn her arm up against a hot skillet—never heard a peep out of her."

"They don't come much tougher." Swaine flipped my hand over and poured more on the back. The pain went from terrible to merely awful. "Just ask the man who strangled her last year."

I blinked away the tears and opened and closed my fingers when Swaine released my wrist. "Mr. Twelves is rather fond of tough women," I said, working to keep my voice steady.

"Make the best wives," Twelves said.

"Now don't the two of you start," Swaine said. He put the bottle away and handed me a clean fold of cloth. "No one's getting married here, tough or otherwise."

"What—me and Finch?" Twelves said.

"There's already altogether too much gossip flying between the two of you. No need for anything else to be flying. And even more worrying, you'd gang up on me."

"No need to fear, sir," I said, dabbing my hand with the cloth. The pain subsided to a not-unpleasant tingling. "I'm too tough for Mr. Twelves."

"But can you lift a wagon wheel over your head like Anna Tyler?" Twelves said.

"Careful." Swaine wiped his hands together. "With the right spell, she can lift an entire wagon over her head, if that's your standard for marriage." Swaine took up a quill and scratched out a quick message. He folded it and handed it to me. "Here. While your hand heals—and it should be fine by the morning—why don't you ride to Boston and give this to Mr. Broone while you get some proper silver. I'm sure he has some that he's more confident in. Take whatever funds you think necessary from my billfold. It's in my study."

Inside the manse, I crossed into Swaine's study, opening the curtains to chase back the gloom. His writing desk was littered with a steady accumulation of books and notes that required my periodic reordering lest the stacks bury every last flat surface. One precarious tower of books drew me to dismantle it. Halfway through the pile was wedged a sheet of notes. I glanced over it to see where to put it—then paused. My master's harried scrawls filled the top half of the page, something about temporal manipulation. What caught my eye was instead a small drawing at the bottom of the page of what appeared to be a mule. Not particularly well-executed (one can only have so many talents), it was nonetheless interesting in that I'd never seen Swaine draw anything, nor could I easily picture him absently scratching out a crude drawing while lost in thought or frittering away a spare moment. My master tolerated no spare moments. Curious, I scanned the top of the page more closely. It read:

Time is peculiar. An arrow that points but one direction. Your next moment unwritten, as open as the sky—the moment just passed as sealed off as though by a six foot thick wall of iron, a boundary never to be crossed again. What if that arrow could be bent? What if that arrow could be drawn into a Burnsian channel? What if in doing so, the forces bearing upon it grew so great as to form what Flüsse envisioned in his concept of the Spiegel Verstärkung ? What might that do to the arrow of time? Might it be enough to pry loose the diaglamourous energies manifested—or not? A point of focus worth exploring, closely. Worthy of the sorcerous mind.

I didn't see what any of that had to do with a mule, so I placed the paper on a stack at the side of his desk and finished moving the books to safer homes. I didn't see the *Occultatum Ostium* anywhere, and assumed it locked within the cabinet in the corner. After another pass around the study, I found Swaine's billfold and took out a handful of notes.

After packing up a small meal to take with me for the ride into Boston, I grabbed the rest of my travel attire, including the pistol I wore, and headed for the stable. As I passed by the door to the workshop, I glanced in to see Swaine looking over the gearing that so bedeviled Twelves. Twelves consulted a drawing next to it, explaining something to my master. Swaine's eyes caused me to stumble a step. Once past the doorway, I stopped, returning to peer around the corner of the doorway. His eyes darted back and forth in their sockets in an alarming manner. Twelves, from his vantage, couldn't see it—but I could. Swaine didn't appear to be inspecting the gearing as much as trying to look at every spot on it at once. Or following the crazed flight of an injured fly. My pulse quickened and I ducked back, out of sight. When I looked back in, Swaine nodded, looking steadily at the drawing Twelves proffered. His eyes were back to normal.

I backed off, hurrying for the stable, convinced I'd just seen yet another of the Five Vile Signs: the swift shifting of the eyes an uneven intervals known as *Oculi Malignus Spiritus*, or "eyes of the fiend."

6

BLACKEST MAGIC

"Good citizens, subjects of this great empire," Royal Governor Lionel Sackville said, raising his voice to carry out over the square before Boston's Town House. "I stand before you with a heavy heart, for this colony suffered a grievous blow with the loss of our beloved Hamilton Whitelocke. It is only with the deepest humility that I receive this sacred appointment from His Majesty George II to fill the seat left vacant by a man of such honor, courage, and duty."

Sackville stood on a small wooden proscenium set before the doors of the long brick building. Dressed in a rose-colored coat and waistcoat of embroidered silk, white lace cuffs and matching cravat, a white powdered wig gracing his high forehead, he looked every bit his new role. Flags of the empire flapped in the breeze where they'd been hung from the roof's edge behind him. Spreading out into the square, the gathered assembly strained to hear his words. An impressive array of officer staff occupied rows of seats beside him, generals, colonels, majors and more from the colony's various regiments, including the Governor's Own, extending to other regiments of what I took to be infantry, cavalry, and artillery, each distinguished by the various insignia on their collars. Extending out from the officers sat every Abbot, Winslow, and Prescott in the city. Bankers, merchants, lawyers. Thinkers, buyers, lenders. I spotted well-known portraitists, tailors, haberdashers, wig-makers, and cobblers who had no doubt been decades in the patronage of the late Hamilton Whitelocke.

Farther afield stood significant men and their wives from around the colony. Judges and whale merchants, men who owned smithies and mills, ship makers and printers, men of business, industry, and trade. Craftsmen, laborers, women, children, and other curious onlookers formed the outside ring to witness the official inauguration of their new Royal Governor. I hung back, once again obscuring my appearance, this time with Howell's *Deflected Guise*, the same spell I'd once used on Francis and Clara to steal them into the late Governor's ball. In such a crowd as gathered before the townhouse, the effect was maximized, liberally borrowing features from nearby persons to disguise my own. Eyes, nose, chin, shoulders, gait, all drawn from those around me in a combination unlikely to be noticed by anyone giving me even a close look. I slipped through the outer ring of the audience, keeping my eye out for Mary Whitelocke.

"Yet I assume the mantle of His Majesty's authority with a steely commitment to keep this great Province safe from the infernal threat which menaces our people. Those whose treachery might bring great peril to us all, those traitorous elements determined to strike at the heart of our vigilance against the scourge of blackest magic," Sackville continued. As he spoke, regulars stood alert at the edges of the square, watching people's eyes, looking for any signs of hostility.

I thought it might be an opportune moment to set his attire ablaze—but I weathered the temptation.

Mary sat off to the side wearing a demure outfit of dark plum and charcoal, while a great hat kept the sun from her face as she regarded her father's replacement. She, along with the other members of the extended Whitelocke family, wore the signs of mourning: black ribbons in the hair of the women, black armbands for the men and boys. I sidled up behind her, the nearest guard no doubt mistaking me for a family member or person of otherwise sufficient prominence. Mary's gaze sharpened as I leaned in by her shoulder and whispered, "Mary, it's me. Finch."

To her credit, she kept a faint smile on her face. "You're saving all the good techniques for yourself, clearly."

"We have to talk."

"And miss this riveting spectacle of leeches letting go in search of warmer blood? Yes, please." She stood from her seat and slipped back to the row behind. "Half of them won't even meet my eye. I hadn't given them that much credit for shame, so I suppose that's something."

We moved back through the crowd, her hand on my elbow. "They say Grayson has fled to New York," she said. "Scandalous cur that he is, no one doubts it. Embezzlement. Caught *in flagrante delicto* with a pastor's daughter. Selling away the spiritual tether of the province in collusion with Doctor Rush, making a deal with Lucifer himself in exchange for wealth and flesh. Those are merely the tales I've heard since arriving this morning."

We came to a stop at the edge of the crowd, spread more thinly on the cobbles of the square. "He's safe," I said. "Or, somewhat safe."

"Maybe he *should* have gone to New York."

"I'm doing what I can."

"Of course you are, darling. I'm sure he's being as unhelpful as ever."

"He's helping."

"I wouldn't put too much faith in that. Not for long."

"We need your help, too."

"Coins that need to be bobbled about? Candles which require a flame somewhere near their wicks? Count me in."

"Not that kind of help. Help with distraction. Help with your specialty."

"Dresses? I'm not sure how that will help, but I'm always game."

"No—with this." I motioned to the gathering of Boston's most influential society. "With your connections. Surely you can keep the new governor off balance, wondering how much support he has."

"He has His Majesty's support, and that's the support that matters most."

"Is it? What do you see when you look at this crowd?"

She paused, seeing where I was going with my question. "More than anything, I see *uncertainty*," she said. "Where up until a few weeks ago my family was indisputably the hub of influence and power, where weaving through a room or marketplace would draw obsequious flattery and a single-pointed focus as a magnet draws iron filings—there's a subtle change in the attraction. Believe me, I have enough years' worth of experience of the unalloyed draw of power to know when it's changed. They don't know where to cast their lot just yet, with all of our new governor's talk of damnation. Their doubt will evaporate quickly enough—and take with it the influence of my family name with nearly as much rapidity as my father's problem with his molars turned into his funeral."

"But there's time," I said. "And that's all we need. Time."

"I might be able to slow things down. Sackville doesn't come with much warmth, or money, as far as I can tell. The man's eyes light up with the sort of militant religiosity that Boston's moneyed class finds off-putting."

"Can you do something to make it hard for him?"

Mary smiled. "I can do all kinds of things. With the web of social connections I've woven, I can have half of Boston believing *he's* a warlock himself by week's end. With unsavory predilections. Ghastly table-manners. Habitual lying. Terrible breath. Piles of debt. Hanging in the King's graces by the barest of threads. A helpless need for fawning and flattery. A loathing of exactly that. A few well-placed whispers here, another set there, still more over there, and soon enough no one will know what to make of our strange new governor, let alone trust him. More importantly, he'll be rudderless in building up his personal store of loyalty. Vexed by the peculiar reactions of his new charges. Driven back on his heel."

"Genius," I said.

"I told you—we can play at the highest levels of influence. Not just look divine and smile prettily when called upon." She adjusted her hat, her gloved fingers tilting it just so. "When I'm through with him, he'll be begging His Majesty to be called back to London."

"And no magic," I reminded her.

"It will be magic—my sort of magic."

"Exclusively."

"You don't sound particularly confident in your best pupil."

"It's not that. Just promise me."

"Fine. I promise. I shall keep my efforts restricted to the earthly realm of human nature."

As we spoke, Governor Sackville reached the conclusion of his remarks. "...and with unmatched vigor, we shall reclaim the moral fabric of our blessed land, stamping out the spreading fires of Satan and those who traffic in his will. May the Lord continue to protect this city and this Province. God bless His Majesty George II."

With that, Sackville turned. A pair of officers helped him down the steps. The gathering fell back some, the edges thinning, merging with the market stalls lining the square and nearby establishments as people returned to business. The new Governor headed back toward a waiting carriage, shaking out his cuffs as he strolled amongst a retinue of advisors and officers. One of the officers signaled to the footmen and coachmen, who made ready. An object shot from the crowd in a low arc that clipped the new Governor's shoulder. It glanced off him and landed by the door of the carriage: a horse dropping.

The crowd hushed. The Governor spun, his face flushing.

"Oh, dear," Mary said, watching intently.

One of the officers said, "Get him to the carriage."

"Probably more worried about what Sackville will do than the mob," Mary said.

Voices rose up across the square. The front line of regulars used their muskets to shove people back, while a second group of soldiers closed in around the Governor, who craned his neck to see who had the gall to hurl dung at him. They led him to the carriage.

Someone shouted, "There's room in the burial yard for more than one governor!"

At another officer's hurried signal, a group of horsemen moved into the throng, breaking it up. The shoving and trampling broke backward in a wave. Officers took their pistols out, one keeping a hand firmly on the Governor's collar. Alongside them, the phalanx of horsemen turned for a second pass through the assemblage, sending men and women alike pressing back, some losing their footing and slipping to the cobbles. An old man shouted "For shame!" as he fell and disappeared into a mass of fallen bodies. A woman with a baby raised an arm to defend herself against the push of a musket. A stack of chicken crates toppled over, and a number of birds flapped out squawking. The officer nearest the Governor managed to shove him inside the carriage. He slammed the door closed and banged his hand on the side.

"Go!" he yelled. More soldiers turned and waded into the melee. Mounted men filled in around on both sides and the wedge of soldiers sliced along the side of the square.

I watched as one soldier, at the point of the wedge, went down at the hands of a brute of a man, well over six feet, with the build of a blacksmith and undressed to his waistcoat. The regular cried out as two more louts set upon him, kicking him in the side and head. The crowd disintegrated into chaos, breaking apart, people running toward Market Street, leaving a pair groaning on the ground near the soldier who'd fallen, who cradled his own bloodied head.

"I see your friends bore no personal grudge against my father," Mary said as we hurried off in the direction of her own carriage. "They hate any governor."

I knew Francis was behind the protest that sparked the violence. "They intend to keep his attention elsewhere while Doctor Rush and I take care of our little problem."

"Yet you're currently in the middle of elsewhere," Mary said. "Come."

As the crowd thinned down to clutches of three and four people heading away from the square, I worried the spell disguising me grew less effective. Regulars stood on nearly every corner. I took Mary by the arm and slowed her. "I'm going my own way from here."

"I should think so—you're starting to resemble me a touch too closely," she said, staring at my face. "I know, a compliment under most circumstances, not that you don't possess a certain aloof beauty on your own, mind you. But still—even I'm finding it unnerving, say what you will about anyone glancing in our direction."

"I'll be in touch," I said, giving her arm a squeeze. "And be careful. My master—while no fan of Lionel Sackville—credits him with a certain feral cunning."

"I'll have this haughty little alley cat chasing his own tail before long, cunning or not."

I peeled off from the side road where a line of carriages waited, cutting down a dirt path between two shops. My actual errand— procuring silver of the proper purity for the sorcerium's glamours—

still beckoned. Keeping the spell intact, I hurried on to quieter streets, the residual commotion from the incident at the inauguration dwindling behind me. By the time I slipped out next to the establishment of George Broone, Silversmith, it appeared a normal weekday in Boston, the length of Hanover Street flecked with people going about their early afternoon beneath a cloudless blue sky. Before I reached the door, a movement drew my gaze to a barrel of water snugged against the corner of Broone's. A raven perched on the rim, sooty lines of shadow unfurling from its feathers.

"Miss Finch," the raven whispered in a voice very unlike the guttural croak of an actual raven.

Try as I might, I don't think I succeeded in hiding my surprise. Yet with forced ease, I turned and approached the barrel, blocking it from view from the passersby on the opposite side of the street, a pair of lawyers from the look of them. I turned back to the raven.

"Doctor Rush?" I said.

"You've made yourself difficult to find, my dear," the raven said in a hissing simulation of Rush's voice.

"Largely intentional, sir."

"Of course." The raven moved its weight back and forth on its legs, shifting its grip on the rim of the barrel. "We have a problem."

"I'd say we have more than one."

"Indeed. Yet the one I fear most involves your master. He hasn't listened, has he?"

"No. He hasn't, sir." It pained me to speak so bluntly about Swaine.

"My latest set of readings confirms as much. Two instances of *omnis lux solis* in the last forty-eight hours. Much higher than before and centered in the vicinity of Salem. What is he doing, Miss Finch?" The raven eyed me.

I lowered my voice, making sure no one was near. "Tampering

with the demonmere. Attempting to harness the planar energies within."

"Madness."

"You're right, sir—I don't think he's in his right mind."

"Obviously not."

"No—I don't mean stubborn, or thinking unclearly, or deceitful. It's worse than that." I hesitated to say the words aloud for a moment, then let them out. "I'm afraid he's falling—or fallen—under the influence of a demon."

"Are you suggesting he's possessed?"

"I'm not certain. But he's showing signs."

"There's a reason why sorcery is the most perilous of the unseen arts, not that the time for lecturing isn't well past. This may well be catastrophic, if true."

"Well that's just it—I'm not certain."

"The strategy of demons lies in ambiguity. Is he aware of your suspicions?"

"He doesn't know I know. Or suspect. I don't think."

"And the demon?"

"I'm not sure."

The raven turned its beak one way then the other. "That may be to our advantage."

I looked at the hanging wooden sign in front of Broone's shop. "If I slowed him..."

"Slow him? How?"

"The work he's doing—that he's got me helping with. I could slow it down. Sabotage it."

"Wouldn't he know right away?"

"Not if I'm careful, sir."

"I don't like the sound of this, Miss Finch—you'd be putting yourself at tremendous risk."

"I'm familiar with demons."

"As was your master."

"He's not a witch, sir."

The raven shook its feathers. "Yet you are. Forgive my bluntness, for I know the regard you hold your master in, but I believe you are more important to our hopes than August is precisely because you *are* a witch. We can do this without him if need be— yet without you, I'm afraid our chances dwindle to the point of zero."

"I'll be careful. I'll slow him down, enough to buy us time."

"But you absolutely must flee at the first sign of personal danger, Miss Finch."

"I understand."

"Are you sure?"

"Yes." My next question hung behind my lips for a long moment. "And my master? Can we save him?"

"Demonic possession is not kind, even to those who survive it," the raven whispered.

"Surely you must know some way, sir."

"I've only known enough to stay away from demons in the first place, I'm afraid." Perhaps sensing the sting in his remark, he added, "But I will scour my books for any possibility, Miss Finch."

"Thank you, sir."

"Now do what you can—but remember, your safety is paramount. Much depends on it." In a flutter of wing and inky shadow, the raven lifted off the rain barrel and into the sky above the shop, leaving me to confront the noxious blend of worry and betrayal I'd just mixed for myself.

7

A BRAVER SOUL

I knelt on the floor of the sorcerium's grand summoning chamber, deep in concentration, tuning the valences of the one hundred and eleven glamours that marked the circumference of the massive *Graves' Countervalence*. Arranged at equidistant intervals, the six-inch channels carved into the wooden floor designed by Robert Twelves, each no wider or deeper than a four-penny nail, contained a line of *fine*-grade silver filings thrumming with magic. Incanting the glamours had taken several fifteen hour days. The pattern was absurd: three *grand loci* of 37 individual glamours; each *grand loci* containing a symmetrical array made up of three sets of 12 separate mirrored glamours called the *stations*; the center of the arrangement of *stations* contained a lone glamour known as the *crown*; those three *crowns* formed a powerful strand of magic called the *truss*. The *truss* then ran behind a panel that held five dials and ten levers, engraved and calibrated to manipulate the valences in any number of combinations.

Charts, notes, and checklists had been the order of the day, for one errant glamour and the entire countervalence would have to be started again, from scratch. I didn't dare make such an error, as badly as I wanted to slow down the work, for Swaine barely trusted me to tune the glamours in the first place and was ready to do it himself if I couldn't handle it. I'd finished each day drained from the effort, dreaming of yet more channels, yet more glamours. Checking, double-checking, triple-checking every step of the way. Still, I managed to stretch the task out as far as I could without drawing Swaine's ire.

Twelves emerged from the doorway leading to the stairs carrying a set of handles for the dials. "He's in a mood."

I paused from my work. "What's it this time?"

"Everything."

"Wonderful." Swaine's temper, always unpredictable, had darkened into a heat just below the surface, always at the ready. I attributed it to the influence of the demon—yet could do nothing about it for fear of risking my ability to slow the work on the sorcerium down. The feeling was intolerable, but I shouldered it. I got off my knees. "You might want to check the last lever over there, Mr. Twelves. I noticed it's not lettered." All the other levers bore an engraved letter atop the handle, lettered *A* thru *H*. "Why give him something else to grow furious about?"

"I did," Twelves said. "I made the proper handle. He wanted that one without and didn't care for my suggestions to the contrary. I'll not be pressing the point again."

"I won't mention it to him, then."

"No. I wouldn't." With a sigh, he went into one of the side chambers and set to work.

I turned back to setting the valences of the glamours. The further I went, wild ejections of magic buffeted the grand chamber as the diaglamoured forces built upon one another, layers of force and repulsion vibrating in a complex series of frequencies. The more potent the forces became, the more diffi-cult it became to tune the final glamours. I checked off: *Glamour 104 (grand loci 3, station 12a)* on my sheet. Getting the proper valence involved three spells—one for establishing the current valence, one for linking the glamour with its mirrored twin, and a final one to set it to the precise value called for in the overall scheme of the countervalence. I'd found that my witchcraft gave me an advantage, in that each glamour shone with a particular hue, and as I tuned them, the pattern they made became apparent, which allowed me to save time in the first of the three spells, as I knew within a degree how close the glamour was to where it needed to be. I wondered how anyone could perform magic without that extra sense.

And so passed the early hours of the morning. The strain grew as I made my way through the final seven glamours. My hair and dress lifted on the gusts of energy that crashed throughout the chamber, and a pervasive nausea grew, paired with a leaden headache. Little sparks danced in the corners of my vision, ones I knew weren't in the chamber, but in my eye. The final two glamours before I got to the *crowns* were so difficult I worried they were impossible, beyond my reach. Graves had cautioned that the closing few glamours would be *"girded and stubborn as steel that refuses to bend, refusing to settle into their proper demeanor, all the while expelling remarkable force against their fated cohort."*

I struggled. My ears filled with the crackling of energies that leapt through the air before me: a terrible thunderstorm in miniature. The penultimate glamour before I dealt with the *crowns* refused to pair with its twin. Every time I spoke the proper incantation, the pressure of the air in the space shifted, stealing my breath, pushing me away. Magic flared, straining the bindings I'd put in place. Three times I tried, and three times it got away from me. I found even moving through the space difficult at that point. Knots of pressure and gravity created invisible barriers, unseen spheres of resistance.

Sitting back on my heels, I considered reversing the pairings of the final two glamours as a way to slow down the work. Nor would it be an obvious error, given the complexity involved.

"Fine," I whispered.

Unfortunately, doing it the wrong way proved no easier than doing it the proper way. I couldn't get the glamours to pair in either configuration. That, at least, slowed things down. Still, knowing Swaine was in a foul mood wouldn't make it any easier to tuck my pride and tell him the countervalence still wasn't finished. I smoothed down my lifted hair and clinging skirts as I left the wild energies behind me. At the bottom of the stairs, I paused before crossing the main room. *Bear his wrath.* I put my shoulders back and took a steadying breath before starting for the door.

Swaine sat behind a makeshift table of planks spanning two sawhorses outside of the sorcerium. Twelves leaned over next to him, tapping various points on the drawings with his finger. Neither one of them looked happy. I remained off to the side, girding myself for what was to come. Every time I looked at my master, I sought more signs of possession, a habit I found horrid. My trust, loyalty, and devotion to him crashed headlong against the dread I felt at the thought of a demon winding its way slowly into Swaine's will, coiling into and strangling the man I regarded as family. As much as I wanted to grab him by the collar and plead with him to help me figure out how to help him, I knew I couldn't without risking a greater catastrophe—both to my master himself (for who knew what the demon would do to him if it sensed its presence was known), and to the colony (for keeping the pretense of ignorance was the only way I might retain any influence over the progress in Salem). My heart wanted to help him, yet my head knew I couldn't.

"Finch." Swaine's voice was sharp. Both he and Twelves stared at me.

"Sorry, sir?"

"It's not too much to ask, I trust, that when we review our work, we can pay attention for up to a full quarter of an hour. Repetition, lack of clarity, the wrong focus—all cost us. Do you understand?"

"I'm sorry, sir. It won't happen again."

"Best see it doesn't. Now—for the second time—when is the shipment from Hamburg supposed to arrive?"

The shipment contained an expensive relic known as the *Hand of St. Gretchen*. Swaine was less interested in the storied hand itself than in a strange ring of bronze documented to occupy one of the fingers. I'd retrieved it on the day of Governor Sackville's inauguration and hidden it away beneath the floorboards of my room beneath a web of glamours and witchcraft.

My cheeks grew flushed, a nice unintended touch to my deceit. "This week or next. Mr. Winslow is looking out for it."

"I don't want it sitting in his warehouse."

"He's promised to get word as soon as the ship reaches the docks, sir."

He was less than pleased with my answer and turned back to Twelves. "How long will it take from then, assuming we ever get it?"

"Hard to say."

"Be daring." He said it as though he were being light, but Twelves and I both knew his fuse had been lit.

"The problem is that I'd be guessing. It could be anything."

"If there are no significant complications."

"With everything else, weeks. Easily."

"Everything is weeks, and everything takes longer than estimated." Swaine leaned both hands on the board. "We're losing *months*, and if either of you think this trajectory is in any way acceptable, let me be clear: it's not." He pounded his fist on the map to emphasize the last word. "I want solutions, not continually to be presented with the problems. Solve the problems, don't simply announce them. Announcing a problem is for cowards and shirkers. It makes *your* problems *my* problems. Solve them, and let me carry on with my work, which, need I remind you both, is crucial to this entire undertaking."

Twelves and I both held our tongues. I felt as though guilt

radiated off me like heat, but Swaine's fury no doubt projected all that and more across both of us.

Swaine waved his hand over the map. "There is a colony full of individuals who will gladly watch us fail. Who will find a thousand reasons to disparage us. Who will think they know better, even as they blunder through their days of leisure, never once engaging any more will than what it takes to decide what to have for dinner. Yet they'll be eager to tut-tut over how foolish we are if we don't prove them wrong, and quickly. Don't think word hasn't gotten round. It has." He straightened. "And if the two of you don't believe what I'm telling you, I'm not sure why I'm even bothering." With that, he swept the maps off the boards and turned, heading back to the lane that led to the manse. Once he'd reached the turn in the lane, I knelt and retrieved the maps, putting them back in place.

Twelves muttered, "Can't make the impossible possible by claiming it's unacceptable for it to be impossible."

"I know," I said. "And he knows."

"Does he?"

Of course he does—but he's possessed by a demon. I couldn't say the words. Twelves, despite his many notable qualities, had a pronounced flaw I couldn't ignore: he was incapable of keeping a secret. His words flowed straight from his heart to his mouth, most often skipping his mind altogether. Any promise to discretion he made would be forgotten within minutes. I would have to say something eventually—but not until the time was ready.

"He's frustrated," I lied. "He puts himself under so much pressure."

"And us."

"We get off easy compared to what he does to himself." We passed back into the queer chill of the sorcerium.

"Still. Can't say I share his belief that misery is the price of excellence." Twelves retrieved a set of calipers. "But at least we got this week's tongue-lashing out of the way early."

"Well there's one area we're ahead of schedule. Shall I run and tell him?"

"You're a braver soul than I if you do. A braver soul."

I was never sure how long these moods of Swaine might last. Minutes weren't unheard of, yet neither were days. He could squirrel himself away in his study, he could disappear into the sorcerium, he could ride off into the countryside and return to the land of the reasonable without warning, pleasant and cheerful. The best policy was to keep one's head down and carry on with the work. So it was that I saw nothing of my master until late in the afternoon. I'd returned from the glamour work in the sorcerium to gather more supplies when Swaine called for me, outside the workshop.

"Finch!"

"Is everything all right?"

"Of course it is. It's brilliant. Come here—post haste." He stood in his waistcoat and breeches, his hair loose. He clutched a piece of paper. "Ready the wagon. I want to ride down to the far side of the harbor mouth. If I'm correct, I may have just located a secondary source of energy capable of evening out the potential load required to stabilize the countervalence."

"Of course, sir." When I had the horse hitched, I brought the wagon around to my master, his impatience eclipsed by his enthusiasm, thankfully.

Swaine climbed to the driver's bench next to me. "Down past that tumbled bit of foundation where we found that skull." The skull in question had, curiously, been the only human remains we'd encountered in all our explorations of Salem. What tale explained it remained a mystery.

I let the brake free and flicked the reins. "I thought the point of the countervalence was that it stabilized itself, sir?"

"To a point, that's true. Past that point—well, I've run a

number of calculations that aren't comforting. Not all of them, mind you. But enough."

"Not comforting in what way?"

"In the way of initiating an uncontrollable planar breach."

"But isn't that just what Doctor Rush is worried about, sir?"

"Yes, and no. In the good Doctor's mind, *any* planar incursion —or breach, if you must—is cause for alarm. His myriad fears are informed by the faulty premise that no planar breach is capable of being controlled. That's nonsense. Now, should a breach pass a critical level—well of course there's a danger. Collapsing planes. Hordes of demons. Unimaginable energies feeding on themselves, drawing in yet more planes. Terrifying. That's to be avoided at all costs. But below that threshold lies an unending reservoir of energy, capable of powering an entire new chapter in the unseen arts. Would you rather grind corn by hand, one cup at a time—or in a grist mill, bushel after bushel after bushel?"

I looked at him out of the corner of my eye, but his gaze was down by the harbor. Why would he mention a grist mill?

"Would you rather row a boat across the Atlantic with a paddle —or with sails in full flight, drawn by the wind?" he continued. "Harnessing the power of the natural world, seen or unseen, is the future, revealing horizons undreamt of. Bringing them within reach."

I breathed a little easier, grasping the analogies he offered. Swaine explained in some detail how he might pair the energies of the countervalence with this secondary source in order to ensure nothing spiked above the threshold levels he deemed safe. Even as he explained it, I wondered how safe Doctor Rush would find any of it; unsafe all around, I suspected. Still, I didn't bring up the obvious objections Rush would interject with for fear of souring my master's mood. When we reached the area Swaine indicated, I slowed the wagon. Wind gusted in from over the water, carrying with it flecks of sea-spray from where the waves bashed the rocks, the harbor restless. Unkempt vines and grass scrabbled down to the high tide line, replaced with translucent brown seaweed lying in clumps along the water's edge.

Swaine climbed down. "It said it should be somewhere around here."

"It, sir?"

"The book."

I needed no further clarification as to which book he referred to. He consulted the scratches on the paper he held, retrieving a planar compass from his waistcoat pocket. From the wagon, I gazed about, matching the location with the maps I'd put together showing the handiwork of the witches. Soon enough, I was certain we weren't far off from one such spot. In fact, a shimmer in the air lined with faint hints of color confirmed it. Swaine headed straight to the spot.

"Come look at this," he said. And there it was, a squat cairn of stones with two low walls extending half a dozen paces from it— clearly another witches' seal. He paced around the stones, stepping over the walls with care, glancing down at the planar compass. "Yes, it's here." He turned to me. "Is this one of the spots you noted during our experiment?"

When we'd lit up the skies over Salem with the massive Holzian half-life energies released by Swaine's device, the various seals had been perfectly revealed.

"That's one, sir. Yes."

"How odd. I'd expect the opposite—but I trust in the book. Here—help me move these."

"The stones?"

"Not all. Just a few. It should be right here."

"What exactly is it?"

"Not what was shown, that much is clear." He started to push aside some of the stones. "As far as I can see."

"Is that wise, sir?" The stones themselves were no more than markers, for the most part. But still.

"It makes a certain sense, if you think about it." He ignored my question, straining as he hefted a larger stone and rolled it off to the side. "Various seams. Planes bursting through, exerting pressure. The witches do what they think is necessary. It works, to some degree. Time. Age. Renewed pressures. A hand, Finch. A hand."

Not happy about it, I helped him move some of the smaller stones. The area around the seal hummed with witchcraft—but it felt solid to me, not like the frayed and damaged seals I'd repaired at other locations. All the more reason *not* to tamper with it.

"Ah, here we are." Swaine dropped to his knees and clawed at the dank soil revealed by the stones. He only dug for a few moments when he evidently found something, leaning in closer, his fingers scrabbling at something in the soil. "By God, it was right."

"What is it?"

"Look. Feel it."

He sat back and I peered at the spot he'd been digging. A small nub of what appeared to be metal protruded from the ground, no more than an inch of it. When my fingertip made contact with it, a wave of chills ran up my arm, all the way to my scalp. I pulled back.

"I don't understand," I said.

"It's the tip. The very tip."

"Of what?"

"Of this." He handed me the paper. Scrawled across the top were notes as to the location we'd reached, but below it was a sketch of a building resembling a church, a tall steeple rising from the end of the main roof. Swaine tapped the steeple's highest point, where a thin line extended. "I'm not sure what to call it—a spike of some kind. How perfect."

I looked over the drawing again and then down at the nub of metal in the earth. "It's under here—the building?'"

"Clearly."

"But couldn't that be something else?"

"Such as?"

"I don't know—just a bit of metal? A rod? Anything?"

Swaine took the paper back from my fingers. "Doubtful. The coincidence would be too great. The book told me it was here, and here this is. Alternate explanations would seem to strain credulity even more, wouldn't you say?"

Everything about the *Occultatum Ostium* strained credulity, but I didn't think it the right moment to say so. "Is there a way to be certain, sir?"

"Now you're thinking the right way." He paced around the spot. "I've a feeling that it's close to driving out of the earth in the same manner of the sorcerium—but I don't want to have to count on that. Revenants. I'll set some revenants to digging. If the drawing is accurate, it won't take much to confirm the larger structure beneath the spike. Still, it would be easier if it breached the surface."

"And nothing else."

"Ha! Indeed. Nothing else. No, Finch. This is a moment to appreciate. Everything is coming together. I've all the tools at my disposal to realize a new age of the unseen arts. These things don't happen by accident. They require a vision. Hard work. Sacrifice. Single-pointed focus. The heights of effort. But isn't it worth it? What else might one do with the miserly allotment of days in this world if not strive to make a mark and better mankind? Stop at the foot of the mountain because it looks daunting? Pause halfway up because it's exhausting? Retreat? No. We've set our sights on the peak—and that's where we're bound." He started back to the wagon. "Marvelous."

I soon had the wagon turned around, heading back up the manse. Shadows stretched long across the silent meadows. Rich sunlight leant Salem clarity. Swaine folded up his paper and crossed his arms, looking out over the abandoned town.

"Do you know what Mary Whitelocke told me back at her recital?" he said.

My breath catching in my throat couldn't have been more obvious. "Mary?" I repeated.

"Yes, Mary." He was silent for a few moments as the wagon banged through a rough patch of washout. "I'm not sure whether to be angry, flattered, or paranoid."

Little of that sounded good. "What on earth did she say?"

"She suggested I consider the post of Royal Doctor of Magickal Sciences."

"I'm not sure that's worked out particularly well for Doctor Rush, sir."

"Well of course this was prior to Governor Whitelocke's death."

"Do you think Governor Sackville might continue the post?"

"The obvious answer is no. But I do wonder. If the promise of our work comes to fruition, he may not have a choice but to acknowledge it."

"He sounds quite opposed to any dealings in the unseen, sir."

"At the moment."

"But would you wish to be given such a post, sir?"

"Well of course not, Finch. Parading about the colony, reassuring the citizenry that all is well, an expected presence at public events—I couldn't imagine anything worse." He rubbed his chin. "No, not for me. That said, my accomplishments may carry with them a certain prestige."

"Except no one knows about them, sir."

"For the time being. But were the secrecy drawn back at some point, I would have access to the right people of influence and in such a position might properly influence their views of the arts. Pry it out of the darkness of ignorance and into daylight. In time, create a center of learning, right here. Think of it."

He said nothing further, his eyes closed, the fields passing by unnoticed, my presence forgotten, as was the case when his thoughts bore down on a single point.

I brought the wagon across the river. Sunlight danced along the ripples, reflections of clouds on the surface of the water.

"You may have competition," Swaine said. His eyes were open again, and he leaned forward, hands on his knees.

"Sir?"

A tight smile appeared for a moment. "Madam Whitelocke suggested, none too subtly, that should I raise my profile, she would endeavor to study with me."

"Mary? Study the arts?" I was terrible at lying and felt as though my response came out with all the artifice of a bad actress reciting a banality over-seasoned with melodrama.

"Now, now—no need to get your plumage up, Finch."

"I wasn't."

He glanced at me. "Behind the protest often lies the truth."

"Now you're teasing me, sir."

He honked a laugh. "Well, who knows? She told me she's learned many techniques studying under Doctor Rush, a tableau I find preposterous, frankly. She said it all with a wink and a pursing of her rosebud lips, which could very well have been a titillating intimation of something of a more seductive nature, for all I know."

Doctor Rush? Ridiculous. All that she'd learned, she learned from me—I'd been there for every trying moment spent corralling her flitting attentions to achieve even the most basic techniques.

"You could always try it, sir," I offered. "Perhaps she'd have the same facility at the unseen arts as she possesses with fashion. Or singing."

"Stranger things have happened, I suppose."

"Although speaking from personal experience, you're not particularly easy on your apprentices. That might pose some difficulty, sir."

"Are you suggesting that she might not possess the grit and fortitude I found in the person of a nearly-strangled orphan with but one eye?"

"I'm only offering the possibility. Something tells me that Madame Whitelocke would expect an order of magnitude more deference than you might offer."

"She is a Whitelocke."

"So she'd have *me* doing half the work. Doing her practicing for her. Summarizing Gardener, Hume, others into bite-sized bits. Doing her summoning exercises while she chooses the best outfit for the occasion."

Swaine nodded along, chuckling. "She'd demand her own revenants."

"She would. Then she'd demand her own copy of the *Occultatum Ostium* the next time it found its way into the hands of one of them."

Swaine fell silent. The mirth drained from his face. He stared at me. "Sorry, the what?"

"The *Occultatum Ostium*, sir." Without warning, I felt that I'd slid out onto the weak pond ice of March.

"I heard what you said. What did you mean by that? Answer me." His tone sliced through whatever light mood we'd conjured.

"The—with the revenant, sir. The book."

"Why are you babbling? Give me a complete sentence. What are you referring to? Now."

My gaze went from his face to the approaching bank of the river, then back to him. "How the *Occultatum Ostium* appeared in the hands of the female revenant, six—no, seven days ago. I told you about it. Right away. I gave the book back to—"

"You told me no such thing," he said, raising his voice and staring at me with as hard an expression as I'd ever seen on him.

"I did—I absolutely did, sir."

"No. No you didn't." He pounded his fist on the seat of the wagon. "Inexcusable. How dare you try to hide this from me?"

"But I didn't, I'm not hiding anything. You were at your writing desk, and you bade me to put it on the corner. You even said that—that it was to be expected, from time to time. Or something to that effect."

He glared at me. "Expected? Not likely. And if you think you can put words in my mouth, then you're just digging yourself into a deeper hole."

"That's what you said. It's the truth, sir."

"It is *not* the truth," he said, emphasizing the *not* with yet another slam of his fist. "And the gall you have getting so brazen with me about it. Who do you take me for?"

My mind locked up then. Guilt seeped in from all corners, more than I could've imagined, and with a shock I felt my eye fill with tears. I seemed to have lost the ability to put together a full sentence, even a small one. "No—I don't take you for—it's not —when I—"

"What did you do with the book?"

"I did nothing, sir. Nothing. I took it from a revenant who'd wandered out past the
field—"

He lifted his hands up as though I'd just vomited into his lap. "You took it from the manse?"

"I didn't *take* it anywhere. A revenant—"

"Stop this ridiculous story, right now!" he shouted at me. His voice echoed out over the desolate landscape as the sun neared the western hills. "Do you expect me to believe such pathetic nonsense? No, no, no. I can't abide any of this, Finch. How long have you been waiting to tell me this?"

"I told you when it happened, sir." My hands trembled, and I couldn't stop blinking. "The very moment."

Swaine grabbed the riding crop we kept tucked under the driver's bench. "You've set fire to my trust in you. Now tell me the truth before I have to ask you again." He held the crop up, as if to strike me. I tried to calm my thoughts.

"It was by the edge of the lane at the gate, and I saw her crouching by that large

granite—"

The crop stung the tops of my hands, brought down like lightning in Swaine's grip. "The truth!"

I cried out, shocked. The backs of my hands stung, the right one so much so I clenched it into a fist. I wrapped it in the other hand. "It's the truth, sir. I'm not lying."

He hit me again, this time across the front of my chest, just beneath the angle of my chin. "You wanted to look at it, didn't you?"

I shook my head, my voice having retreated into my throat like a frightened animal leaping into its den. He whipped me with the crop again, across the back of my left hand. Terror and disbelief crowded out all other thoughts. I dropped the reins and the wagon slowed to a halt.

Swaine stood over me, panting, his shoulders shaking. "Do you know how much I've put into my work with that book? How I've wrestled with it? Night after night, turning the delicate springs and notes, progressing only an inch an hour, a day? How much all of my work depends on it? And you take it from me? Prance about the fields with it? *Lie* to me about it?"

All I could do was shake my head: *No, please, I didn't.* I felt as though I'd fallen off a cliff.

"That book is *never* to leave my custody. *Never. Ever. Ever.*" Each *never* and *ever* came with more whips, on my arm, my chest, the top of my head, the side of my face. Everything turned white in my vision, and it was as though I were watching it from a distance. Time stretched out like thick molten glass. I recall thinking *He will take out my other eye* with a strange calm, each blow leaving me with plenty of room to marvel at how the afternoon had turned into something terrible. The last strike, to my face, sent me tumbling from the driver's bench to the ground. My head stung, my face burned where it had been sliced open. I covered both with my hands. They couldn't stop shaking. I fought back a retch.

Above me, Swaine gathered up the reins. He leaned over.

"You break my trust after all I've done for you? I bring you into my home, into my work. I hold nothing back from you. I let you see it all, hear it all, absorb all I say. You read my books. Profit from my studies, taking it all for granted." He slammed the crop against the side of the wagon. "Pay attention. Holding every gift, gifts excluding none. Feel I never cared—helped?" He hurled the crop at me. "You make your own bloody way back. I expected better of you, and shall now question all else that you've said, and that you've done. *Everything.* You'd best think hard about what that means. And one more thing—if there's anything amiss with the book, don't even bother showing your face again."

With that, he called to the horses, starting them off along the lane. The ground shook beneath me with their steps, with the rolling of the wagon's wheels. I sat up. Swaine didn't glance back, setting the horses to a fast pace. I put a hand to my face. It pulled away with a speckling of blood smeared on my palm. The entire side of my face and my head throbbed. My eyepatch had slipped to the side, and I straightened it with fingers that didn't want to work. I dabbed my cheek with the hem of my skirt. Warm blood seeped into the cloth.

Swaine and the wagon crested the hillside, merging with shadows as he rode into the lowering sun. My knees shook as I got to my feet. Still, I forced myself to walk, stepping over the crop where it lay in the dirt. The late spring breeze, the blue sky, the lapping of the river mocked me, revealing themselves as uncaring as they'd ever been. As I held the cloth to my face, I looked at the welts rising on my other hand, and I wept.

8

MIDNIGHT STAIRS & DOORS

They say water, given enough time, can wear away even the stoniest earth. Change landscapes with its relentless passage. Grief, too, irrevocably alters the contours it meets, save if the landscape is your heart. Yet grief is worse, for it never flows away, but rather collects in depths unsuspected—until fresh grief adds to it, and the immensity of that bleak ocean below reveals itself yet again. Grief consumed me as I made my wretched way back through Salem. My body knew it even before my mind did. Clenching. A hollowness. Vision blurred by tears. A sensation akin to rising laughter, but one that leads instead to wracking sobs. The afternoon fled before the blaze of sunset and I wandered, my face swelling, my hands bruised, my chest aching, plunged, once again, into the dark and blurry fathoms of loss.

It wasn't the blows that had stung. I may not have been a beauty of the caliber of Mary Whitelocke, but neither was I delicate. Over the months, I'd banged my head, hammered a finger or two, cut my face on a stray nail, got stepped on by more than one horse, burned off a patch of hair and an eyebrow, and more. I'd lost an eye to the kick of a mule as a young child, after all—I started out tough. Nor was it Swaine's fury, for I finally accepted the truth that blazed so glaringly before me: Swaine was gone, lost to the clutches of the demon who possessed him. I'd seen it as he'd leaned over the side of the wagon, shouting at me. *Conspicio Homicida*, the murderer's gaze, the fourth of the Five Vile Signs I'd seen in my master.

What took me, rather, was grief. Grief, for what Swaine had done for me. Rescued me when everyone else around me fell prey to a demon. Discovered who I really was, identifying the witch-blood coursing through my veins. Grief for what Swaine meant to me. The inspiration for my dedication, to the exclusion of all else. He'd called for a discipline within me I'd never known, one that fueled me during the long days and grinding nights of work in his service, more often than not up earlier and awake later than he himself. From that, I'd mastered what he'd taught me, and more that he hadn't even suspected. The running of the household, the attiring of the revenants, the caring for the animals. Sweeping, painting, cooking. Errands, the organization of the workshop, the library. I'd built a root cellar myself. And I'd never once complained—because of what it meant to me.

I'd watched out for his health, the soundness of his thoughts, the integrity of his will in his dealings with scores of wretched demons. August Swaine was a singular genius—and I would be the first to laud his brilliance, without question—but who else but me knew how to support his best energies while sparing him from his own worst impulses? He could work himself into ill health, into inarticulate solitude, and, yes, into mistakes when left to his own devices, while I'd learned to keep him from his worst excesses.

All worth it.

My commitment to being the best apprentice possible knew few bounds. Yes, yes, I know—I'd kept secrets from him. Guilty. Yet I'd done it out of a hard to replicate set of circumstance, uncertainty, and shame—not out of faithlessness or duplicity, not out of avarice or lowness.

By the time I reached the manse, I was worn out by grief. Night settled over the land, the moon in full flight and the stars silhouetting the trees. I stared at my home. Swaine's rooms were aglow with light, while the rest remained one with the darkness. Had that been what it looked like, night after night, before I'd arrived there the year before? Would it look so again were I to turn around and disappear? If I slunk off, defeated?

I wasn't going to find out. For as I'd walked each step through the lonesome roads of Salem, another emotion had taken the grief, the hurt, the fears to flame within my thoughts.

Anger.

I faced the manse. Its dark shape silent before the towering hemlock. A curl of smoke drifted from the chimney. The floorboards creaked as I passed through the entry. At the foot of the stairs, I paused, listening. No voices, no sign of Swaine or of Twelves. I checked the study, the library, and the kitchen, finding them likewise empty. Curiously, I saw none of the household revenants.

I climbed the stairs to the second floor to the far end of the hallway where Swaine's room was. The door was closed. I knocked. "Master?"

No response. Frowning, I knocked again, then tried the latch. The door opened, and I peeked inside. His bed was unmade. A fire in the hearth had burned to dull embers. He wasn't there. I was about to turn to leave when I paused, my eye caught by something on his writing desk, something I'd never seen.

"Master?" I called. No response, the house was empty. I stepped into the room and neared the desk. A map of Salem stretched across the whole surface. What caught my eye stood above the map. Scraps of paper of varying sizes stood on copper pins and lengths of wire, affixed with small daubs of wax, forming a third dimension to the map itself. I leaned in and looked at the nearest piece of paper. It resembled two rainbows crossed over one another. Others had symbols—and I was shocked to see ravens on one, a key on another, a coffin on yet another. Lone letters, whole words, and glyphs covered other pieces. Many of the words were incomplete, the missing letters nothing but hash marks (a common practice within sorcery, where a particular word might prove caustic.) Seeing that, I stepped back and extended my senses, feeling the delicate strands of magic wound within and around the strange map.

What exactly was I looking at?

As I traced the general topography of the raised pieces of paper, I realized they didn't quite follow the various lines of the bindings wound in and around Salem, the work of the witches. I knelt and looked at it from the side. One of the nearest scraps on a copper pin had the words *Mitternacht Treppen und Türen* scrawled across one side, along with the number 7. On another label was written the phrase *die Beschatteten Tal* next to the number 23. I glanced around to find what the labels referenced. One of Swaine's books sat off to the side of the map, several ribbons marking various sections. Frowning, I looked toward the door.

"Master?" I called again. Hearing nothing, I reached for the book, recognizing it as the work of the great Gustav Koeffler. Opening to the first ribbon, I found a description of what Koeffler identified as the Seventh Plane, named *Midnight Stairs and Doors,* or *Mitternacht Treppen und Türen.* Swaine himself had scratched a note in the margin of the text that read: *Flüsse's passion—interesting.* The reference meant nothing to me. Flipping the pages to the next ribbon, I came to a comparable text describing the Twenty-Third Plane, the *Shadowed Vale,* or *die Beschatteten Tal.* The note along the side simply read: *Corner?*

I looked up at the map again. The corner of the map was empty of pins or labels. My gaze went to the corner of the room. A cracked bit of plaster decorated the ceiling above it, extending past the hearth. Beneath it stood a large trunk. I didn't remember it occupying that exact spot, so I went to push it aside, but it remained in place as though nailed to the spot. Grunting, I tried harder. Nothing.

Squatting, I discovered a spell holding it in place. I guessed he'd used a version of Summerfield's *Unyielding Repose*, considered the standard of the spell. There was a relatively easy negation to the spell—it wasn't intended to be used against someone versed in magic, but only against the unmagical—which I'd learned as part of his tutoring me in the *Circle of Countering*. I sat back and spoke the incantation known as the *Avulse Deviation*, and watched as pale yellow light skittered across the surface of the trunk, growing brighter along the edges that touched the floor and wall. When it finished, I pushed at the trunk. It still didn't budge. The tightness in my chest cranked a notch further.

He'd used a spell to counter *me*.

A simple *Unyielding Repose* would have been more than enough to prevent Mr. Twelves, the revenants, or anyone else who might find themselves in his room from being able to move aside the trunk. But no. He'd gone farther than that, clearly intending that should I stumble across the trunk, I couldn't do a thing about it. I was, after all, the only other person in the colony (save Doctor Rush) who might conceivably know how to counter the emplacement spell. I felt the sting of betrayal, for such a glamour had been cast with only me in mind. My heart ached at the realization of just how great the distance had grown, in secret, mine and his, even as we'd worked side by side for so long.

Of course, I wouldn't settle for one more secret. There was more I could do beyond displacement magic. I let my other senses expand outward, over the trunk, in and around the magic that sealed it in place. I located the lines of force—how they bound the material of the trunk with the wood of the floor, the plaster of the wall. A fine stitching, wound through with a bright gold force. Something in the magic rang a bell—something from the German school, I suspected—but I wasn't looking to figure out the proper counter to whatever it was. I would break it, unstitch it one wind at a time, rupturing the energies that bound matter to matter by manipulating the space in between. After a few moments, my witchcraft snipped the magic in one spot. I repeated it in another. And another.

It took time. How much, I wasn't sure, as my concentration deepened to where I knew nothing more than stitch and weave, directing my awareness and energy to break the bonds that held the trunk. When the last of Swaine's spell was sundered, a satisfying release coursed through my body. The surfaces of the trunk were free of magic. I opened my eye. It looked no different. I gripped the top edge, pulling—and it slid toward me, empty.

Shoving it aside, I stared at the hole in the floor it had covered: three boards, pried away, leaving a hole only a foot and a half across, and twice that long. A rope hung into the gaping opening, nailed to the floor next to it with a thin silver spike. The sight of that hit me like a bucket of ice water.

The demonmere.

I glanced at the book again, and at the strange map on the writing desk. Was I kneeling before an entrance into the Twenty-Third Plane, *die Beschatteten Tal*?

Frigid air wafted up, the touch of it disquieting. With my hands at the edge, I leaned forward. Space opened beneath me into a wide emptiness. The rope stretched down, knotted every two feet for gripping. I was shocked to see that it had to be at least one hundred feet of rope, dangling to what appeared to be a platform of stone that topped a pair of arches. Within those, corridors extended into darkness. At the floor of one opening, a lantern burned, a small point of gold. My fingers tightened on the edge of the floorboards.

Was Swaine down there, even at that moment? And if so, what did he have in mind? More worryingly—what did the demon have in mind?

Lifting myself up and out of the opening, I sat back, stunned. My mouth went dry, and my heart told me to flee, beating as hard as it did in my chest. I shoved the trunk back into place over the opening. For a moment, I stared at it, wondering if I ought to recast an emplacement spell on it. I shook my head as though to shake such a stupid idea out of it. No.

I locked my fingers together to stop them from shaking. The map taunted me—it was so obvious then that it wasn't the product of Swaine's orderly mind. Another will leaned against his own, pressing in, blinding him to what he was doing. Eroding the foundations of his identity. Eradicating his natural caution. Something else about the map caught my eye. Having extended my senses unbinding the trunk, I became aware of magic whirling over the map itself. Getting to my feet, I stepped to the map and leaned over it. The pins and wires vibrated. Thin beams of light swept the surface of the map, projecting from the unseen sphere that bloomed around it. Strands of light reached through the writing desk, through the floor below. Something about the power of the magic set me on edge—where was it coming from? I realized the spot was directly over Swaine's study.

And then I knew: the *Occultatum Ostium*.

I could leave it be—all of it. I could slip off, leave altogether. Flee. Take those I cared about with me. Go to New York. Philadelphia. Why, even back to London. I wasn't a frightened young woman anymore, incapable of bending Fate to my will. Or I could do something beyond risky, with no certainty of success, and—if I was being honest—a high risk of costing me my life, or worse. I stared at the map. I glanced in the corner. An ember huffed in the hearth.

I decided.

Time was my enemy, overtaking me faster than I thought possible, blinking past in chunks of five, ten, twenty minutes. In my room, the precious minutes hurtled past as I stuffed items into my haversack—a few books, ingredients, random clothes, eyepatches. Panic and shock dulled my wits as I stared at a pair of fancy leather shoes suitable for a ball, wondering if I ought to bring them along or not. Pure foolishness.

Shouldering the sack, I tested its weight. Fair. I looked around the room. The first time I'd seen it, it had been disused, home to a few lonesome pieces of broken furniture, mildew, and dust—and yet I'd turned it into a place of comfort, challenge, and solace. How many nights I'd spent practicing and learning, still thinking of spells as I lay in bed, the candles snuffed, the light from the stars revealing the sills, silvering the boards on the floor. I'd stare at the faint light, alive with the excitement of what I'd accomplished, imagining everything that lay beyond the ceiling, the roof, the manse. All that beauty. And as the stars shifted toward the dawn, I'd fall asleep.

I shoved aside such thoughts, and hurried from the room, my stomach a knotted cramp. I ran down the stairs. As I passed Swaine's study, I faltered. Reaching out one hand, I steadied myself against the wall.

Do it.

Each doubt knocked down was replaced by three more, nothing certain. Instead of trying to find solid footing on logic or clarity, I decided that I'd best rely on instinct—for it had done more in the service of the truth than my thinking had managed. And so instinct guided me into Swaine's study, despite the rush of moments roaring by, each one bringing him closer to returning from wherever he was. I ran past the bookshelves and the hearth, his desk and small workbench, dropping my haversack and stopping before the cabinet.

I reached out and tried the handle, knowing it would be sealed, but I was desperate. My footing slipped and my hand skimmed the handle, as before. My skin crawled with whatever bindings he'd wound round the doors. As expected. Fine.

I stared at it, chewing my lip. Could I break the seals as I'd done with the spell on the trunk in his room? Possibly. It was likely the case that his protections were more involved—much more involved—that the simple emplacement glamour he'd used upstairs. I summoned all the witchcraft that flowed through me. Stepping back, I closed my eye and held both my hands before me, palms out, pointing at the cabinet. After a moment, I let my senses flood with energy. Where witchcraft differed from sorcery or magic was this: one came from within, the others originated without. They were all energy, true—and all relied on manipulating such energy. Yet there was a difference between being the boat, and being the river.

With a long exhale, I brought the energy up through my torso and to my arms. As it poured forth from my hands, my emotions released with it, as though swept along with no say on my part. The dam burst, in a real sense, and everything I'd held in check, everything I'd tried to deny, the grief and fear and anger roaring up along with a massive coil of witchcraft. The glare erupted from my hands. Tremendous coils of magic filled the air before the cabinet, extending through the ceiling, through the floor, snapping and hissing. Red lines like windings of super-heated metal glowed from the top of the cabinet to the legs. Wisps of ethereal flame scurried across the surface of it, and I sensed the strength of the bindings. I didn't care how strong they were, their inflexibility served only to enrage me further, and my witchcraft howled in blinding streams across it.

I focused my efforts to an unstoppable stream.

The glamours around the cabinet flew apart, sending bright streamers of light out across the study to collide with other magic, a bombardment of energy that rocked the room. I raised my arms to the sides of my head as the air filled with whizzing bolts that bounced off my cloak. When the air cleared, I flung open the doors of the cabinet. Thick strands of strange magic stretched out from the *Occultum Ostium*, the webbing of a vial spider extending beyond the cabinet, beyond the room, deep into the puzzle of the demonmere. How much trouble had it already caused me? I didn't think about it—because I knew how much trouble it had caused Swaine. I reached in and lifted it with both hands. Heavy as a fieldstone. Grunting, I tucked it beneath my arm and flipped open the top of my haversack, then shoved the book inside amongst my other things. I tied the top and hefted the haversack up over my shoulders. Nothing untoward happened—no slamming shut of the doors of the manse, no rushing footsteps of the revenants, none of the more outlandish fears I'd entertained about what sorts of magic Swaine might have applied to the tampering of his glamours around the book.

I closed the cabinet. Swaine would know the moment he stepped into the study. Nothing I could do about that. No time to waste. Hurrying out the front door of the manse, I sprinted to the workshop, looking for Twelves, prepared to take him with me, whatever urging and cajoling it took. Not finding him, I called for him. No answer. I approached the manse again, shouting his name but hearing nothing. My stomach fell as I realized he was probably out at the sorcerium—and I didn't dare ride out there. No, I'd have to get word to him some other way. Rushing into the stable, my pulse banged away in my ears, my breathing shallow and quick. As fast as I could, I saddled the horse. Leading her outside, I climbed to the saddle and looked back at the manse. The way the moonlight landed on the gables of the manse itself, the dark of the hemlock rising behind it, the faint murmur of the harbor. This place, this time of night—everything sang of *home*.

And I was leaving it.

A tiny voice in the back of my mind offered that there was still time to put the book back, that there was a better way to handle the situation, a smarter way. A safer way. A more honest way. That Swaine would know what to do. That I'd leapt to the wrong conclusions.

Do you know how much I've put into my work with that book?

The welts on my face and hands were testament enough.

That book is never to leave my custody. Never. Ever. Ever.

No, I hadn't—and no, there wasn't. Gripping the reins, I gave the horse a word and my heels, and got her to a trot, then a gallop. I didn't look back, burning with shame to the roots of my hair. I took a route south we rarely used, one that plunged into the dark wood. The old trees reached out their branches tip to tip, bough to bough overhead. I left the sigh of the ocean behind me. Faint moonlight fell in shafts that skimmed across the ghost of the road, itself barely distinguishable from the surrounding forest. How many times had I ridden that way? When might I ever ride it again? I resisted those thoughts and the feelings that crowded my heart and kept my attention on the surrounding forest. The night swallowed me whole.

9

WOLVES OF MY OWN DEVISING

Dawn's first light sketched in the trees. With it came some measure of relief, for my exhausting flight from Salem had taken on the qualities of a nightmare. Hour after hour, alone on one empty road after another, straining my ears for sounds of pursuit, wary of the darkness of the forest on either side, cautious of those open stretches where the moon and stars might reveal my passage. All the while, aware of the *Occultatum Ostium* weighing down my haversack. Bowing my shoulders even more: guilt at my betrayal. Not solely that I'd stolen the book—for that was, in the end, a blow to the demon, not to Swaine. No, the weight I carried whispered of how I'd failed my master by not recognizing what had happened to him as it was happening. I'd been too distracted with my own secrets and deceptions. Spent too much time making and then covering up for my mistakes in judgment. Failure stalked me, wolves of my own creation.

Steering the horse off the road as the black ribbon of the river came into view, I hitched her to a slender birch tree. With aching legs and a sore back, I pushed my way along the gurgling river, bending back underbrush and the branches of saplings as I went.

Birdsong greeted the coming sunrise. Not far from where I left the horse, the first brushes of magic registered in my senses. Shrubs and thickets slowed me down even as the magic grew in strength. I finally shouldered my way through a patch of hazel and spotted the tiny house, tucked against a bend in the river. The walls wore a weathered white-washing beneath a thatched roof. Smoke curled up from the stone chimney. I studied the house and the path leading to it carefully—it matched Doctor Rush's description.

"Hello, Miss Finch."

Staggering forward, I raised my hands in defense. Doctor Rush stood by my shoulder, a pipe clenched in his stained teeth, dressed in a plain set of breeches and a loose shirt of linen.

"How did you—I didn't—" I sputtered.

"I did invent the witch-pole, after all."

"But I didn't see you."

"You wouldn't have." He smiled. "I see you're alone. And rather jumpy. Come."

He led me to the house. As my heart slowed back to normal, I told him about what I'd done. He puffed thoughtfully on his pipe as he went through the small door, so low I had to duck my head to enter. The house had but a single room with a hearth and chimney rising in the middle. A pair of spindle-backed chairs and a slender table occupied one corner, books and papers arranged on most of their surfaces. A trunk sat near the hearth. The other side of the room was home to a narrow cot and a rocking chair hung with bedding. Utensils hung on the stone of the chimney. The smell of the fire just about covered up the musty scent seeping from the roof and floorboards.

"My great-uncle built this," Rush said. "Lived most of his life here. Hunting duck. Fishing. Growing a firm set of opinions as to the corruption of mankind. Yet he was kind enough to leave it to me, a clear emissary of mankind—though I perhaps had a greater sympathy for his opinions than he knew."

He offered me a cup of water and a bowl of porridge, which I gladly accepted as I finished my tale.

After a minute of silence, Rush spoke. "Remarkable. And the book is in your bag?"

I nodded. "You may take a look at it, if you wish."

"I might also shove my hands into the fire, if I wished. I wish neither." He looked darkly at the haversack. "Of all that you've told me, Miss Finch, I find that vile book to be the most disturbing element, by far. I cannot fathom how any modern practitioner of the arts would risk so much as cracking open its covers, knowing the history behind it. Yes, there are the alleged breakthroughs, dramatic innovations—yet the trail of mayhem left behind tells all the tale that any wise individual might need to know."

"It told me things that were true."

"And you have showed remarkable fortitude in resisting its allure—I don't believe most experienced practitioners could have done the same. Nor is it a coincidence that such overtures were made to you in particular because of your nature. That said, I wouldn't trust any perceived motives of it. It's likely that you've frustrated its true plan."

"I don't understand how a book can have a plan," I said.

"It's no ordinary book. The tales vary in the telling, yet it's clear that its true nature falls in the center of a potent intersection of curse, of some form of planar intelligence, and of malign personalities—possibly several of those. I suspect that its origins lie in the form of a quest for some fashion of eternal life." He tapped out the ashes from his pipe. "A goal I'd say best avoided altogether. Eternal life means eternal troubles, if one gives it more than a moment's thought. Better to drink life to the dregs and then get some rest."

"What should we do with it?" I said.

"We will need to hide it, without question. Physically, magically. I know several techniques which should render it unseen from any avenue that your master might pursue—and we must assume that he will pursue all of them. No delay. Come." He motioned that I should take the haversack, which I did with all the eagerness of lifting a bag full of serpents.

"How close is August to finishing the grand summoning chamber?"

"Very. I ran into trouble with the last glamours of the *countervalence*—but as soon as he finishes it, which I believe he's capable of, he could use it."

Rush put a hand to his chin. "But will he? In the condition under which you suspect he has fallen?"

"I don't know." The words broke my heart. How far had Swaine gone? How deeply had the demon wound its way into his thoughts, his soul? The closeness we'd had for so long—was it gone, vanished? That I couldn't find a confident answer to the Doctor's question told me how vast the chasm had opened between Swaine and I. How unthinkable that would have been at any point over the past year—and how cruel the universe was for having turned so. "But we have to do something. To help him."

"The situation may well be dire."

"I know. We can try."

"You understand the difficulties of possession."

"Of course I do—but there may still be time."

"And there may not be. Your master has been rummaging about in a powder house, waving his torch to and fro, convinced how marvelous it all is. Until the flame touched the powder."

"He's always been so careful."

"Powerful demons are subtle," Rush said. "I recall reading of the possession of the great Moulay ibn Muhriz of Marrakesh, long regarded as the most accomplished sorcerer of the last century. In addition to penning three of the art's most detailed compendiums of planar demons, travelling to four continents and in those locales tutoring apprentices who would later go on to make significant names for themselves, Muhriz was known for his extreme precautions. Yet for all that, the demon that eventually destroyed him seemed to have taken well over a decade to insinuate itself into control over him, leaving few signs that Muhriz or his close associates were able to recognize. When his acolytes later gathered to investigate the obliteration of their master, they identified the demon as an entity so powerful that over the centuries it had earned the sobriquet of *Prince of Wretchedness*, one of the three most powerful demons ever recorded. Muhriz was careful—all the good it did him."

My stomach sank as he spoke, for I knew how true his words were. My master was a genius, it was true—and he had the genius' ability to skewer most arguments he didn't care for, and the genius' lack of insight where pride blinded him. Even minus possession. "The book," I said. "It made it worse. It got in the way of his better judgment."

Rush looked over his spectacles at me. "And yet he will fight us every step of the way in order to get it back. We must be prepared to take matters into our own hands." He motioned for me to put the haversack to the table. "As you already have. Your decision to abscond with the book may prove itself to be one critical turn of events in our favor. It was driving his thinking, which could only lead to worse and worse choices on his part. In addition, his desire to get it back may buy us some time for him attempting any larger magic or summonings that might tip the delicate balance that appears to hang over us. Set it upon the table if you would."

I slid the book from the confines of my pack. "He's frantic. I know it."

"All the more reason to cloak it as completely as possible. While we can assume that your witchcraft has been sufficient until now, a moment of distraction, a lapse in effort, slumber—anything might make its location vulnerable to detection." Rush went to his trunk and rummaged through it, coming up with a pair of thin chains. These he spread out on the floor, forming a circle with them. "Place it there, please."

As I brought it to the chains, the book grew restless in my grip, exhibiting a peculiar lightness, as though it was a falcon that wanted nothing more than to launch itself from my hands. I laid it within the chains. Letting go of it struck me as portentous: one more link in the terrible chain that was the history of the *Occultatum Ostium*.

Rush leaned over it. "Very good."

"What spell are you going to use?"

"It is of my own devising, related to my studies of panlocational cartography. I start by imbuing the chains with a charged enchantment similar to a *Beadle eyelet,* if you know the technique."

I nodded. "Recombinent elemental energies."

"Yes. Once activated, and wrapped around the book, I shall excite the state of the energies in such a way as to enfold them in upon themselves, thus creating what you might think of as a planar sequestration."

"The *eaves* of which you've written."

A quick smile flashed across his face. "Under fairer circumstances, knowing my work had been read would have elevated my mood for a day, Miss Finch. Yes, you're correct. Now let's hope that this damnable book isn't laden down with centuries worth of counter-spells."

"My master found it missing anything of the kind. It bothered him. At first."

Rush looked at the book's cover, and where the binding was broken. Frayed bits of string and cloth hung from the spine. Stretches of the top had cracked and buckled like broken ice. He moved his hands just above the surface, whispering what I assumed to be a spell of detection. After a moment, he pulled his hands back and frowned. "Strange—but we lack the requisite hours or more to investigate further." With a grunt, he folded back the cuffs of his shirt.

"Do you need any help from me?" I said.

"Thank you, but no." He rubbed his hands together. "Simple enough, even for one as ancient as myself."

I stepped off to the side. As Rush began the lengthy incantation, I watched the chains brighten, and the air above the book shimmer with faint washes of scarlet, deep as the final rays of sunset on a humid summer day. He continued, and the magic flared. While it did, a sound caught my attention, coming from inside his trunk. A row of glass beakers in a wooden stand sprouted fine scribing, as cracks releasing various stains of leaking fluids discolored the trunk beneath. A glass rod broke into segments. An hourglass grew jagged lightning bolts of cracks on both domes.

Rush finished a section of the incantation.

"Doctor—I think there's a problem," I said.

"I'm not finished." A note of irritation sounded in his voice. Interrupting a spell or a summoning was a profound breach of etiquette.

Holding my tongue, I instead extended my senses, once again encountering the strange energies coming from the *Occultatum Ostium*—twists and arcs of planar force reaching from the book into the surrounding room. Distortions in the air wound up and away, probing. Looking for a way out. Lifting my left hand, I widened my fingers, generating a stream of energy. As Rush continued his incantation, I attempted to draw the planar extensions of the book to me, hoping to contain it until the Doctor's spell took hold. Whatever the energy around the book hoped to reach, I didn't like it. Was it some of Swaine's magic at work? That of the book itself, sending out a flare to its most recent owner? Neither prospect would do. When my energy collided with the distortions emanating from the book, the air in the small house shuddered. The fire shifted in the hearth, embers lifting up in a spiral. A window pane shattered. I gasped, forced back a step by the intensity. Powerful currents of energy whipped about the open room, stirring papers, knocking objects from the shelves, books from the table. Rush raised his voice, his hands lifted over the circle of chains and the book. Timbers creaked and flecks of wattle and pitch fell from the planks of the roof.

"...*proferat, staminis, atque subtegminis, omnisque tenetur in abscondito obumbratio,*" Rush finished. Strands of magic rose from the chains, shifting like the reflections of sunlight on the surface of a fast-moving river. With a shimmer, both the book and the chains vanished from sight. The air pressure within the house trebled, wreaking further havoc with the Doctor's equipment and items, making it difficult to breathe or hear. For a moment, I feared the spell had gone fatally awry. An instant later, the precarious balance shifted as the magic rising from the chains twined together in an intricate pattern and collapsed, taking the powerful energies of the book with them. The chaos ceased. A few last falls of dust sprinkled the stones of the chimney. A lone book tipped off the table and landed on the floor with a bang, causing both Rush and me to jump.

"I like this book even less than before," Rush muttered.

I couldn't disagree. "How did it do that?"

"Unknown—though I suppose not unexpected. That said, I believe it to be well hidden now."

The floorboards appeared free of any signs the book or chains had been there. "Where is it, sir?"

"It's still here. And *not* here. I've tucked it away within an interplanar fold, one not likely to be found or even noticed." He looked over the ruined glass in his trunk. "Rather quick thinking on your part, Miss Finch. I didn't dare stop halfway."

"It was the book, sir. Reaching out, I think."

"Your master's handiwork, we must surmise—though I will say the counter-magic was subtle enough to elude me." He turned. "How did you do it?"

"I—well, I can't quite put it into words, sir. I just knew that a certain kind of energy would attract it. Or distract it. I can't even say. I just knew."

"Your quick thinking may have saved us, allowing me to complete the spell. Magnificent," Rush said. He shook his head, wiping his hands on the tail of his shirt. "If only we had weeks to do nothing but study your talents—I could think of nothing more satisfying. But as it is, time is our enemy, devouring minute by minute the diminishing opportunity we have to prevent a full breach of the planes. Even yesterday, I received reports of what I believe to be yet another demonic incursion in Cambridge. That's the fifth such incident in nearly as many days. The ferocity seems to range from minor—a milliner and his family tormented with flying plates and books in their home—to more significant presences. In Tewksbury, the disruption has been noteworthy. Corpses disinterred, animals turned vicious, several residents gone missing. In Cambridge, a demon appears to have taken the life of one of the city's most active pastors, Benjamin Richards. They found him in the belfry of his church. It looked as though he'd been pulled through the cracks between the floorboards, right in the corner. Rolls of skin, shreds of clothes. A shoe. Wig. Splinters of bone. All the boards sucked in and broken. Stones had scrapes of blood and hair. Even the bells had shattered."

It reminded me of what had happened to the late Governor Whitelocke.

"The public profile of Pastor Richards makes this last incident particularly fraught," he continued. "Word has spread, rumors of how he died. And of course Sackville has the gall to intimate my involvement in the man's death. I never thought much of the pastor, in truth—but now my name is being sullied as a way to rouse the people. Our challenge is difficult enough without the citizenry being told I'm stalking the darkness like Lucifer."

I stepped over to the map on the table. "That would be near the 17th and 19th seals."

"Indeed."

"The first section we need to repair."

"Exactly where we didn't need extra attention."

"Yet if Grayson and Francis keep to their end of the plan, the Governor's men will be drawn off to the shore to the south of the city."

"If they can manage it." He didn't sound convinced.

"They know what they need to do."

"Let us hope," Rush said. "Sackville is a man full of guile—which he subsequently imagines all his enemies to possess in equal amounts. He is, therefore, not a man easily deceived."

Could Grayson and Francis compete against such an opponent? I pushed the thought out of my mind before the answer could land on the wrong side of my question. They had to—there was no other choice. "Well I see no reason to wait, sir. I can't return to Salem now."

"I agree, Miss Finch." He leaned on the table, looking at the map. "The damage to my materials, while unfortunate, shouldn't cause a delay. My remaining supplies shall be sufficient."

As he turned to gather up his equipment, a quartet of shadows swept through the open window and into the interior of the house, whirling counter-clockwise—they appeared to be birds of some kind; not ravens, smaller. A frantic chirping accompanied them, filling my ears as they circled us. Shadow-sparrows?

Rush seemed neither surprised nor startled, but his gaze was sharp and he spoke in an urgent whisper. "Someone approaches." With that, he closed his eyes and raised both hands, speaking several quick phrases. The light from the windows dimmed. I felt a powerful magic engulf the house as I stepped to the window the shadow-sparrows had flow through.

I shrank back, for just past the edge of the clearing strode a revenant from Salem—a man of thirty or so who'd drowned after falling off the pier near one of Boston's waterfront taverns while drunk, revenated the previous September.

So that was that: Swaine knew I was gone, and what I'd taken. He'd sent his demons—revenated, and likely otherwise—out in all directions, searching for me, taking the routes I'd most probably have taken. And while I'd been on horseback, a revenant could run nearly as fast, never tiring, never struggling, bound in speed only by the mechanics of bone and flesh. If I'd still been on the road, if the Doctor's cabin had been much farther, he might very well have caught me unawares, flying from the lane behind me, or leaping from the woods.

The revenant scanned the house and pushed his way through the nearest trees. With a gentle release, I let my witchcraft seep from my palms, wrapping myself in an unseen cloak. Between that and Doctor Rush's magic, the revenant paused, frozen as a statue. Even his eyes remained still. I didn't dare breathe. After half a minute, the figure continued along in the thick woods that bordered the property, parallel to the river. When at last the gray of his tunic and black of his breeches disappeared in the underbrush, I lowered my head with a sigh. He'd lost my trail and any sign of the book.

When I explained to Rush what I'd seen, he set his mouth in a grim line. "We're now being sought on all sides. Are you ready, Miss Finch?"

With one last glance at the trees by the river, I nodded. "Never been more ready, sir."

10

HUNTED

Dusk found the streets of Cambridge nearly barren, a few straggling passersby the only other traffic on the streets between the river and harbor beyond. A distinct chill rode a northeasterly wind. I bunched my fingers together, keeping them warm. Doctor Rush and I made our way through the empty streets on a wagon, our cloaks hiding our faces. We stopped one street over from the church. The final rays of sunset lit the underside of fast moving clouds and gleamed on the brass cross atop the steeple. Across the way, the cupola atop one of the houses at Harvard College faded into the blue gloaming. I pulled the wagon to a stop, eyeing the brick houses and thick hedges for signs of revenants. Or soldiers. I saw neither.

"We'd best start at the church," Rush said before climbing down. "I've no recollection of anything resembling one of the witches' seals in this part of the city. It's quite possible that it was moved or built over in recent decades."

I helped Rush down. The cool wind groped his cloak and coat. We cut between an iron fence and the edge of a burial yard, soon reaching the back of the church. No lights shone. No guards. Glad for the cover of deepening twilight, we slipped in through a door and found ourselves at the back of a large congregation hall, silent and still at this hour. Light from the rising moon brightened the walls to one side, catching stray dust motes as they lazed over the wooden pews. Our footsteps echoed as we hurried alongside the walls to the front. I recalled Swaine's comments to me on the subject of churches: his astonishment that people saw fit to build such inspiring spaces—tall, pleasing, grand—for such unimaginative and tepid purposes. He was even more cutting in his estimation of pastors, men whose egos, humble to the undiscerning eye, were in fact as rapacious as that of any aristocrat or governor, constantly fanned by those who saw a stiff collar and stern countenance as a righteous figure to uphold in their lives. No, my master didn't think much of the whole enterprise. He longed for the time when such respect and architectural endeavor was raised to celebrate human achievement, to honor the mysteries of the universe. The thought darkened my mood, for I had little doubt that it was through Swaine's grandiose sense of self that the demon insinuated its will over his own.

A loft rose above a receiving room and a pair of alcoves, and at the side a narrow door opened onto steep stairs leading up into the belfry.

"It happened up there?" I said.

Rush leaned on his cane. "By all accounts, yes."

"I'll take a look."

"And I will search down here. My hips have complained enough without a climb up a steeple," Rush said. "But be careful. I fear even simple use of magic is leaving a trail of dangerous disorder."

I nodded and started up the steps. Extending my sensitivities, I felt nothing of concern. The stairs rose, angling by ninety degrees every half-dozen steps, eight flights of them in all. At the top, I reached a door in the ceiling. I leaned my shoulder into it, lifting it with a squeal of metal hinges. A pair of ropes stopped it from slamming down. With a steadying hand, I stepped through the floor and into the belfry.

Above my head, the mounts for the bells were empty of their contents. Narrow windows looked out over the city in all four directions, the easterly one brilliant with the rising moon. The small room had unfinished floorboards grown rough and warped in the heat of summers, the frost of winters, and smelled of weathered pitch. Shards of the shattered iron bells littered the floor, pushed into the corners where a broom had left them. The gore of the pastor's demise had been cleaned away—but the stains remained. A wave of gooseflesh broke across my neck and shoulders. As I moved about the tight space, an uneasy energy put me further on edge. More than just being the site of a demonic murder, the belfry felt wrong—that if I looked closely, I'd see that the angles were queer, that the corners held living shadows. That if I would only kneel down and lean forward—

I stepped back just as one of the great chains, freed of its bell, whipped down through the darkness, screaming through the air and splintering the floorboards before my feet. A demon lunged at me, a slender collection of limbs and angles, its winged and barbed shape expanding as it dropped from its hidden perch at the peak of the steeple. Staggering, I lifted my hands and released a blast of witchcraft, enough to send the fiend crashing against the far window. I shouted Hume's Seventh Ward, striding toward the demon with my hand making the proper gesture. A fey light filled the space, running across the hideous face of the demon, goat-like eyes leering at me, a slim mouth extending to reveal rows of fine, pointed teeth.

"Miss Finch?" Rush called from below.

I couldn't spare him an answer, instead crouching and using the residual feeling of the ward to shape another burst of witchcraft. With a hideous cry, the demon turned to shadow, vanishing into nothing like an exhalation fading on a frozen winter's morn. Just as I was about to breathe again, the floor shuddered beneath me. I scanned the belfry for any sign of the demon, or others. Dust tickled my nose and the remaining bell mechanisms rattled overhead. Pulsing waves of planar energy weighed in on me.

"Miss Finch?"

"I'm fine," I called down the stairs. I straightened. The vibrations grew more pronounced. Part of a window frame snapped. I stepped back. Who was I? A barely trained apprentice with raw witchcraft, in the company of a hobbling magician in his ninth decade—the two of us alone in trying to turn back a tide that had been building for decades. The surging planar energy towered around me, convincing me that we were on a fool's course. A hopeless fool's course.

"I'm registering a spike in energies," Rush yelled.

Another chain slipped from its pulley and snaked into a heap in front of me. "Yes—I'm seeing it here."

I tried to connect with the energy as I'd done at the previous seal locations, but it buffeted me about, driving back my attempts. Massive flares of pale light tore the air, tracing arcs and seams that eluded my witchcraft. The temperature dropped. Already exhausted from banishing the first demon, I didn't know if I'd have enough strength to fight a second so soon, so I retreated to the stairs. The walls shook and steps rocked with tremors as I hurried down, one hand on the walls in order to stay on my feet.

Stepping out into the congregation hall, I found Rush crouching by one of his devices: a small brass tripod mounted with a pair of dials and a spinning plum-bob. "I don't like the looks of this at all," he said.

"There was a demon," I said. "Another might be coming."

"I'm not surprised—this seal—wherever it is precisely—seems to have sundered completely. Tremendous flows of planar energy. Tremendous." He tapped one of the dials as though not convinced it was displaying the proper levels. With a glance in my direction, he said, "Could August have attempted to use the sorcerium?"

"I don't think it's ready yet."

"He knows the peril—or at least he *did*—but who knows how much, if any, will he has left. If he or the demon has started tampering with large flows of planar energy, our task will be infinitely more complicated. In the state they're in, the remaining seals won't sustain their integrity. This is precisely what I feared."

An icy draught of air rolled from the stairs leading to the belfry. "I'm not sure it's safe to stay here, sir," I warned.

"Only as long as it takes to get a definitive reading—we need to know what we're dealing with. Without the proper data, we'll have no choice but to fire blindly in our attempts to repair the seals that are still salvageable. Time is slipping through our fingers. We may have none to spare." He peered at the dials. "Almost there. Do what you can to hold the fiends back."

I moved down several rows of pews. The darkness within the stairwell deepened. A pale tentacle slipped past the threshold, followed by another, hard spikes scraping the floor. Curious shadows flitted along the walls and high ceiling, splotches of deep black—ones I recognized from the previous year.

"Doctor—a planar umbra!" I hissed.

"I need more time."

Not shrinking back, I put myself in between the demon and Rush, my hands aloft. Lengths of shadow stretched from ceiling through the walls at strange angles. To my left, sections of a stained glass window crashed to the floor. Reaching deep into my reserves, I drew forth as much witchcraft as I could and projected it like a shield. Faint lines of witchcraft rose through the floor and joined with my efforts—the remnants of the original witches' seal nearby, I assumed. Wherever it came from, I was grateful for the help for the planar umbra swung its attention in my direction, reaching for me with hideous limbs bursting from the steeple stairwell like pale worms, spinning shadows around me like a web.

A terrible wave of nausea swept through me, tilting the congregation hall around me, making my eye hurt, pushing my gorge up into the back of my throat, sending a split down the center of my skull and face. The air around me warped, twisting the darkness in moving spots—one here, one there, sliding from the doorway. I forced myself forward.

"Another minute," Rush said.

The air grew chill as if a sudden winter wind blew. Hymnals lifted, Rush's hair rose, as did mine. Without warning, the candlesticks on the altar lifted off and flew across the church. All around, the space erupted—the ceiling groaning and cracking, another stained glass window shattering. I slid sideways as something grabbed me by the leg. I cried out and flares of crackling bolts shot from the uplifted palms of my hands. In the sudden light, I was face to face with a nightmare. Half-solid, half-shimmering, the demon materialized in front of me. Its central torso and head reached as high as the windows, while the rest of it extended out into fearsome appendages. It was coal-black, a foul bat with the orb eyes of a spider, while the snaking limbs were something dragged up from the depths of the sea, dark and corrupt: bloodless, pale streaks bore hundreds of moving finger-sized tentacles. All around it, the air warped in on itself, bending the walls behind it, twisting the doorframes, stretching it all into a bent glass distortion that seemed to fall into an unimaginable depth.

My witchcraft shot through the air and ran along the grotesque edges of the thing. It thrashed. Behind me, Rush straightened, turning from his device. Limbs tore at the pews and swung through the air. I kept myself between the nearest ones and Rush, who scrambled back. No matter how I positioned myself, the monstrosity came at Rush, backing into him until he was pressed up against the steps to the pulpit. Cracks ran along the ceiling and walls, filling the air with splintered wood.

"*Sumum stōwum swā brād swā man mæg on syx dagum ofer-fēran!*" Rush yelled. A pulse of light burst from his hands and the church shook, grinding bricks and tearing at beams. The beast rocked back, withdrawing its limbs.

I pried my leg loose from the grasping tentacle and released a more powerful burst of witchcraft. The hall went dark again, wisps of shadow and movement all around, somehow nearly as bad as the actual sight of the beast. Around Rush, a glow rose as he whispered, gesturing with his hands, tracing figures, his fingers crossing and curling in strange combinations. I scanned the darkness.

"We have to leave," Rush said. "Keep watch while I gather the equipment."

I moved between the pews into the processional between them, not staying still. "It's still here."

The floor trembled as the fiend came at me, a feint here, a dart there, limbs striking forward like venomous snakes. Each time, I loosed a blinding burst of witchcraft from my hands. The energy blew forward, powerful enough to hold back the fiend, strong enough to shift rows of wooden pews. Above our heads, the beams ran bright with spidery lightning, extending out over them in a moving halo. Rush staggered toward his gear.

"I don't know how long I can do this!" I shouted.

He grabbed the tripod. "To the door," he said.

Before he could take another step, all the doors flew wide open, then boomed shut. All of the glass in the windows shattered, falling to the floor in a song of broken shards. Beams groaned overhead. I leapt to Rush's side, taking his satchel. An icy touch gripped my ankle. I jerked back, seeing a vile coil of shadowy flesh reaching from the center of the hall.

Rush lifted his hand and yelled: "*Ataat da duma frisin cubat atuaid. Dall! Dorcha acht nad fail múr eturru! Na clocha cubat.*

Dorcha ainm in dumai iartharaig. Dall! Dorcha dano ainm in dumai airtheraig!"

The air pulled from my lungs. Everything in the church that could move, did. The chairs in the vestibule, the Bible on the pulpit, the crucifix on the wall, the very timbers all shifted. A thrumming shook the space. The air wound and twisted on itself, forming a giant distortion between us and the planar monstrosity, leaving everything beyond warped, as through a sheet of thin March ice.

"Now," Rush said. We ran for the side door, but two of the pews spun across the floor, careening into the entryway, blocking it. From beyond the wall of the spell came furious movement. A sharp sound grew. Shadows pressed into the half-seen wall, glowing cracks spreading out from half a dozen points, hammer blows onto thick glass. I didn't think we'd be able to make it to the door, so I turned to the nearest window and knocked out a pair of wicked shards.

"Doctor—this way."

Rush kept one eye on the spell he'd cast and allowed me to help him up to the sill. I grabbed the tripod from him and steadied him. He swung one leg out, ducking his head to avoid the broken bits of the frame above. The drop to the soft ground beside the burial yard wasn't quite five feet and he managed it without slicing open his leg or forearms. I shoved the tripod and satchel through to his outstretched hands and clambered up onto the sill myself. A high-pitched squeal, delicate and quavering, sounded from the congregation hall. Shudders spread across the magic behind me, growing ever more intense. Darkness seeped from the cracks, black and blossoming out as ink in water. The darkness was alive; nothing was still. Tendrils of blackness reached for me, swirling, wrapping, spinning.

"Miss Finch, quickly," Rush called.

Horrible thuds and slams filled the church. Laughter erupted behind me. I lowered myself down to the chilly ground, staggering away from the wall. Flashes of light burst from the ruined windows. Holding onto Rush's arm, I helped him as we hurried along the burial yard.

"I was hoping our initial outing would be rather more successful," he said.

"At least we managed to leave the church mostly standing, sir."

We came to the edge of the fence around the graves. The sound of hooves reached us, galloping down the street.

"Wait," I said. I saw nothing at first, but as the sounds grew louder, two mounted soldiers came into view, filling the middle of the street. A large wagon followed, filled with regulars. Four more soldiers on horseback followed. As the sound of the wheels grew, I spotted more soldiers on foot coming from the other direction, all of them moving quickly. They'd spotted us—drawn in by the ruckus, or our passage along the streets noted by the new governor's network of informants, it hardly mattered.

The church seethed with shadows—we couldn't go back that way. "We have to get through the soldiers."

Rush narrowed his eyes. "You handle the ones on the right— I'll take the men on the left."

As the soldiers on horseback neared, I waited until they were closer and then let loose a fire spell, mostly harmless. I hurled the energy down the street, as did Rush in the other direction. With a blaze, my spell released a bloom of fire to spread out across the cobblestones, just before the lead riders. Their horses reared up in fright. Rush's spell—one of chain lightning—erupted behind the last riders, pinning them all between two columns of bright magic. The horses stomped and rolled their eyes and the wagon driver yelled, pulling his horses up before they smashed into the riders in front. The wagon shuddered to a halt. As they struggled the get their horses under control, the soldiers shouted back and forth to each other, some of them reaching for their weapons. A clatter of gunfire exploded from the side street.

In the chaos, Rush and I slipped off parallel to the main road, hurrying to the side of a nearby building just in time to see the soldiers regroup. Behind us, soldiers swarmed, searching for us. One of the horses, riderless and spooked, trotted past us. I reached out and took it by the reins, stepping into the stirrup and dragging myself up onto the saddle. Reaching back for Rush, I grasped him by the wrist and hauled him up after me, his equipment clutched in his other hand.

"Come on," I grunted.

Windows opened up along the street, voices calling out.

"Go," Rush said. It only took a touch of my heels to send the horse into a gallop, flying off away from the flames and noise. I craned my neck, looking behind us. Soldiers regrouped among tattered billows of musket smoke wafting through the street. A lone bell tolled, soon joined by another. As we got further away, I took the horse through a series of narrow streets that led into the wider meadows that bordered the center of Cambridge.

"They'll find us," Rush said.

"Not if we stay off the main roads." As I found a smaller lane, I let up on the reins and the horse slowed, his barrel chest pumping like a bellows. I looked all around, keeping my eye out for patrols. The streets of Cambridge crawled with regulars, patrolling on foot and on horse. We stayed close to the buildings along Water Street, passing by shops closed for the night, taverns shining with lanterns and filled with patrons. Almost everywhere I looked, soldiers—I'd never seen so many, and that they searched for *us* tightened a spring inside me, one turn after another, after another. A large group on horseback appeared down the lane. I took the horse off to the left, along a footpath that led down to the river. Soon enough, the water stretched, drifting and reflecting lanterns across the way. I brought the horse down to the silty banks. Low granite posts marked a slipway. A small boat bobbed against the bank.

"That might be our best chance," I said.

"Agreed." Rush let go of me and I helped him down. Once he was firmly on the ground, I joined him, giving the horse a swat on the flank to get him to disappear out into the darkness alongside the river. Rush hurried to the boat and I helped him in, steadying it. I lifted the equipment in, settling it on the wooden bottom. Rush reached out and took me by the arm. "We need to hurry," he said. I stepped to the side of the rocking boat.

A voice called out behind us, "There. It's them!"

I turned and looked back. Two soldiers stood at the granite posts. More hurried up alongside them. They raised their muskets, steel bayonets fixed on the ends. Rush didn't hesitate— he raised his hands to let fly another spell. But no matter how good a magician he was, we were badly outnumbered, so I turned and shoved the prow of the boat off into the river with my foot, sending it off into the current.

"I'll catch up with you," I said, then turned and filled the narrow footpath between the boat and the soldiers, buying him a few moments.

"Keep an eye on him!" the nearest soldier shouted, pointing at the boat as it left the bank.

I raised up both hands and whispered, "*Nubes nocte carbones.*" The air before me filled with a billowing black cloud. I sprinted off to the left, racing along the river in the opposite direction that the boat was going. Shouting rang out. I stumbled to a halt and looked back just as the boat swamped, Rush fighting off the group of soldiers who'd leapt into the river after it. A spell flared bright blue, but it wasn't enough to keep the boat from capsizing, sending Rush into the water, and into the grasp of the regulars.

Footsteps raced after me. More soldiers charged. I sprang away, and didn't slow. As the path veered away from the water, I tripped over a rock. Staggering out into the street above the footpath, I ran straight into more soldiers. I was trapped. One soldier exploded forward, grabbing me by the back of my cloak and yanking me off my feet. I landed hard and gasped as the air was punched from my lungs, even as more soldiers who'd chased me from the slipway came out next to me.

The man who'd downed me slammed me to the ground with his boot. I lay in the path, half a dozen muskets pointing at me. Raising my hands, I let fly as much energy as I could summon— and with a fuel of fear and frustration, it was potent. I cried out, and the soldiers lifted into the air, shouting. I hurled them back, and they crashed into the ground a good ten strides from where they'd stood, grunts and cursing accompanying their broken wrists or collarbones. Ignoring the pain in my own ribs, I got to my feet and darted right past the groaning soldiers. One of them caught my cloak on the tip of his bayonet, but I tore myself loose and ran faster than I'd ever run. Shouts and the crash of musket shots followed me, but I made for a grazing meadow and then through the woods, grasping for every opportunity to lose my pursuers, darting between stands of oak and stretches of meadow, leaving all paths behind. Eventually I came to a road and paused, panting, holding onto the weathered fence that bordered it. A stitch in my side doubled me over.

I scanned the darkness. Nothing. They'd lost track of me. I let go of the fence, my hands shaking.

He's fine, I told myself, repeating it over and over. I let out a shaky breath. *He got away.*

I turned it into a prayer, repeating it as I raised my cloak and hurried along the empty road. Not far along, I heard the sound of horses. A quartet of cavalry rode out of the night, looming from high on their mounts, their scarlet uniforms dark in the moonlight. I slipped back into a copse of birch trees and crouched, motioned with my hand, and muttered a spell of concealment. The regulars rode two abreast, the hooves of their mounts loud as they ambled right past the spot I'd just stood. They didn't pause, and at least two of them stared right at where I crouched— without seeing me. Once they'd gone, I leaned back, drained.

I felt my way out of the underbrush, soon stumbling across a dilapidated barn, the boards missing from some of the walls, a portion of the roof open to the sky. The fields near it stank of bog. Twenty yards away, the foundations of an old farmhouse gathered moss, the blackened ruins half-buried in the ground like bones. Deer paths crossed through the thickets that kept the entire location hidden from the road. Starlight shimmered in the canting doorframe of the barn. It was as good a place as any to wait out the next few hours.

With a glance in the direction of the road, I ducked my head and passed into the old barn. I was being hunted.

11

CONFOUNDING THE STRIKE

There exists in sorcery a technique known as *confounding the strike*. It works thusly: in the battle of wills that takes place once a summoning has begun, the sorcerer presses and retreats, each press designed to drive the fiend into a defensive crouch, each retreat allowing it to sense a vulnerability. An opening, a lapse. The demon will lunge for that point of weakness. The sorcerer anticipates just such a strike, yet is not there at the moment it's delivered—and is instead closer to the demon than at any prior point in the summoning. No longer out of reach, the sorcerer is where the demon least expects her to be, and in that moment of confusion, has created the greatest opportunity.

It's not for the faint of heart. Yet as Swaine told me when describing it, "Being where you're not expected can yield the richest rewards of all, if you have the courage to commit to it."

Courage. Maybe I had it, or maybe I had nothing more than dressed-up desperation—but I committed to my plan the moment I came within sight of the house just up from the corner of Queen Street. The new home of the Whitelockes, in the heart of Boston. More soldiers near it than practically any dwelling in the city, and certainly under the eye of Governor Sackville and his men. A wrought iron fence enclosed the property. I scanned the dark gables that topped the house, watched windows light up with the dawn. Regulars manned a perimeter around the property; I spotted them one after another.

I reminded myself: courage. With that, I settled in to wait, maintaining a minor enchantment to blend in with the trees across the way. As I'd hoped, I didn't have to wait too long before I saw my opportunity, for not long after the city's bells marked half past eight, a well-heeled carriage behind two horses was brought around to the front door. That was my chance. At a side gate in the fence, a pair of soldiers stood watch. Just steps away, I released the enchantment. One soldier held a hound at the end of a chain, an enormous white beast with mottled scars around its muzzle, black eyes ringed in pink. The dog bristled, and leapt toward me, only to hit the limits of its chain, straining and gasping as the collar bit into its throat. The soldier holding him pulled with both arms, "Back, you bloody monster."

"I'm supposed to report to the kitchen," I said without preamble.

The dog growled, yellowed teeth showing beneath a curl of his black lips, eyes locked on me.

"Not without Mr. Hartley here, you're not," the soldier said, grunting as he held the dog back.

"Not even with this?" I said. I motioned with my hands at both guards. "*Mancynnes weard ece dryhten, teode firum foldan frea almigtig.*"

The guards' faces went slack, and they collapsed to the ground. The air around them flared a pale blue for a moment. Unfortunately, the sleep spell didn't work on dogs, and the beast hurled itself at me. Holding out my hand, I stopped him at the last moment, pouring forth a stinging energy that snapped and popped around the face and chest of the hellhound. He snapped at the air, shaking his head as though being stung by a swarm of yellow jackets, pawing at the ground.

"Go," I whispered, giving him a hard shove with my foot. Tail between his legs, the poor thing scurried off. I dragged both guards into the hedges. Taking my time, I spoke the words of an Italian spell, straight from the school of *Magia Nera*—and watched as streaks of shadow sped out over the ground, along the branches and leaves of the bushes, the stone, the flagstones, carrying with them a potent dollop of vague fear powerful enough to dissuade anyone from approaching. That done, I waited by the open gate.

A moment later, the carriage rocked forward, the driver steering the team back toward the gate. Staying out of sight over the bodies of the sleeping guards, I waited until the horses passed before stepping out, reaching for the handhold alongside the carriage door, swinging up onto the runner. Before the carriage pulled out onto Queen Street, I had the door open and slid myself inside, unnoticed by either the driver or the postilion who rode alongside him.

Mary Whitelocke sat on the cushioned bench opposite, voluminous skirts of ruby silk over a deep black petticoat, black embroidery and lace climbing the waist and sides in a flowery pattern, matching the white ruffles of the low-cut collar. I took a seat across from her, my finger to my lips as I quietly closed the carriage door. The driver started the team forward onto the main road, setting the carriage to rock on its springs, the wheels to raise a din against the cobblestones. I cast my eye to the gilded ornamentation of the carved mahogany, the fine joinery, the velvet of the cushions. I imagined the carriage had cost more than most Bostonians earned over several years. "You're becoming as bad as Doctor Rush," Mary said, one hand to her chest. "And what happened to your face?"

My fingers brushed the fresh scar on the side of my face

where Swaine's riding crop struck me. "This—nothing. They have Doctor Rush. The Governor's men."

"They do—but that's not everyone they have. They have Grayson. They have that—*Rattlesnake* leader."

"What?"

"Both of them, plus some others. They raided the powder house at the end of the Common, or tried to. Just last night. And every last one of them was either captured or killed. I learned of it practically before the Governor did—my eyes and ears are all about, none of them much fond of our new leader."

No wonder there'd been so many soldiers about the city when Rush was captured. "They weren't supposed to be anywhere near there."

"This is Grayson we're talking about, darling. My late brother was the tactician of the family. An officer worthy of the name."

Francis. It was Francis' idea, I was sure of it. "This is bad."

"Do you think so? Because it gets worse," Mary said. "They're bound for London on the morrow. Word is they've already been brought out to one of the ships in the harbor, readying to set sail."

"Which ship?"

"I don't know." She frowned. "But I aim to find out. Sackville likes to think he's serving the Lord's purpose. He likes to imagine he's rock-ribbed, steely-spined. The King's right hand. But I've noticed the man is distinctly afraid of women—so he ought to be terrified of me."

"Terrified enough to clap you in irons along with the others."

"He wouldn't dare."

"I don't think shame is his strong suit."

"Shame has nothing to do with it," Mary said. "It's all politics. He can abscond with Grayson and very few feathers are ruffled. A few more with the Doctor—but no one was ever really at ease with the old gentleman. Boston's elite can rest easy with those two languishing in a London prison. That calculation changes with me." She adjusted the curls in her hair. "If Sackville so much as hints at dislodging me from my perch, he'll immediately lose the modicum of trust he's been granted by everyone who matters in the colony. He can't afford it. Shame or not, he can read the political ledger well enough, I presume."

"Let's hope you're right." I wasn't convinced, remembering the look on the Governor's face as he'd scanned the inaugural crowd for the person—elite or not—who'd tossed horse dung at him.

"I have a gift, darling. Rather as magical as yours—just not involving magic, sadly. Or sorcery—which reminds me: with Grayson and the good Doctor checked off Sackville's list, August is no doubt left at the top, all on his own. He needs to know."

I must have flinched under the memory of my master's blows, for Mary sharpened her gaze on me.

"Is he all right?" she said. Then, leaning closer, "Are *you* all right?"

She had a gift indeed. "We had—a falling out. A terrible one."

She pointed at my cuts. "Tell me those aren't from August."

"It's not—not really."

"Not really? I don't like the sound of that. What happened?"

As the wagon crossed from Queen Street through one of the market squares, I gave her a brief version of what I'd told Rush, what had happened in Salem. With a question here and there, she pulled more out of me. After a minute, it took all I had to keep my emotions in check, for even relating Swaine's brutal treatment of me on the wagon brought it all back to me. The sting, the shame. The confusion. Words poured from memory.

"What does that mean?" Mary interrupted me as I relayed what he'd shouted as me while I was lying in the road.

"What?"

"*Holding every gift—gifts excluding none?*"

"It means—well, all he's taught me, I suppose."

"It's a strange way to say it."

"He was furious."

"Even stranger, given that."

The image had seared into my memory, my master leaning over the wagon's side, smacking it with the crop as he shouted, "*Pay attention. Holding every gift, gifts excluding none. Feel I never cared—helped?*" It *was* a curious construction, now that Mary pointed it out. Even the end phrase, *Feel I never cared—helped* was choppy, unlike Swaine's normally fluid diction. And curiously, when I'd seen him angry—though, to be fair, not nearly as angry—in other moments, his words typically grew more clear, not less.

Feel I never cared—helped? The phrase circled in my head. *Pay attention...Feel I never cared—helped?*

Mary leaned forward. "Why would he—"

I held up my hand, shushing her.

Feel I never cared—helped?

And I saw it: *Feel. I. Never. Cared. Helped.* The first letter of each word. F-I-N-C-H. *FINCH.*

"But—" Mary tried again.

"Wait." I closed my eye, recalling the rest of the phrase after *Pay attention: Holding every gift, gifts excluding none.* H-E-G-G-E-N.

In other words: Pay attention. Heggen. Finch.

Heggen? I opened my eye—I'd heard that name before. Heggen. Heggen. A proper noun, not the name of a person, or a technique, or a spell. Heggen? No, it was a place. My thoughts raced this way and that as Mary stared at me. A place—a Scandinavian place. A village: Heggen.

And then I had it, I remembered where I'd heard that name.

"My God—he's giving me clues."

"Clues? Why not just tell you?" Mary said.

"Because of the demon," I said, seeing it clearly, my heart taking sudden flight. "My master is still there, somewhere—not all the way in the thrall of the demon. And he's giving me clues, clues the demon won't see, won't understand. Can't. Clues for me to help him. He knows—he knows what's happening."

And he trusted I'd figure it out.

That he had such trust in me struck me with the force of a cannonball. All he'd shown and done for me, the miserly compliments I'd wrung out of him, the uncomfortable moments of genuine affection—none mattered more than Swaine's trust that I would hear the message he was hiding from the demon, and that he expected me to know what to do with it. I explained the code to Mary.

"What on earth is a Heggen?" she said.

"It's a village. In Norway. Deserted, abandoned—somewhat like Salem. My master visited it two years back, before he left London."

"And?"

"And—I'm not sure what to make of it. But there's an answer. I feel it."

"He's not suggesting a trip to Norway is required?"

"No. It's something else." I put my hand to my forehead, thinking. I cursed myself for not taking more books when I'd left Salem—returning to do research in the library was out of the question. As was returning to the Andover house, which still held a small selection of my master's library. No, both those options were no good. I lowered my hand. "Doctor Rush's house."

"What about it?"

"Drop me off near it."

"It's being guarded."

"So was this carriage."

"If you're caught by Sackville's men, you won't be able to help August."

"I don't plan on getting caught—just drop me off nearby."

Thinking back to Rush's secret hideaway on the harbor island, I'd seen a handful of books, a dozen at most—those he'd brought with him on his flight from the Governor's attention. Even fewer had joined him in his great-uncle's small house in the woods. The bulk of his collection, therefore, still resided at his house on Crooked Lane, guarded or not. It was the best chance I had.

"We're being followed," Mary said, flicking her fingers in the direction beyond the rear of the carriage. "Everywhere I go lately. A pair of men on horseback, sometimes together, sometimes apart. Subtly isn't part of Governor Sackville's repertoire."

"Then we'll distract them—and you can lead them on somewhere else after I get out."

She kept her eyes on mine and reached up and pulled a slender velvet rope that ran above the window. I heard a bell jingle at the front of the carriage. The driver slowed the horses, bringing us to a stop next to a chandler's shop.

"Madame?" he called.

Mary leaned over to the open window, raising her voice. "I've very nearly forgotten—Alice Howe has promised for ages to return the fox-fur cape I lent her at the ball last winter. Perhaps if I darken her doorway she'll finally relent and do so. If I wait until the weather grows chill again, I'll have to pry it from her dainty little fingers. Over to Dartmouth Street, if you would be so kind."

"Of course, Madame Whitelocke."

The carriage started forward again. Mary lowered her voice. "We'll be two streets over, nearer the scrappy houses behind the Doctor's. That should leave you with only four or five guards to deal with, as opposed to the dozen or more you'll find on the side facing the Governor's manse."

I peered out the back of the carriage, soon spotting two riders following us. They wore no uniforms, but their demeanor and physiques nonetheless marked them as soldiers. They kept their distance, six horse-lengths back or so, but made every turn we did. Traffic increased as we drew onto Dartmouth Street. I looked for my opportunity—and it didn't take long. I turned to Mary.

"Be careful with the Governor," I said. "I don't have as much confidence in his ledgers as you. If you find out the name of the

ship, leave it on a note rolled up and tucked next to the sword of
Warren Peabody—you know the statue by the green?"

"Eternally watching against vile devilry? I'm surprised
Sackville hasn't had it moved to his bedchamber yet—but yes.
And I'll find out. What else can I do?"

I moved closer to the door. "Stay safe, most importantly. Slip
away, the evening after next. Alone."

"Should I use magic—for a distraction?"

"I wouldn't."

"Where's your confidence in your best pupil?"

"Spells might draw a demon to you."

"I'd best sneak off, then."

"Exactly. Get to Andover. The tavern—Knox's Tavern and Inn.
Bertram is the owner. Wait for us."

"Us?"

"The Doctor. Your brother. A Rattlesnake. Me."

"And then what?"

I put my hand on the door. "And then we save the colony and
rescue my master."

"Is that all?"

"You said we oughtn't dream small, didn't you? We girls can
make a difference, and all that."

Mary leaned back and smiled. "You were listening, after all."

"Just keep the riders following us as busy as you can after I
cause a little distraction."

"I'll give them a ride around Boston they won't soon forget."

Passing us in the other direction was a slow moving dray,
loaded down with hogshead barrels. As it got behind us, I raised
a hand and concentrated, familiar enough with wood magic that
I barely needed to struggle to connect with it. As soon as I did, I
flexed the staves on two barrels, wrenching them along the length
of their grain, prying at the latent energy still within the wood.
Black liquid leaked from the sides soon enough. I didn't wait, all
too aware of Doctor Rush's observation that moments mattered

even as they slipped away. With a tremendous exertion, I released a massive current of witchcraft into the barrels. They burst asunder with a pair of crackling bangs. Printers' ink spattered everything within a dozen paces, a hundred gallons or more sluicing off the dray and onto the street in ropey strands. The drayman cursed. Horses balked at the sudden puddle of ink. A murmur of voice rose as the people nearest reacted to the strange sight, many shocked to find droplets of black staining their garments.

"Stay safe," I whispered to Mary before swinging open the door and gracefully stepping down from the moving carriage. As I hit the ground, I spun, catching my balance and darting off into an alleyway, raising a momentary blur around me with my witch-craft. With everything else going on in the street, I counted on being no more than an innocuous flash of movement out of the corner of all eyes as I headed to Doctor Rush's house, confounding the strike yet again.

12

BENIGHTED LANDSCAPES

Whatever knack I'd developed for slipping past armed regulars gave me little comfort. As I crossed into the cool shadows of Doctor Rush's house, I was all too aware that it would only take one miscalculation on my part and all of the witchcraft in the world couldn't protect me from enough brawn and steel. Three guards, distracted by the commotion down the street. Two more, senseless and hidden behind a woodpile. Yet how many others watched the other side of the house? How often did they change shifts? Had I missed any? Cordoned off as though a plague house, there was no mistaking Governor Sackville's paranoia in his dealing with the Royal Doctor of Magickal Science's residence, his desire to maintain eyes on it. Every minute I spent in it risked discovery.

Furniture stood in disarray. Shelves disturbed. Drawers rifled through. Those and other signs of a thorough search marked every room I passed through, nothing subtle about it. Staying out of the sight lines of the windows, the fear rose that Rush's entire library had been confiscated—after all, books on magic were illegal in all cases, save that of his appointment. And what might

Sackville enjoy more than stripping Rush of all aspects of his reputation, his books a tangible sign of his troubling expertise?

Scraps of paper and remnants of glassware littered the hallway between his workshop on the top floor and the stairs I climbed. I explored the second floor until I came across the Doctor's library, tucked into a slanting room beneath the eaves on the northern side of the house. Currents of magic crisscrossed the doorway. I'd noted much of the magic Rush kept in place was still quite active, despite the raiding of his home. Not that it would do him any good.

His library impressed me after a single glance across the two walls of books, taking in the arrangement. Whereas Swaine's collection of books existed in an ever-changing landscape carved by his immediate fascinations, his argumentative debates with theories he questioned, and his habit of dropping one pursuit for another regardless of where he might find himself—thus my unending shepherd-like mission in keeping the books at least somewhere near at hand—Doctor Rush's shelves stood neat, each volume labeled with the author's last name, A occupying the highest left-hand shelves, down to Z on the bottom right of the second set of shelves. No dust dimmed head nor spine. Where a book had been taken down, its home was left open. All stood at attention, no laggards allowed to slant or rest horizontally, save for those stacked on a nearby reading table.

When I examined those, I felt a pang of gratification. One stack of books contained *Memorable Provinces Relating to Witchcrafts and Possessions, The Atlas of the Sight Beyond,* and *The Spirit Treatise of Isaac Levy, Esq.* Next to those stood H.S. Spenser's 1723 volume *English Civil Law and the Restrictions on Magicks,* which posited—incorrectly, it seemed—that with the eradication of the Settlers in Salem, the British Empire had seen the last of witchcraft. There was John Bartlot in his 1599 *Witchcrafte for the Versant Magickian,* a ribbon left by the Doctor at a page noting that witchcraft as a magic bore a strong, natural femininity, using words such as *pungent, fecund, pliant, rich*, and *nurturing* to describe the blending and transformation of elements that suffused it as resembling "*...leaves rotting into soil, from wherein springs the shoot from the seed, and the bloom opening as an expression of the water, the air, the sunlight...*" Bartlot wasn't far off.

A further ribbon left by the Doctor in Giles Wren's *Unknowne Manifestations of Magicke* indicated a passage proposing the traits that marked witches arose in isolated populations subject to frequent planar incursions, and what witches possessed were heightened versions of senses innate within all people. Beside this was one of Emelie Du Marien's works, *Le Royaume des Ombres* (*The Realm of Shadows*), and a page outlining her compelling supposition that certain female sorcerers were, in fact, witches. Beneath this lay a battered edition of Angus Hume's translation of the *Srávobhiśśravasíyas*, in which Rush had marked a passage referring to the "*... layer upon layer of meaning in the sixth through ninth series gestures, designed to echo the subtle manipulations of planar streams accessed by witches.*"

Finally, I looked at a page marked in Doctor Rush's own *On Planar Cartography*, wherein he detailed the workings of the witch-poles:

Thus harnessing the central transferrent principles with the alchemical blending of recombinant energies, the application of such efforts to the object-based binding of the witch-poles throughout the Colony render them critical in the detection of witches. A lantern of silver and pewter and steel, forged and shaped (by the noted silversmith Apollos Rivoire), imbued with a sequence of spells that work to redirect the forces and energies of a second-order plane into a pattern that loops in on itself in seven folds, creating an effect as though curving mirrors expand outward in such a fashion as to tune the witch-pole to the specific currents of planar force that all witches, by their nature, must possess.

"All witches," I whispered. "By their nature."

The wind rattled the shutters outside the library. *Their nature.*

And what was *my* nature? Did I know—had I *ever* known? A child, a sister, a daughter. A Finch of the well-stationed Finches of Mayfair, weaponsmiths to Kings. Were those my nature, or were they costume of the sort Grayson Whitelocke had insisted so many mistook for their authentic selves? Certainly, when they'd been torn from me—wrenched away by the demon—they'd been revealed as every bit as fragile as a mask of papier-mâché. Orphan, indentured servant. More horrid conditions thrust upon me by chance. Apprentice? Student of the unseen arts? Yes, closer, I supposed, having taken those on of my own volition.

But underneath, who was I?

Pay attention. Heggen. Finch. The clues from my master echoed in my thoughts.

In that moment, I decided I was Katherine Patricia Finch: witch and apprentice. And I was going to save my master, August Swaine.

Thus armed, I descended upon Doctor Rush's collection of books, searching for answers—starting with the only clue I had to go on: Heggen. For Swaine to risk giving the name to me, it had to be the key. Yet the more I searched, the less confident I grew. For half an hour, I searched book after book. A passage here, a chapter there, commentary after commentary—and came up empty. Scandinavian authors. German. English. Desperation took hold. And all the while, I listened for signs that the missing guards had been noticed. Keeping panic at bay, I scanned quickly through the shelves, no longer even sure what I was looking for. I found no almanacs. Nothing helpfully titled *The Story of Heggen, Norway.*

Running my finger along the spines, I paused when a particular name caught my eye—Heinrich Flüsse. Where had I seen that recently? I pulled out the book and flipped it open. My German was passable. As I read through various descriptions of planes, I recalled that Flüsse was one of Gustav Koeffler's apprentices, one whom my master had great affection for. I was just about to put the book away when my gaze stopped on a particular phrase: *Spiegel Verstärkung*. I'd seen that recently, as well. Where?

Closing my eye in concentration, I thought back—and then I had it. When I'd looked in Swaine's room I'd found a note he'd written, the page marked with a curious drawing of a mule in the lower corner. At the memory, my breath caught. *A mule.*

It was another clue—one that would, or ought to have been, clear to me, but one that would mean nothing to the demon slowly throttling my master's will. The mule kick I'd received as a two-year-old had cost me my eye. Was it yet another example of my master saying *pay attention*? It had to be. What was it he'd written?

It'd been about time—the arrow of time, peculiar in that it only points in one direction. And what else? The hundreds of hours of study I'd done with Swaine had strengthened my memory enormously—the spells, the references, the theories he'd expected me to master. I thought back to the note he'd written. Fragments came to me. *What if time could be bent? Drawn into a Burnsian channel? If the forces could be great enough to form what Flüsse envisioned in his concept of the Spiegel Verstärkung? What might that do to the arrow of time? Might it be enough to pry loose the diaglamourous energies manifested—or not? A point of focus worth exploring, closely. Worthy of the sorcerous mind.*

While it was fresh in my mind, I wrote it down, scratching out the sentences on a paper taken from Rush's writing desk in the corner. I read them over. What had Swaine wanted me to notice? I wasn't sure what a Burnsian channel was, though I suspected it had to do with Elwood Burns, a magician of Knightsbridge who, after Edward Neile, was generally considered to be the most influential name in the realm of magical metallurgy. And how did that relate to Flüsse and his *Spiegel Verstärkung*? What was it even saying? I kept returning to the final phrases. *A point of focus worth exploring, closely. Worthy of the sorcerous mind.* Those were clearly Swaine's message to me—for how often had he told me that the sorcerous mind has but one point of focus? Hundreds. More. A point of focus worth exploring. One point of focus.

I still didn't understand. I reread the sentence preceding them: *Might it be enough to pry loose the diaglamorous energies manifested—or not?* Something peculiar about the phrasing. I looked more closely. *Pry loose the—diaglamorous energies manifested —or not.*

Diaglamorous. Energies. Manifested. Or. Not.

DEMON.

Might it be enough to pry loose the *demon?*

Swaine was pointing the way for how he might be rescued, I was sure of it. I didn't know enough of sorcery to drive off the demon on my own—but Swaine did, and counted on me to decipher the method from his clues.

Heggen. Flüsse. *Spiegel Verstärkung.* One point of focus. Burns. It was in there, somewhere.

Trying to keep my thoughts clear, I pored over Flüsse's book, trying to see what I could make of the *Spiegel Verstärkung.* Translating roughly into *Mirror Amplification*, it appeared to describe the phenomena of magic's strange behavior when attempted in close proximity to a planar boundary, likening it to the visual curiosity achieved by aligning two mirrors such that they create the illusion of a never-ending hallway arching into the distance in both directions. In the case of focused magic, he noted that each subsequent reflection increased the raw energy, quickly rendering it too wild to control.

But how might that affect time? A demon? The near-certainty that I was in well over my head closed in on me. I put the book aside, chewing my lip, staring at the shelves. Looking up, I stretched to the top shelf and read the names—and found *Enchanted Properties of Various Metals*, by Elwood Burns. Yanking it down, I brought it into the light. It wasn't a small work.

What I was looking for—a *Burnsian channel*—was almost certainly not even referred to as such in Burns' own book, the sobriquet likely bestowed by later practitioners.

I leafed through the pages. "Where? And what?" I whispered, as though imploring Swaine to give me something more specific to go on. Much of what I skimmed dealt with the rigorous study of the properties of metals with a particular focus on their application in glamours. Fine: glamours. Swaine used them all the time. The grand summoning chamber of the sorcerium thrummed with glamours. I paused, thinking of the various tuning rods Twelves had installed. I quickly flipped back a dozen pages, having seen the word 'rods' moments earlier. One page, another, another—none of them correct.

From outside the house, a voice called out for someone named Eagleton. With a glance at the window—and the sinking feeling that one of the guards behind the woodpile was named Eagleton—I returned to the book.

There. Rods—and mention of a channel. I didn't do more than read it quickly—"...*the creation of such a channel to link disparate glamours by carefully modulating the planar deportment of each via calibrated tuning rods embedded with specific purities of metals, activated into a state of sync through parallel enchantment...*"—before realizing it had to be relevant. I took the book and laid it atop the volume by Flüsse, certain I was on the right path, even if I couldn't put it all together yet. Pieces of the puzzle.

But what about Heggen? Nothing I'd found seemed to connect to it. Burns was English. Flüsse German. Had they ever traveled to Norway? How could I ever know it if they had?

"Private Eagleton!" came a call from what sounded like just beneath the window to Rush's library. I stayed out of sight, rather than leaning out and helpfully offering that they might find their missing private behind the woodpile around back. A gasp of nervous laughter fluttered from my lips. I bit it back and considered the haul of books spread out before me, their pages marked with scraps of paper and ribbons. I stared at them with growing panic, sorting through what I'd read, fitting it together with Swaine's clues.

Heggen. Still nothing. I shut my eye, thinking. Swaine had traveled there. An abandoned, accursed village in the depths of a Scandinavian forest. The sum total of what I knew of Heggen.

A door banged open on the first floor. "Take a look around," someone said.

I cursed under my breath and crouched behind the mostly open door. What sounded like a pair of soldiers tromped through the rooms below. "Eagleton? Murray?" One of the searches started up the stairs. Feeling once again the magic Doctor Rush had lined the doorway with, I used it as a boundary for an expression of witchcraft designed to keep me hidden from all but the most direct observation, blending in with the shadows behind the door. The regular reached the hallway and started down it, stopping at each room, presumably peering in. When he neared the library, I went as still as I could, concentrating on nothing but my witchcraft. He stepped into the room, his weight creaking the same floorboards I crouched on from the other side of the door. He didn't linger, not finding his brother in arms perusing Rush's collection. Turning on his heel, he continued along the second floor and finally up to the third, calling out to the other one downstairs that he'd found nothing but the curse Doctor Rush had clearly levelled on anyone foolish enough to intrude on his premises. His footsteps passed by the library one final time before heading back down the stairs.

I relaxed my witchcraft. Before I got up, my gaze landed on the spine of a book level with my eye, toward the end of the second lowest shelf opposite. In Rush's spidery handwriting: *Maxwell Gordon – Benighted Landscapes & Abandoned Regions.* Listening as the soldiers talked and made their way back outside again, I leaned over and plucked the book from the shelf.

A slender volume, the book had a dusty ribbon inserted in the pages towards the end. Carefully cracking the book open, I saw a chapter entitled "Salem: A Tale of Devilry". The first few paragraphs outlined the incidents leading to Salem's abandonment— a fair enough rendition, for the most part free of the hysterical nonsense of Major Thomas Abbott's ubiquitous *Accounte of the Defeat of the Infernal at Salem*. No surprise that Rush would have marked the chapter.

Flipping the pages, I went farther back in the book, my pulse quickening. One chapter focused on the bleak haunting of the Bábolna Forest in the Kingdom of Hungary. I knew that tale: a cruel demon so spiteful that even after its summoner—a would-be sorcerer whose name was lost to history—was flayed, tortured, and obliterated, it continued to wreak horror on the region wherein it had been bound for decades. Fanning the prior pages, I also found a chapter on the *Devil of the Three Rivers*, recounting the infamous disappearance of an entire village near the town-land of Lusmagh in King's County in Ireland in 1577 (the attribution referred to the three rivers bounding the area, the River Lusmagh, the River Shannon, and the Little Brosna River.)

And then I came to the chapter on Heggen.

My frown deepened as I read. Gordon's account began with legends of a local physician who was purported to also be a sorcerer, a man by the name of Arvo Kühlewind. Kühlewind stumbled across a particularly baleful demon, an arch-fiend, bending him to his will in the depths of the nearby forest. The demon in question rather cleverly tricked his aged master into allowing his young granddaughter Ágnes to play with the accursed glass music-box that he'd been bound into. The villagers recounted how poor Ágnes had appeared to sponta-neously sing in a tongue she'd never learned, one comprised of the demon's true name—*Svaradallanave*—sung over and over. The child had unwittingly weakened the bindings—perhaps aided by the failing senses of Kühlewind himself—and the demon wasted no time in possessing her. Under the demon's thrall, the child flayed Kühlewind and seventeen other members of his family, murdered sixty-four other people in Heggen, and set fire to every structure in the village before disappearing into the Skygget Mountains. The child's body was found staked upside down to a stout tree branch that reached across the opening to a cave known thereafter as *Djevelens Hul* ("Devil's Cave"). More alarming, the region around the village displayed concentrated demonic activity at such a level that all inhabitants within a twelve mile radius either fled or disappeared over the next six months, leaving that section of the valley abandoned for nearly a century. Rumor spread, eventually attracting the attention of one of Gustav Koeffler's brightest apprentices: Heinrich Flüsse.

My eye widened. I read on.

It seems that Flüsse investigated the village in the year 1651, soon identifying the presence of three separate planes, using their full names as designated by Koeffler: *Mitternacht Treppen und Türen* ("Midnight Stairs and Doors"), *die Beschatteten Tal* ("the Shadowed Vale"), and *Wo die Sterne Flüstern* ("Where the Stars Whisper"). It was in conjunction with this latter plane where Flüsse claimed to have encountered an enigmatic realm of endless staircases, stairwells, doors, landings, and corridors.

I paused—the demonmere.

Intriguing, yes. As intriguing, no doubt, as my master had found it when he'd decided to travel to Heggen himself to explore.

And what had he brought back with him from Heggen?

I flipped back to earlier in the chapter, to mention of the arch-fiend.

Svaradallanave.

From outside the house came raised voices. I knew immediately—they'd found the soldiers I'd stunned. While they were distracted, I had a chance. I swept up the books I'd gathered, jamming them down into a leather satchel I found wedged next to Rush's writing desk. Racing down the steps, I ran to the side door to the kitchen, on the opposite side of the house from where the searching soldiers gathered. With a quick peek outside, I sprinted from the doorway, keeping near to the hedges, unseen for a precious few moments. By the time I reached the next lane over, I clutched not only the satchel of books, but the one thing I hadn't had enough of lately.

Hope.

13

SOMETHING TERRIBLE

I stood at the foot of Fort Hill, on a grassy slope not far from the South Battery. In front of me ran an empty street, beyond it wharfs and docks spread out on either side, faint beneath the moon. Out in the harbor, the hulking ships rocked at anchor. Any one of them might have held Doctor Rush, Grayson, and Francis—and I had nothing to go on. The statue of former governor Warren Peabody had contained no note from Mary Whitelocke telling me what she'd learned. Perhaps she hadn't learned the name of the ship. Perhaps her note had been snatched away by one of the many spies of Governor Sackville after she left it. A darker thought was that she'd been apprehended, her calculation that Sackville wouldn't dare disproved. I scanned the harbor, desperate.

A company of soldiers occupied the Battery, a fortified two-story building across from one of the larger wharves. Only a few guards stood watch at that hour, outlined against the lantern light coming from within the building. Sticking to the shadows, I skirted the building and followed the road, clambering down to the water's edge. A dock jutted out into the harbor. Larger wharves extended on either side, fishing boats lashed to the pilings, the lap of the water beneath the wooden planks echoing, a lonesome sound.

I stared out at the ships. Some were dark, but a few shone with lights through their small windows and portholes. Which one? A large one caught my eye, though I had no way of knowing if it held the prisoners. My exhausted mind skirted over spell after spell, but came up empty. Most of the larger ships were far enough away I wouldn't be able to read their names even if I knew my target, in any event.

Steal a dinghy and paddle across the harbor, searching one ship at a time? Hours. Swim out? Not after my near-drowning in the river—I hadn't taken more than a bath since then and slipping into the black water of the harbor filled me with an unsurmountable terror. I paced back and forth, my steps shifting the smoothed stones that marked the high tide's edge. After a minute, I stopped. What might Doctor Rush do? That I wasn't there with them would, at the least, give him hope that I hadn't yet been captured. And while he mightn't know for certain, it was the only hope he had, for the new Governor's men would have stripped him of all but his clothing, bound his hands, and gagged him, all to prevent him from casting any spells. That would be a sound strategy on their part—but not all magic required voice, ingredients, or gestures. If he believed I was still free—again, a rather presumptuous *if*—he might reveal his location in some fashion hidden to any guards. But what? I recalled various spells of beckoning, of flares, of unseen bells, though I couldn't account for how *any* of them might be executed without full freedom of word and motion, let alone the component materials. None were trivial incantations. No, it would have to be something different.

I resumed pacing, casting my memory back through book after book, spell after spell. While Ephraim Rush was certainly familiar with many such books, more than I was— he'd *written* one of the most well-regarded texts in the field, *On the Principles of Planar Cartography*. A book that explored, at remarkable depth, a vast spectrum of concepts pertaining to *location*. At Swaine's insistence, I'd read the book. And out of my admiration, I'd read it a second time, the moment I'd finished the last page. I scanned the dark harbor. Doctor Rush was out there somewhere, and I was certain he was signaling his location. Would he expect that I might have any instruments with me? Of course not. Requisite materials for the experiments and spells of which he wrote? No. He did, however, understand that I carried something just as sensitive to the planes, something that didn't fit in a haversack or case: my nature, my witchcraft. It hit me like a thunderbolt.

That's how I'd find him—if I were clever enough to follow his lead, and do something about it.

Fine, a signal. A planar signal. What? I let the water roll up across my shoes. Could Doctor Rush create disturbances at the border of the one plane where it met with our own? He'd mastered a technique of accessing the *occulta proluo*—the *planar eaves*—at will, having studied them for half a century.

If I concentrated, opening and extending my hidden senses, what would I see? I hesitated, still uncertain, and aware that doing so might put me at tremendous risk, what with Swaine searching for me, and with demons about.

Demons.

I stopped my thoughts there, mid-step. That was it—it had to be. If Rush had found a way to disturb another plane enough to attract the interest of a demon or two, I might deduce his location from their reaction to my presence. Setting aside for the moment the danger, for such a move on my part had the potential to tip my hand to Swaine, I thought it possible.

So with everything to lose, and no promise of gain, I stepped back from the water to a place of firm footing, and readied myself. I settled on Hume's Fourth Ward, the most potent—and fastest—ward I'd mastered, placing it in my mind, within easy reach. With one long glimpse across the harbor before me, I let out a long breath, and opened my senses.

When the attention of a demon swings in one's direction, an unnerving sensation crawls across the back of the neck, a sense of directed malice grips the heart, a sudden alarm sounds deep within the mind. What happened when I revealed my full nature wouldn't have stunned me more than if I'd been drenched head to toe in icy water. I'd expected one, two—a handful, at most, but more demons rushed me in that instant than I'd ever seen at once, or ever *thought* I'd see at once. Demons—scores, more— prowled the harbor like monstrous sharks, circling around, above, and underneath a large four-masted ship that rode at anchor several hundred yards from where I stood, a pair of windows at its stern lit up. And half a moment later, the fiends flew at me, their new prey, shadows ripped from the water, hurtling through the air, all desiring to devour me.

The water's edge around me exploded when I pulled back my senses, spray and stone filling the air, water spouts rising in an instant. I was knocked from my feet, a pressure wave of planar disruption hitting me so hard that I flew a dozen yards or more before cracking against a retaining wall by the lane, the weather-worn timbers bearing the brunt of my impact. I cried out. Furrows in the sand and stone raced as the demons tore up the shore searching for me. Harbor water whirled and spun, rising into swells fifteen and twenty feet high, dark shapes visible in the crests, bucking into the troughs. A vile illumination seeped through the surface, darting above the water. The small dock near where I'd stood burst apart, ravaged by the planar entities.

The air howled with demons, filling my nose with their terrible stench, buffeting me with frigid gusts of air as they scoured the water's edge for me. I put everything I had into strengthening my cloak as I darted to the right, following the narrow strip of stony shoreline, my feet slipping on strands of kelp left by the high tide.

Back at the Battery, voices of soldiers called out. A pair of them approached the harbor's edge with lanterns. A door opened in the main building, and more soldiers came out. I paused, sensing the demons spreading out from where I'd been, hunting. I eyed the ship where the demons had been circling.

Rush was there.

The wharf nearest me had a pair of vessels lashed to it, neither of which was a rowboat. No help there. Fine. Witchcraft wouldn't do. I would not swim out there—so magic it was. As the group of soldiers reached the shoreline not fifty yard from where I stood, I turned to the water.

Water, my bane. It had to be water.

I pushed aside my feelings concentrated my mind on the recombinant elemental energy incantation I'd need for my desperate plan to work. Water was fickle to begin with, and sea-water more so, but I would force it to do what I damned well needed it to do. I shook out my arms and concentrated on the specific form of transferrent adaptation. One key to such magic was that some versions of it required no specific ingredients as long as the spell leveraged the most basic and natural expression of the energy. Lighting a wick with but a word, for instance, was feasible; causing a stone to dance with flame was not. And what were the most essential qualities of water? It flowed—and it froze.

I raised my hands, standing in the water, the gentle waves grabbing at my ankles. I brought my awareness to the water, and allowed my thoughts to match the fluid nature that touched my skin. It took grace to manipulate the subtleties of water, for water would just as soon push as follow, always ready to elude the will, happy to find any way out of the magician's grip.

Could I find such grace?

I whispered the words. "*Gif þæt gegangeð, þæt ðe gar nymeð, folces hyrde, ond þu þin feorh hafast.*" My will extended into the water, flowing, and the connection spread.

The ice formed first just before where I stood. Pale blue,

glowing from within. It spread out, groaning and grinding, rocking side to side until it was six feet wide and six feet long, a foot thick, mostly underwater. A blast of frigid air washed over my face and hands. I stepped up onto the ice, and it held. Moving my hands, I repeated the incantation, modifying the end of the phrase with the words *adl opðe iren ealdor ðinne*, which directed the transferrent energies in the manner that was the key to my plan. I took two paces forward. The water froze before me, while behind me, the magic released, trails of steaming condensation marking the shift from solid back to liquid. Keeping my cloak up while managing the most audacious display of elemental energy magic I'd ever attempted was as difficult as keeping my balance on the groaning ice. Larger now, extending half a dozen paces from where my feet skidded, the entire raft tipped and dipped like the bed of a dray stripped of wheels and harness and tossed into the water. If I stepped too far to one side, the plate of ice tilted, submerging the edge, and threatening to send me sliding into the black water. I tried to make the ice larger, thicker, or more stable—but I'd reached my limit.

Still, it worked. Ice formed in front of me, and melted in back of me, and I strode across it, arms out for balance, stomach clenched, panting from the fear of it. Step after step after step, maintaining the magic, gaze fixed on the front of the ice as I led it farther out into the harbor. After a grueling effort, I'd only closed the gap between shore and ship by a third—and already my energy flagged, my skull seeming to press in on my brain. The ice shrunk, the effect of the magic diminishing as I pulled more from my dwindling reserves. I ignored everything else: my terror of the deep water; the awareness of the nearby demons that kept my hackles raised; the shouts of the soldiers back at the shore who had yet to notice a strange pale patch of ice seeming to move of its own accord across the harbor, a desperate shadow astride it.

As the size of the ice platform grew smaller, navigating it became impossible. Each step tipped. I tried to keep my weight in the center, but even that wasn't a guarantee, as the crests and undulations of the water kept it moving in unpredictable angles. Halfway there. To my right, something splashed out of the water, a dozen yards away, causing my concentration to slip. The ice crumbled at the edges, steaming and crackling. I lost my footing, the ice now the size of a writing desk. It turned sideways, and I wheeled my arms, flailing as I slid into the chop, crying out as the cold water enveloped me.

In the muffled dark, terror swept through me. My dress tangled around my thrashing legs. I imagined limbs and tentacles, eyes and teeth, dark forms twisting toward me, slicing through the depths. My head crested the surface, and I clawed at the ice. I whispered the spell while kicking my legs, using the ice for floatation, aiming my efforts toward the ship, now a looming silhouette against the stars, thirty yards ahead.

The magic failed. Whether it was my concentration—broken, given how I was attempting not to drown—or that I'd burned through the reserves I'd had throughout the course of the previous thirty hours, it failed. I lost the connection. The ice shrunk until I grasped a circle of ice no bigger than the seat of a chair. Even that sunk as I tried using it to keep me afloat. A ghostly circle, made murky by the harbor.

"*Gif þæt gegangeð, þæt ðe gar nymeð, folces hyrde, ond þu þin feorh hafast.*" I paddled my arms, kicked my legs, whispering the incantation around mouthfuls of saltwater. "*Gif þæt gegangeð, þæt ðe gar nymeð, folces hyrde, ond þu þin feorh hafast.*"

I was so desperate that witchcraft seeped out into the words, for I sensed the awareness of demons turning my way. I cloaked myself.

Beneath my weight, new ice spread forward with the sound of grinding glass. I kicked, pushing it ahead of me through the water. It extended even farther and grew more difficult to push. Before I knew it, the ice stabilized. I hung on the edge of it for a moment, trying to catch my breath, a desperate rat clinging to a scrap of a wreck. With a grunt, I clambered up onto the edge, my muscles shaking as I heaved myself from the water, my clothing seeming to weigh a hundred pounds, sodden. Still on my hands and knees, I looked up and saw that the ship was only twenty yards away. So close that the sound of the ice echoed off the side of it—crackling, snapping, a glassy hissing sound.

Drips and rivulets fell from me as I got to my feet. The ice spread in crystalline patterns in every direction, churning through the black water.

It wasn't my magic that did it: I hadn't the strength. Yet the ice thickened and spread. It wasn't my witchcraft, either—for I wasn't swarmed with demons, although I still sensed their nearness. No, something – or someone – else was at play.

Doctor Rush. It had to be.

The how and why of it eluded me, but in that instant, I didn't question it. I hadn't drowned, and my path to the ship grew by the second. I followed the spreading ice until I stared up at the starboard side of the great ship. Ice spread out beyond the length of the ship. Between the ship and the leading edge of the ice, water splashed. Hurrying, I scanned the side until I spotted a coiled rope ladder.

Rope magic had always come easily, and it only took a moment before the ladder shook and trembled, then released itself to where I stood. With one last glance at the surrounding ice —now looking like a snow-covered meadow that bordered the ship—I grabbed at the rough hemp of the ladder and pulled myself up, swaying to and fro, bashing my fingers a few times as the ladder swung me onto the deck. At the top, I paused, peering over the rail. I saw no one on watch—I even craned my neck and looked at the rigging above, but still didn't see a soul.

I lifted myself over the gunwale, shivering and dripping, pushing locks of hair from my face. I expected a sailor or soldier to come investigate at any moment. I cut alongside the rail, stepping around coils of rope, block pulleys, and heavy iron rings set into the wood. Towards the stern, a small flight of stairs led to another deck, and beside it stood a doorway leading between decks. The door was open, so I slipped inside it, running a hand along the wooden wall to guide me forward, as there was no light —which was why I didn't see the body of the sailor before I tripped over him.

I'd been around enough corpses to know one when I felt one, so I had no worries I'd stumbled over a drunken sailor. I pushed myself off him and risked a touch of light, whispering the spell that flared up in my palm, pale moonlight. The young man stretched out underfoot, his neck broken, head twisted around. That alone told me I wasn't looking at a murder mystery—for it was the work of a demon. Another body sprawled a few yards beyond the first. An older sailor, maybe even the captain himself, in shirtsleeves, the back of his head crushed by the small cask a few paces away, smeared in gore.

It didn't take long before I found two more bodies. Had anyone on the ship fled once the demons had breached the planar boundaries? Hopped over the rail, swam frantically for land? Had enough time to lower a dinghy? Was there anyone else, even then, cowering below decks? The ship was as silent as the inside of the Whitelocke crypt.

Doctor Rush's plan—part desperation, part genius—had proven treacherous. More than a signal, whatever he'd attempted allowed demons to slip into this world, and they'd rampaged. I ducked back into the doorway and soon found the narrow stairs leading to the 'tween deck. Light shone from the far end of a passageway, where a lantern burned, hung from a hook. I approached it, listening for any signs of life, or of demons. All I heard was the hull scraping up against the ice outside, a sound that, given the circumstances, filled me with dread.

Just past the lantern, I found a door, a wooden bar across it. I knocked out the bar and pulled open the door. A stateroom greeted me, in darkness. Pulling down the lantern, I stepped inside, prepared for the worst.

"By God, Finch—if you had a bottle of brandy in one hand and a meat-pie in the other, I couldn't be happier to see you," came the voice. Grayson Whitelocke sat on the edge of a small bunk, squinting at the lantern, wearing only breeches and a loose shirt. His bare feet showed beneath the iron shackles that bound them. They'd given him only six feet worth of chain, enough to reach a bucket of water, and another bucket for relieving himself. "Doctor, I take back everything I said about your inane plan."

In the far corner, Doctor Rush sat with his back to a wooden column. Bound, blindfolded, gagged. I ran over and knelt beside him, putting the lantern on the floor. Gently, I slid the blindfold up over the old gentleman's brows. His gray eyes blinked, wrinkles spreading from the corners as he kept them narrowed to slits and turned away from the lantern light. I worked on the cloth they'd gagged him with. "Is Francis onboard?"

"No," Grayson said. "Jailed in the Battery. Not notorious enough, apparently, for a berth bound for London. The snub clearly stung the fellow. In another blow, he's missed what's surely been the longest time anyone's spent in the good Doctor's company without him saying a word."

The knot came loose in my fingers and I removed the cloth from Rush's mouth. He stretched his jaw, opening and closing, working his tongue. "If only they'd had a second gag," he croaked.

Grayson sniffed. "Ungenerous, sir. Ungenerous." As I untied the ropes that bound the Doctor's hands behind the beam, Grayson continued, "Why, you're soaking wet, Miss Finch. Did you bloody swim out here?"

"Don't ask," I said. The knots were stubborn, so I whispered a quick spell, and they wriggled themselves loose. I was down to my last drops of magic, for the time being. "There we go."

I helped Rush sit. It took a minute to get his hands to his lap, his arms had grown so stiff.

After a few moments, he looked at me. "It worked."

"Somewhat too well. They almost got me," I said.

"The demons."

"Hundreds."

"I beg your pardon?"

"Hundreds of them, Doctor." I told him of the crew.

If Rush hadn't already looked pale, he might have grown even paler. "I had no other course."

"Well I'm here," I said. "And it was clever of you."

"A dozen or more dead crewmen might beg to differ." He rubbed his wrists, working the circulation back into his hands.

"Sod them," Grayson said. "And everyone associated with Lionel Sackville. Chained and bound. Starved. Every bit of dignity stripped away, pissing and shitting in a pail. En route to be hung, no doubt. They deserved it."

"I for one will not blame the men who had no choice but to follow orders," Rush said.

"Save for that fellow who got a taste of your magic just before he tied you up."

"Well, I didn't kill him."

"He only looked like he wished you had."

Rush looked at me. "And you, Miss Finch? You are all right?"

"I'll do what needs to be done—but you will have to deal with these chains, I'm afraid," I said. "It's taken everything I have to get this far."

A chill seeped through the wood of the hull beside us, accompanied by odd water sounds. I looked back at the porthole. A lace of frost skimmed the glass, growing thicker even as I watched it. The air in the hold grew noticeably colder. Noises from the deep below sounded. The ship shuddered. Rush and I looked at one another.

"Can you break the chains?" I said.

"They're only iron." With that, I stepped back. Rush closed his eyes and lifted his hands. Coils of light spooled from his hands, accompanying the spell he cast—I didn't recognize the specific words, but the energy of the magic was familiar. As the iron shackles on his ankles sundered, I stepped over to the wall and peered out of the porthole. A pale light shone from beneath and I realized that the ice surrounded the ship, for we were on the opposite side from which I'd climbed aboard. The strain of planks let out quiet groans somewhere between bow and stern. A creak of end grain against end grain.

"Doctor," I said. "I think we'd best hurry."

The ship bucked. A grinding noise pressed it, just on the other side of the hull.

Grayson got up into a squat. "Did we get rammed?"

I pivoted back to Doctor Rush and helped him to his feet. Shards of the shackles and iron slid across the floor as the ship canted.

"Chains, Doctor—chains," Grayson said, his voice rising to a higher pitch.

The banging and snapping of timbers grew. A more disturbing sound joined in: water, rolling in somewhere nearby, unseen. The ship tilted, sending me tumbling up the wall. Rush lost his footing. The light from the porthole warped, and water sprayed in. Behind me, the wall buckled with a series of shuddering cracks and bangs. Pieces of plank and board slid across the tilted floor of the hold, landing on Grayson. The wall behind us crushed inward. I got my feet beneath me and helped Doctor Rush back up, an arm underneath his shoulder.

He stood over Grayson and said, "*Conteret ferrum, et vade tibi, audi me!*"

The shackles burst apart. Grayson tore at the chains and flung them away, free. He staggered to the door as the ship continued to roll. Distressing sounds filled the air, creaking and breaking.

"Out, now!" I helped Rush to the door of the stateroom,

catching a hold of the buckling wall. The two of us scrambled up the incline. Ice-cold harbor water splashed across my feet as the ship keeled further, by that point approaching sideways. The noises were deafening, an agony of wood surrendering to thick ice. Once Rush and I were in the hallway, I reached a hand back for Grayson, hauling him out of the room as water filled in the space behind him.

The three of us crawled along the wall of the dark passage-way, the lantern extinguished in the depths. After ten paces, the ship rolled the other way, rising with the sounds of crushing. We slid off the wall, and hobbled along through one door, then another, until we reached the 'tween deck stairs.

"This way!" I shouted.

Grayson and I helped Rush along the steps, bashing into walls as the ship rolled again. The terrifying sound of gushing water followed us up onto the deck where the stars filled the night sky. We stumbled out, tripping and sliding on the iced-over deck until we crashed against the gunwale. More, the harbor itself had frozen, the ice reaching all the way to the wharves in one direction, halfway to the distant harbor islands in the other. Dozens of ships listed, some with their keels clear of the ice, others flipped onto their sides and lifted onto the unbroken field of ice. I heard the shouts of sailors grasping at masts, ropes, anything; many prayed, others cursed.

Demons rampaged. The more I looked, the more carnage I spotted: a head, missing the body it came from; a huge smear of blood, clear against the ice; a man stripped of his clothes, yelling like a wolf, running himself over and over into the trunk of a mast, his face and forehead a bloody mess. Not fifty yards away, a body dropped from a high mast onto the ice, bursting with a sickening thud, sending a spray of black-looking blood across the ice.

"What on earth has happened?" Grayson said.

"A planar breach," Rush said, holding fast to my arm. He

looked around. "We need to reach the shore. This is all highly unstable."

Even as he said the words, cracks appeared throughout the ice, spreading faster than a man might run. Quicker than a horse might gallop. Grayson lifted himself over the gunwale and slid along the outside of the ship. It was a fast ride, covered as it was with ice. He came to a bone-jarring stop on the ice at the bottom.

"Help him down—I'll catch him," he said.

"I'm not a bundle to be tossed about," Rush said, swinging one leg over the rail. "Now out of the way."

With that, he careened down the side of the ship. Grayson ignored Rush's wishes and slowed his impact by allowing the old gentleman to crash into his arms. Grayson had him on his feet in spite of the protests of being *fine without his help, thank you.* I followed and as soon as I landed, we set off, half-running, half-sliding away from the ship. We sped up, the ice rumbling and shifting beneath our passage. Fierce winds swept over the icy harbor, while giant cracks, black water beneath, sprang open in lengthening fissures. I leapt from one section across a two-foot span, to another, and yet another. Gaps yawned farther and farther apart.

"I feel like a bloody ant running across a porcelain plate being cracked to pieces," Grayson said, steadying me as I landed from another jump. We both helped Rush. The waters between the cracks grew violent, breaking in stinging, salty spray. The great plate of ice tilted and then broke free like a large flat-bottomed boat. We jumped off the far side, stepping up onto a firmer stretch of ice and hurrying from ice shelf to ice shelf, the air filled with the sound of shattering ice, huge pieces of it grinding together, bangs and groans carrying to the depths of the harbor.

"No dawdling, Doctor," Grayson said.

The ice behind us vanished. Black shapes of ships slipped under the water. We were still forty yards from the shore when we ran out of ice ourselves.

Grayson slid to a stop. "Sod us."

Roiling water separated us from one of the storm breaks of piled stone before the wharves. Our feet sunk into the water, the ice we stood on tilting as it grew thin. The water grew rougher, and the winds kept us struggling for balance.

"Bugger it," Grayson said. "In we go. I hope you both can swim." He gave a loud curse as he plunged beneath the surface.

I turned to Rush. "Doctor?"

Rush nodded. Holding his hand, we both leapt into the murk. The water was so cold that it punched the air from my lungs. I clung to Rush. After a moment, our heads broke the surface. Grayson bobbed just in front of us, and we all gasped. The waves tried to drive us under, but we paddled to the shore. Currents tugged me in one direction, while the waves battered me in another, yet I stayed right next to Rush. I didn't allow my mind to conjure images of sharks, of eels, of my foot bumping against something in the black water, a demon coming up from the deep.

It seemed to take an hour, but I suppose that it was in reality only ten minutes until my feet connected with the silty bottom. Grayson reached the stone first, then helped me pull Doctor Rush out, sputtering and shivering. We hauled ourselves onto firm land. Gusts of warm air blew as the last of the ice in the harbor broke apart with the force of glacier and berg, splashing and roiling as the water churned. The ruined ships sank beneath the surface left by the vanishing ice. Behind us, a bell tolled in alarm, soon followed by another, then a third. Above the harbor, a swirling pattern of light the color of skulls turned, flashing as though with distant lightning. It was massive, filling the sky, brighter to the north. The power of it prickled my frigid skin.

Rush looked from the harbor, to my face. "What do you sense?"

"My master," I said. "He's done something terrible."

14

STRAIGHT INTO THE FIERY MAW

Over the harbor, the shape loomed—a crack of some kind, spanning the sky from one side of the harbor to the other, bent and twisted, a quarter of a mile high. All along its length, a queer glow peeked through. The light within pulsed and shifted, spreading out, veining further along the length of it.

"It's moving," Grayson said.

"Then I'd suggest we hurry," Doctor Rush said, leaning on my shoulder.

We left the water's edge, passing alongside a stable and on to the next street. Just two streets over, flames and smoke filled the air. Voices called out. We moved quickly, sticking closely to the backsides of the homes and businesses along the way. Up across one street, and then across the dark yard of a sawmill. A company of soldiers came around the corner, heading right for us.

Rush stepped to the doorway of the nearest building. The door was locked. He held his hands out before it. "*Ferrum audire, ferrum torquent, ferrum adspiret. Liberare ignem penetralibus.*" The black metal of the latch and lock flared and shook. With a hiss, they went from black to deep red, setting the wood in the door to smolder. As he spoke the final words, the metal shattered, dropping in red hunks to the threshold. I pushed the door in and kicked the glowing shards inside before me. Rush and Grayson hurried inside. I shut the door behind us.

We stood in the kitchen of a bakery, the floorboards scuffed with streaks of flour. Stacks of cordwood lined one wall, and above them hung bundles of drying herbs. I grabbed one chunk of wood and placed it next to the door, to keep it from opening without the latch. As the soldiers neared, we ducked down out of sight, listening as they passed by the bakery. When they moved out of earshot, I stood, looking around.

Only the ghost of heat from the fires of the morning remained over the gray ashes in the ovens. Stacks of platters, metal tines, and wooden peels leaned up on the wall next to three long oak tables where dough was kneaded. It reminded me how strange and otherworldly my life had become—where were the corpses, the magicked metals and other ingredients, the glamours? I shook my head and peered into the bakery's front room. All was still. Empty shelves, baskets, more platters. I went no farther, for the windows in the front gave no cover from being seen by the passing soldiers who swarmed the streets leading to the harbor, along with half the city's residents, by the looks of it.

Back in the kitchen, Grayson knocked a loaf against the edge of the table. "Stale. Dismal selection. Still." He leaned his weight on it, and the hard crust crushed and broke. He tore it into thirds and handed the pieces out. "And a fire might be nice. Can't stop shivering."

"We can't afford to be seen," Rush said.

Grayson gnawed at a piece of bread. "A fire that burns unseen, then. Surely that's a spell."

"A spell for those who wish to burn their surroundings down with no chance of extinguishing the flames."

"I *would* make a terrible magician."

I took a bite of the bread—stale indeed, but that didn't deter me. "The crowds might work to our advantage," I said around a mouthful of the reluctant crust.

"Save when everyone else is moving toward the harbor, and the three of us are the only ones heading in the other direction," Grayson said. "Soaking wet."

I rubbed my temple. "So we'll wait half an hour."

"Then where?" Grayson said.

"We go after Francis."

"That might not be wise," Rush said.

"And you said yourself you couldn't muster the witchcraft— spells—whatever it was—to break the Doctor's chains," Grayson said. "Knocking down the walls of the Battery? Well, I imagine that's even harder."

"No—we should head north," Rush said.

"North? Whatever for?"

"Equipment."

"As long as this equipment is the sort with four feet and saddles, that sounds perfectly reasonable." Grayson rubbed his arms, still dripping seawater. "And dry clothing, perhaps."

From somewhere nearby came the rattle of musketry. We paused, listening.

"And none of Sackville's men," Grayson said. "Let's not forget we were an hour ago on our way to London to be hanged."

"The threat we face has not changed," Rush said. "In fact, it has only worsened."

"Let the bloody new Governor deal with it. It's in his hands now."

Rush shook his head. "Governor Sackville can't help us. He won't entertain more than six words from my lips before sliding the Bible from his coat pocket and chasing me about with it as he calls for his men to chain me up a second time. No, we're quite on our own."

"We have to get into Salem," I said. "To stop my master. To seal the planar breach."

"You've both lost your minds," Grayson said. He poked about the pantry off to the side and came out with a white shirt and cloak. He stripped off his wet shirt. "Between demons, mobs of armed soldiers, treacherous governors, planar breaches, and His Majesty's ire, it might be best to quietly slip off. What say? Let them all think we're shark food at the bottom of the harbor. Perfect, really. I've cousins in New York. Friends farther south of that. Money at the ready. That's where we should go."

"That would not be far enough," Rush said.

"Spoken like the tolling bell of doom itself, I note with no surprise." Grayson slipped the spare shirt over his head. It was made for a man wider and taller than he, so he tucked the overhang into his breeches. "So, what then? We're to sally forth— all *three* of us—into Salem? You did both see those bodies out on the ice, did you not? The soldiers, all of whom wouldn't hesitate to apprehend us yet again the second they recognize us, which they surely would? It's utter madness." He looked at us, waiting for us to agree. "Ah, I see. You're *both* mad."

"We can't just leave," I said.

"Why not?"

"No one's forcing you to come with us."

"So you claim as you subtly force me to come with you. Goading me into it."

"You don't need to join us."

"Nice try, Finch. Although you might reconsider." He draped the cloak around his shoulders, shaking fingers getting the clasp after a few tries. "I warned you I was never any good at this. I can't lead men without getting caught. I couldn't save my father from a demon, nor my brother from a bullet. My sister—well, with friends like these, and all that. My efforts would appear to have very little to recommend me. Just being honest. Costume finally off."

"Maybe it's not as much of a costume as you think."

"Oh, it's more of one. Much more."

"We have to try," I said. "It's the right thing."

"Let me be the one to point out that both my brother and my father were certain they were doing the right thing. An admirable quality. And one they took to their graves. Emphasis on *graves*."

The skin of my arms, shivering, cold, rose anew in gooseflesh. "Doctor."

He glanced about. "You sense demons?"

"Yes."

"We'd best not linger."

The crack of nearby musket fire erupted again, closer this time.

"Excellent," Grayson said. "Demons nipping at our heels. Soldiers on the hunt."

As I passed behind him, I put a hand to his arm. "You're not your brother, or your father."

"Not yet. Though we can both confirm there's still plenty of room in the family crypt."

Peering out the door of the bakery, I saw a section of the city to the west burning. People crowded the street. "Come," I said. We left the bakery. The strange deformation in the sky glared, an unmoving thunderhead. Smoke stung my eye. Confusion and fear took the streets. Regulars on foot and on horseback shouted for the crowds to disperse, driving them back inside, only to see them reform again as soon as they moved on. Men and boys darted through the streets, running to find their friends or relations, to help put out the fires. I fended off the searching probes of the demon.

As we approached the town dock bridge, I paused. A line of men clambered up the weathered pilings and beams from beneath, single and in pairs, lifting themselves up to the street. None of them wore uniforms, looking for all the world like laborers or men off fishing boats, yet several carried weapons. That's when I spotted a woman with them, hints of ruby silk flashing in the firelight.

"Mary!" I shouted.

Two of the men helped her to the street. Once they were all up, they sprinted in our direction.

"This way," I said, signaling the line off the main road past the bridge, scanning the street for signs of regulars. Mary ran to me, Francis at her side. The hem of Mary's dress hung tattered, decorated with scorch marks.

"Unbelievable," Grayson said. "She's leading a company of men."

Mary rested her hand on my shoulder, trying to catch her breath. "The bastard—Sackville. Arrested me. The nerve. Tossed me in the jail—but I got us out. Fire spell. Worked somewhat more impressively than expected. Whole jail roof burned. Four or five buildings near it. Burning still."

"Did you say *spell*?" Rush said, cupping a hand to his ear.

"And they're chasing us. Not being very nice about it," Mary said, giving me a smile.

"But we have men," Francis said. "Friends of mine."

"Plus a dozen former members of the Governor's Own," Mary added. "Sackville didn't trust them. Put them in jail, too. Thought they were too loyal to my father. He's damn right." She looked at the men. "Seem rather loyal to me, now that I got them out from behind bars. Of course, Sackville's men are scouring the city for us. We'd best keep moving."

The main intersections and roads teemed with soldiers. Francis knew ways past the backs of stores, winding alleys, through dung-piled stretches of dark grazing meadows. He and a pair of former Governor's Own scouted ahead to find out the positions of the governor's forces. I raised my hand and halted the rest of us, peering out from underneath a wooden overhang. Heaps of wooden staves with fire marks on them stood next to iron hoops and raw boards.

As we waited for a signal from the scouts, one of the young men stared at Grayson. "Christ in heaven."

"Not quite," Grayson said.

"He's the bloody governor's son."

"Former governor's son. And what—you didn't notice my sister rescuing you?"

"Your father's the reason I've spent four months rotting in that cell."

One of the jailed soldiers nodded at him. "You deserved to be there, Rattlesnake."

"Oh, please," Mary said. "You're both free, for the moment. Let it go."

"Or all go your separate ways," Grayson offered.

"No—don't," I said. "Listen. There's a danger facing us that's bigger than the Whitelockes. Bigger than the new Governor. Bigger than politics, pamphlets, ambushes, or insults."

I glanced at Rush, but he only nodded for me to continue.

"The infernal," I said. "What's back there. Broken bells. Cries coming out from the burial yards. A harbor full of sunken ships. And worse is coming." They all stared at me. "So we can argue about who put who in jail. We can bicker about who has money, and who doesn't. Who knows how to fight, and who is unskilled. But none of it will make a single bit of difference to what's really threatening this colony and everyone in it."

"Listen to her, lads," Grayson said.

"Says a Whitelocke," one of the Rattlesnakes said.

Grayson raised his leg in front of him, pointing to the skin of his ankle, rubbed raw by the shackles. "The irons holding me did this. A rather recent addition to my attire. But in another way, I've had a chain on me since the day I came squalling into this world and had the name Whitelocke bolted to me. I know that must sound like faint punishment—or no punishment at all—to you. Fair enough. But I was raised to think one way about this place. And people like you. And people like Finch here. All that's gone, now."

The men watched him.

"You don't have to trust me," Grayson continued. "I probably wouldn't, if I were you—but listen anyways: a bloody trapdoor to Hell has opened up, and we're all good and sodded if we can't get it closed. I'm not my brother. I'm not my father. If someone wants to take the name Whitelocke from me, fair enough. I don't care much for it anymore. Let's just save this colony. It may be too late —but if there's a chance, Finch here will find it. And I'd follow her straight into the fiery maw if that's what it takes. Best listen to her."

"If it wasn't for her," Mary said, "we'd all still be in jail. Trust me on that."

Footsteps hurried back to us, Francis leading the two soldiers. "They've got patrols everywhere," he said. "Four cannon down on the Neck. Checkpoints at all the major streets."

"We have to get across," Rush said. "Head north."

"Take a boat," Mary said.

"There are no bloody boats," Grayson said.

"No," I said. "We'll have to cross the Neck."

Francis nodded. "We can come out just up from the cannons. Through that gap between the Bunch of Grapes and the smokehouse."

Doctor Rush and I exchanged a glance. "Fine. We'll figure it out."

The message spread down the line, Francis splitting up the rag-tag company into three groups. His would be the primary, and their charge would be to distract the Governor's Own at the cannons. Once everyone understood, we spread out into the night. Grayson went with the group that would approach first, from Merchants Road. Mary, Rush, and I stayed with the second group, while the third paralleled us. We drew closer, keeping out of sight of the main roads. When we reached the corner, I looked the scene over. Four twelve-pound cannons, arranged in a shallow horseshoe shape. A quick count showed about sixteen soldiers, gun crews included. As far as that location, they'd done well. I didn't see how we could get past it.

Just then, Grayson staggered out of the darkness next to the smokehouse. He gazed to the sky, as though distracted by the frightful colors of the planar breach, one hand to his mouth as though stunned. His gait suggested drunkenness.

"You. Get back," one of the soldiers yelled. "Watch where you're going."

Grayson didn't slow. "Did you see it? Bloody cut him clean in half, it did. Took his bloody shoulders and neck and head. Right off. Rest of him stood up for half a minute. Then fell."

Several of the soldiers turned to him. He neared the gap between two of the cannons.

"You've got to bloody help, lads," Grayson cried. "I can't put him back together again after what that devil did to him."

"Back off," a soldier ordered, raising his voice.

Grayson waved him off. He turned his back to the men and the cannon, and began fumbling with the front of his breeches. "Well piss on your bloody new governor. Can't keep us safe from such devils."

That drew the captain out. Grayson swayed back and forth for a moment, as though readying his aim. The captain came up beside him.

"That's enough," the captain said. "Out of here. Now."

Grayson reached over, his hand searching for the man's shoulder, a drunk looking to steady himself. When the captain leaned back, away from the hand, Grayson spun on his heel and planted his foot, driving his other fist, already balled tight, into the man's jaw. He grabbed him by the collar of his uniform with the same hand and yanked him forward, getting a second hand on him and reeling him down to meet his pistoning knee. I heard the captain's nose break from where I stood.

Francis and the rest of the men poured out from their locations, fanning out and charging the cannons. The startled soldiers raised their weapons, but were only able to get off a few shots, filling the street with gray smoke that quickly rose and caught the glare of the fires that ringed the waterfront. The former Governor's Own moved in. Francis ran forward and vaulted over the bricks that had been stacked around the cannon for the redoubt. He dove into the fray, pulling men out of his way until he reached the right-side gunner who was trying to ready one of the cannons to fire. Francis tore him away from the cannon. The soldiers with him didn't give any of Sackville's men even half a second to work at coordinating their efforts as more and more of his men swarmed over the emplacement. They'd made the most of their advantage of surprise. A few of the cannoneers fled, and one of them got onto horseback and rode off north along Orange Street.

"I want men on every gun!" Grayson yelled.

He breathed hard, flexing the fingers on his right hand. Of the remaining soldiers manning the cannons, a few surrendered while the rest were driven back, muskets and pistols now turned on them. In moments, the cannons were all in motion, with other men gathering up the powder and balls, the linstocks, ladles, rammers, sponges, and priming irons.

"Come," I said, leading Doctor Rush and Mary out from our hiding spot. By the time we reached the cannons, a Rattlesnake ran back from up the street.

"More coming," he said, out of breath. "Mounted. Foot."

"Hurry, hurry—load them up!" Grayson yelled. He turned and ordered some of the men to position themselves twenty-five yards up the street, and to clear off any civilians who were fool-hardy enough to step outside or remain on the streets. The rest of the men worked quickly behind him, shifting the guns and readying them to fire. The breach above the harbor reached a new level of intensity, filling the night with howling winds and flashes of pale green light.

The sound of musket shots drew my attention back up

Orange Street. Uniformed soldiers came into view, officers on horseback, the men marching in formation. The officers signaled and those on foot started to form a line.

"Give them a taste!" Grayson shouted.

The men took two of the 12-pounders and lit them, touching the slow torch to them. The sound was enormous, one followed a beat later by the second. When the smoke cleared, I saw that it had broken their line wide open. They hadn't expected that they'd lost their cannon, and many of them broke into a retreat. Our men were already sponging down the cannons that had just fired, filling the air with steam and readying the next powder and munition.

"Heave into it," Grayson said. "We need to keep on them."

Francis took off running up the street as Sackville's men retreated.

"What does he think he's doing?" Mary said.

Grayson wiped the sweat from his forehead. "He thinks he's driven them off on his own, knowing him."

Before anyone could comment further, Francis leapt into the saddle of one of the horses whose rider had been bucked off by the cannon fire. Swinging the reins around, he gave the horse his heels, galloping back toward us. When he reached us, he swung down and handed me the reins. "Take Doctor Rush. Before they regroup. Go—now!"

"We have little choice," Rush said.

I nodded, climbing into the saddle. Francis and Mary helped Rush up after me. "You know where to meet us," I said to Grayson.

"We'll buy you as much time as we can—but numbers are numbers, at some point."

"Just give us a quarter hour, then get away yourselves."

He nodded, ordering the men to move the cannon farther up the street, diving in and helping to lift the tail of one of the carriages himself, wheeling them forward, rushing, dripping sweat alongside the men.

"Watch after him," I said to Mary.

"I always do," she said.

Francis stepped to the side of the horse. He smacked the horse's flank, setting us off. Rush held on tightly to me as we raced off into the darkness. The light of the fires dimmed as we crossed the Neck, while the pale flares of the planar breach loomed over the city in the shape of a mocking grin.

15

KOEFFLER TAP

"Here, Doctor?"

Rush consulted the device in his hand, a brass and steel contraption shaped like a small lantern, a pair of dials on each of the four sides. The needles spun, some slowly, some with vigor. "This should do. The breach is quite apparent, as are the signs of a significant collision of planes. Time to test the theory."

We stood in a grove deep in the woods of Andover, two miles from the tavern, farther still from the house Swaine and I had occupied over the winter and into the early spring. A light rain softened the morning around us. A scant few hours of rest at Rush's uncle's cabin after our escape from Boston had given us the chance to catch our breath, to focus on our next steps. I slung the sack from my shoulders and untied the thin rope that held it closed. Reaching inside, I pulled out a mechanism known as a Koeffler Tap. If Rush's theory was correct, the Tap would stabilize the harmonic order of the intersection of the planes, thus drawing off some measure of the wild energies spilling through the breach itself.

Three legs opened into a tripod that stood a foot high, topped with what resembled a squat telescope with clock faces on either end, beneath convex lenses of glass. A delicate set of gears allowed the tube to swivel and rotate smoothly. I opened the legs and set them into the soil, adjusting the alignment using a pair of disc-shaped knobs and two oil-filled glass levels.

"Very good," Rush said. He searched the sack and pulled out a folded leather kit, tied on one side. Opening it, he laid it out beside the Tap. Three narrow rods of metal sat in a pocket—one copper, one silver, one steel. He placed them end to end, forming a triangle. From a glass bottle, he shook out three pinches of powdered rose quartz he'd glamoured before we'd set out, each pinch receiving a whispered incantation before being sprinkled over the points where the ends of the rods met. Once he'd done the same for all three joints, the metal shone with the third-order harmonic energy each rod manifested: the silver, a pale white; the copper, a molten orange; the steel, blood-red. A wavering of the light extended out from the triangle, making the ground beneath it appear to shimmer and dance in the gray of the forest.

Rush looked up, wiping the residual powder from his fingertips. "Would you kindly commence with the outer glamour?"

"Yes, sir." I'd found the Doctor easy to work with as we'd prepared the necessary ingredients, magic, and instruments: steady as an old clock, methodical, focused yet unfailingly polite. None of the mercurial pressure of working with Swaine, the threat of thunderheads always ready to blow in at a moment's notice, the deliberate vagueness that so often tried my patience, the refusal to repeat himself if he was in a mood. While Swaine might, if he were feeling generous, slide a book across the table at me in response to my questioning, Rush appeared to delight in laying out the clearest, most succinct answers for me. As we'd concluded our preparations, he told me he was quite jealous of Swaine for having had such a focused apprentice. While I'd blushed at the compliment, I'd also unhappily noticed his use of the past tense.

I retrieved the spooled length of twine from the sack, and passed my hand over it, whispering, "*Wuldres eþel, eorþan gefylle. Wide ræce, ofer engla eard. Middangeard ond merestreamas.*" The glamour we'd imbued it with snapped to life, giving it a jittery wriggle. I laid it around us in a circle with care, and bound the ends with the phrase, "*Wundaþ grimme, hrysted fægere.*" A faint circle of light rose from the glamour, starlight on a winter's field.

"Excellent," Rush said. He lifted the triangle—the three rods now bound—and spoke the lengthy incantation he'd designed, turning it three times. When finished, he held the triangle half a foot above the device. After a moment, he released his fingers from the metal, and the triangle remained hovering in the air over the instrument. It turned, rocking a small amount as it did so. "There."

Around us, the trees creaked on the wind, loosing patters of rain from bough and branch. The pale shine of the magic lit our faces as the triangle spun, the rotations getting faster as the seconds passed. Soon, it was a blur, the glow of the harmonic activation blending into a golden yellow. Beneath it, the tube on the stand spun in the opposite direction, the ends rising and falling in synchrony with each turn. As it reached a speed comparable with that of the triangle above it, the air thrummed with a low purr.

"Faster than I'd imagined," Rush said. He scratched out a quick note on a piece of paper, quill and ink bottle retrieved from his coat pocket.

"How long until it reaches the proper frequencies?"

"It shouldn't take much longer. Everything is functioning." After another half a minute, he spoke. "*Spatium.*" The device slowed its turning while the triangle above continued its blurring spin. As the tube came to a gentle rest, Rush asked me to take the readings. I leaned in, and spun one end, squinting at the positions of the three hands.

"First Black, two hundred forty-two," I said. "Second Black, three hundred thirty-seven. Red, three hundred forty-five."

Rush wrote the figures without comment. I spun the scope and looked at the other dial.

"First Red, twenty-three. Second Red, seventeen. Black, two." I released the tube. As Rush recorded the findings, he motioned that I should set it to spinning again, which I did.

"A second measurement?" I said.

"We'd best be certain."

"Where do those readings put our chances?"

"Nowhere good." He offered nothing further, but the tautness of his lips and how his gaze kept shifting from the device to the figures he'd written told me much. Glints of the light from the triangle shone in his spectacles. As the tube spun faster and faster, the air throbbed with the displacement. A flash of light overhead drew my eye. Through the canopy of branches, I saw a line of bright white, jagged and delicate—a bolt of lightning frozen in time, reaching out to us.

"Doctor, there's some sort of—" I got no further before the device flew apart with the sound of a dozen bullwhips, fragments of brass and steel screaming through the air, sticking into trunk and branch, chunking into the ground, shredding leaf and needle. A sharp bite nipped my hand, and another grazed my cheek. Rush flinched, and one of the glass lenses glanced off his upraised wrist. At the same instant, a narrow whirlwind jabbed from the sky, raising twig, needle, and cone like a flock of startled grackles taking noisy wing, extinguishing the magic and plunging us back into the drear gray of the foggy woods. The disturbance settled as quickly as it had come, leaving us with the patter of everything that had been swept up dropping back to earth.

"Doctor—are you all right?" I stood and hurried over to him.

He swept a stray branch from his shoulder. "Perfectly fine, Miss Finch. The numbers—well, I'm not surprised at what we witnessed." I helped him to his feet and checked that he wasn't injured.

"What was that?" I said.

"An unfortunate turn."

"I don't like the sound of that, sir."

"Nor should you." He straightened out his coat and hat, then retrieved his paper. "That was without question a micro-vortex. Common in proximity to an area of significant planar subduction. One plane, or more, grinding beneath another, warping with tremendous force."

"And the readings?"

"More extreme than I'd feared. These are beyond any such recordings I'm aware of. Off the end of Koeffler's Grand Scale of Planar Amplitude, the *Magnifice de Supermundanae Amplitudinem*."

I looked at the sky. "Meaning?"

Rush pulled a scrap of twisted brass from the cuff of his coat-sleeve. "Meaning the planes have breached to a degree almost beyond measurement. Worse, the energy levels are so extreme that the Koeffler Tap can't survive even momentary contact. It's not powerful enough. And I don't know what could make it potent enough in the face of these measurements." He put his hand to his chin, running his gaze over the wreckage of the device. "Going back to the drawing board at this stage frightens me. I believe I understand the problem well enough—and my theory is sound, but it's not sufficient. We're creating a spark in the face of a raging storm—but what we need is a conflagration. Power to match the energies involved."

"What about my witchcraft—can that help?"

"Far too risky, Miss Finch." He pointed to the wreckage of the Koeffler Tap. "Furthermore, we have no time for guesswork, I'm afraid. The hours grow ever more precious. We need power—more power than we have. I'm just not sure how to generate it."

I looked at the distortion in the sky, then down at the shattered wood and twisted brass. "Burial silver."

"I beg your pardon."

"*Argentum inferi*, sir. Burial silver. Would that work?"

"I have none—nor does any exist in the colonies, that I'm aware of. It's impossible to procure, of such staggering rarity that—"

"I have some. Two ounces of it."

Rush stared at me. "Did you say *two* ounces?"

"Yes. Two."

"That's worth a fortune."

"Don't ask how I got it. Would it help?"

"Would it—why, I believe—in some ways, it could function as the perfect accelerant for the harmonic activation. Third-order. Fourth. Fifth. Beyond. With such an extended response, the ability to draw off the upper registers of shadow resonance..." He put his thumb and middle finger to his brows, working through the logic. "Where is it?"

"That's the one problem, sir—it's in Salem. In my master's manse. In my room—hidden away. With glamours and witchcraft."

"Does August know about it?"

"No, sir. At least, I don't believe so."

"It's far too dangerous to waltz into Salem. Very risky."

"Do we have any other choice at this point, sir?"

"We may not." He crossed his arms. "But I don't like it. Not one whit."

Rain fell from the low sky, forcing the trees around us to slouch, the leaves to mutter.

16

BEGONE

While I shared the Doctor's trepidation about sneaking into Salem, he shared little of the faint hope I expressed that we might also rescue Swaine while we were there. The clues I'd gathered did little to persuade him.

"Compelling, yes," he said. Rain channeled from the edges of his tricorn as he peered past me from the back of the horse. We emerged from a grove of birch and rode into the heart of Andover, the road giving way to mud and puddles. Lightning scored the sky, followed by a snarl of thunder. We neared the tavern, hunched against the rain, desperate for a dry spot to sit out the worst of the storm before going any farther. "And yet a demon with enough guile to get past the sophisticated defenses of your master is more than capable of exactly that sort of insidious gamesmanship. Luring you back within its reach would no doubt delight the fiend, proving deadly to you. And to our chances, frankly. The perils of hope are legion in the history of sorcery. I'm sorry for my candor—I have nothing but respect and compassion for your affection towards August."

"The demon wouldn't have known," I said, squinting against the gusts. "The mule. The code. Only my master could have."

"The grip of a demon is beyond intimate. We have no way of knowing what knowledge the fiend might extract."

"But it's something Swaine would have done—it *feels* like him. How his mind works. How he insisted *mine* work."

I could sense Rush's frown without even seeing him. "We have no way to be certain. More importantly, we have no margin for error. I'm afraid that until and unless we can seal off the breach—already a fraught proposition—we can't afford to divide our attention or our efforts, no matter how badly we might want to."

"My master could help us—if he were released. I know he would."

Rush said nothing. I knew as well as he did the tales of wreckage left behind by a demon's possession, even when the grip of the fiend had been pried loose—the stories were ghastly. None came away unscathed, even in the best cases; the vast majority of such incidents gathered at the opposite end of the spectrum, where lay madness, delirium, catatonia, death. He was right. I *knew* he was right—yet I wasn't prepared to consign Swaine to the terrible fate his situation boded. *Spiegel Verstärkung. A Burnsian channel. The arrow of time. Heggen.* I kept the clues rolling through my mind, reassuring myself of their value, of their presence, a jeweler jiggling his velvet sack of gems for peace of mind.

As we drew nearer to the tavern, I saw that we weren't the only ones out in such weather, the mud before the stables churned by the passage of horses. I pulled the horse to a stop. Rush leaned out next to me, peering over his rain-dappled spectacles.

"I don't like it," he said.

"Let me take a look."

"We can't afford to be apprehended again."

"I told them to meet us here." Pulling the horse around back, I clambered down and ducked into the stable. My shoes squelched in the mud, threatening to rip from my feet. Drips of rain bothered the animals. A dozen horses steamed—a mixed selection, several stallions of the sort ridden by the Governor's Own, bearing the proper military tack, a few smaller horses in various condition, a mule, and an old nag with drooping jowls and a bowed back. It wasn't a company of troopers. As quickly as I could, I slid past the stable and up to the side of the tavern, where I looked into a window. Quite a gathering filled the public room. Men and lads standing in small groups, gathering by the hearth, drenched from the weather. Bertram stood near the stairs—speaking with Grayson and Mary Whitelocke. He looked flustered.

I splashed my way back to the Doctor, who looked forlorn and old as he clung to the back of the horse in the deluge. "It's them."

"Thank goodness. I've forgotten what it feels like to be dry."

Leading the horse to join the others in the stable, I helped Rush down. As we hurried to the tavern door, I shook the rain from my shawl and cloak. As I pulled the door open, the ferocity of the storm drew everyone's eyes.

"Ah, Finch, Doctor," Grayson said. "Welcome to the Andover Festival of Mud. Make yourself comfortable—but not *too* comfortable. Half of the Governor's men are searching for us north of the city. The other half are no doubt about to join them as this blasted rain extinguishes the fires they fought to little avail until dawn."

"Where's Francis?" I said.

"Making sure we weren't followed."

Rush took his hat off. "'Tis festive enough for the moment."

I shut the door behind me, surprised at how crowded the tavern was. Every table, every corner, every free space was filled with escaped soldiers and Rattlesnakes. Normally, there might be one or three local townsfolk in the long public room, chatting over an ale, or forking up helpings of sweetmeats, jellies, and squash pie. Such memories only brought on the sharp pang of the death of Iris and her children, cutting deeply as I looked at the spot I'd found their bodies.

"Tell me there are dry clothes for a woman somewhere in this village," Mary said.

"I doubt you'll find much of Mr. Faber's handiwork," Grayson said. "Hope you're feeling rustic."

Bertram appeared slightly dazed. He hurried, trying to get people fed, attempting to carry half a dozen mugs of cider, ale, beer, and tea though the crowd, arms aloft. The sound of thunder and the rain on the windows and roof competed with the talk rising in the crowded room. I slipped past tables, soldiers, printer's lads, and the Whitelocke siblings, turning sideways, excusing myself, leading with a gentle hand until I reached Bertram. His cheeks were flushed.

"Here, let me help," I said, relieving him of half the mugs he carried. "Where's Clara?"

His gaze met mine, grateful. "She's with my granddad. She's fine."

"Good," I said. "Have more drinks ready for me when I'm back."

Bertram nodded, looking for the best routes available to get the remaining drinks in his hands to their destinations. I brought two drinks to the pair of wet and muddy soldiers who sat at a small table near a beam that held a glowing lantern. A flash of lightning shone in the windows, followed by a peal of thunder. The weather wasn't doing much to ease anyone's nerves. I wound my way to the kitchen. Bertram knelt before a cask, filling a series of mugs. The hearth held two large pots over the fire, a kettle, and a tin with cobbler browning, alongside a row of iron skewers with sizzling chicken and rabbit. Wine bottles stood along the large table, next to half-cut loaves, wheels of rich yellow cheese, and a crumb-laden platter of biscuits.

The panic on Bertram's face subsided. "You're saving my life. No one else offered to help. I just came by to check, the whole lot of them came tramping up the street."

"I'm sure they're exhausted."

"And what if they've been followed?" He set aside a third mug topped with foam.

"You heard Grayson—Francis is making sure."

"That one's been jailed twice already, caught by the governor's men, begging your pardon."

"Let's hope he's learned his lesson, then."

"I'm not sure he's the lesson-learning type."

"They made it from the city, so that's something." I gathered the mugs. "Who gets these?"

"Best just hand them out, at this point. Anyone who doesn't have one in hand. Anyone who looks as worried as I am."

I gave him a quick smile, and bustled back into the main room, glad to have a simple task to keep my thoughts from spinning into the bleak outlands of dread. I gave out drinks, and when I was empty-handed, I returned once more to the kitchen. Thunder shook the timbers of the tavern, and a nervous wave of laughter and exclamations passed through the crowd. Bertram pulled chickens off spits, slicing the fowl into steaming strips on a platter. He glanced at me.

"You can put your satchel down in the corner there. No one will touch it," he said. When I made no move to do so, he raised an eyebrow. "Or not. As you please."

The sack weighed on me. As much as I tried to ignore it, the heft of the *Occultatum Ostium* brought forth such an alarm in me I could think of little else. We'd removed it from Rush's uncle's cabin along with his other magical instruments and supplies, worried that the planar instability and influx of demons from the breach might render its presence known. Was this not as it had always gone with the accursed book? Leaving from one place to the next on the back of treachery, of desperation? Driven from its temporary resting place by the encroaching fires of the infernal? As I stood there, still wet from the rains, the straps of my haversack digging into my shoulder, I realized that I was now one in a long line of participants in the unsettling history of the book.

"I just want the rain to end," I said.

He held out the platter. "You're a saint, by the way."

"Hardly." I took the platter anyways and headed into the public room, forking out slices to all who wanted. Some of the men gave me wary looks, but with a few comments here, some small talk there, by the time I'd emptied the platter, most seemed at ease. With the company putting food and drink into their bellies, I gathered with Rush and the Whitelocke siblings at a table off in the corner, sliding off the haversack and putting it on the table.

"We're sure no one followed?" I said, not yet shed of Bertram's concern.

"The only thing I'm sure of is that I've never been more wrinkled and damp in my entire life," Grayson said. He emptied an ale. He looked around for another one, but Bertram was on the other side of the room. "Where's Bertram in the infrequent moments when one needs him?"

Mary and I exchanged a look.

"Maybe it's best if you keep your wits about you," I said.

"I believe the past four days prove rather conclusively that I've left my wits elsewhere."

"Then no chances," Mary offered. "Listen to Miss Finch."

"Precisely what's led to most of my troubles, listening to Miss Finch."

Rush sat closest to the hearth, his coat and cloak steaming in the warmth. "As one who went notably unlistened-to when it might have mattered, I would suggest that once our will is fortified and our cores warmed, we'd best find it in us to raise our performance—whatever is required."

"Then more ales all around," Grayson said. "Neither my will

nor my core is anywhere close to the good Doctor's specifications."

"So no one followed you?" I asked again.

"They'd have to be mad, if they did. Or possibly blind and more intoxicated than recommended. Your friend Francis apparently never saw a thicket, a stretch of woods, a river, a brambled hillside, a bog, fen, or marsh that didn't look more inviting than a simple road." Grayson fanned the edges of his torn waistcoat as though that might dry it out more quickly. "And one might think the concept of *north* was reserved for a singular direction—but not he. Left, right, south, east, west, and other the subdivisions in between were prominently featured in his pathfinding as we made our way here. That we got here at all is nothing short of miraculous."

"Let's not use up all our miracles just yet," Rush said.

"They're searching for us," Mary said. "We didn't make them look good. Sackville's first moves as governor failed rather spectacularly. He's not one to let that go."

"We'd best hope." Rush polished the lenses of his spectacles with a linen napkin. "For in his eagerness to reclaim what he's lost, he won't likely notice a pair of travelers crossing into Salem."

"Salem?" Grayson said.

"Pair?" Mary said.

"Miss Finch and myself."

"That sounds safe," Grayson said. "Reasonable. Oh, and what's the other word I'm looking for? Ah yes: *suicidal*. And, wait —before you treat us all to some version of *To do otherwise is the truly suicidal course of action*, know that we didn't explore the nooks and crannies of the province's least traveled cartography with a horde of Governor's Own tearing up the lanes behind us in order to send the two of you off to toddle into Salem on your own."

"We made it here unscathed," I said.

"Luckily."

"Grayson may have a point," Mary said. "Odd as that sounds to say. Have you noticed that most of our setbacks occur when we split up? Someone, usually my brother, is always captured."

"I'm not the only Whitelocke here who's been captured," Grayson sniffed. "Merely the only one thought worthwhile enough for his own berth on a ship bound for London."

"It's too dangerous for us all," I said. "And we need to be certain we don't draw any attention. The more of a distraction, the farther away, the better."

"Common sense banished yet again," Grayson said. "We're to be lures. Yet again."

"What about August?" Mary said.

I shook my head. "He mustn't know."

"Why ever not?"

"Because he'll try to stop us." I saw her objection forming behind her lips. "It's complicated. And terrible."

"I worry more about him than I do Sackville and his men," Rush offered.

"Then let me distract him," Mary said. "We can leave luring Sackville's men to my brother and that Rattlesnake lad—they've developed an impressive expertise at it, we can all agree. August isn't as immune to my charms as he believes."

"He is now," I said. The appeared to wait for me to elaborate, but I couldn't get the words out.

"Miss Finch is quite right," Rush said. "Circumstances have turned against August at precisely the wrong time. Attempting to reason with him, or distract him, or any other tactic we might consider, is quite likely to make the situation worse. So, no."

"That what?" Grayson said. "The two of you sneak into Salem alone—to what end?"

I leaned forward and told them our plan. Rush added a few comments, but mostly stared at the table, his mouth drawn down.

"You're sure it will work?" Mary said when I finished.

"It's the best chance we've got."

"That doesn't answer my question."

"It's the best chance we've got."

She sat back. "Then we should do all we can to distract August. What if he catches you? Or are you hoping this—Koeffler Tap will be subtle enough that he won't even notice you're doing it? And what of the demons? The planar forces? Whatever else is going on in there?"

"I didn't say it was going to be easy," I said.

"Then let me make it easier."

Grayson tilted his mug on the table as though studying the bottom. "She doesn't want you to make it worse."

"I was the one to get us our burial silver, let's not forget."

"Which nearly devoured the governor's manse, let's not forget," Grayson said.

"Look, I just want to keep everyone safe," I said. "As safe as possible, in any event."

"You think riding around like the hare to the governor's hounds is as safe as possible?" Mary said.

"I think you should stay with Bertram. Clara could use someone to watch over her."

"Children are what governesses and nannies are for, darling. If you don't think I'm quite up to drawing away the attentions of poor August, then I believe that my brother and his Rattlesnake friend could use someone sharp along with them. Someone less prone to panic."

Grayson smiled. "Maybe I'll stay with Bertram's grandfather and the child. Leave the rest to my sister."

"Would anyone be surprised?" Mary said.

I raised my hands. "Fine. Enough, you two. We don't have time for squabbles."

"Always time for a good squabble," Grayson muttered.

As Mary crossed her arms, my gaze snapped to the door a moment before it opened. I wondered for a moment if it were Francis—but when the door opened with a gust of rain, in stepped a man soaking wet, splashed with mud. It took only a moment for me to recognize him: in life, a young carpenter who'd been stabbed in the heart during a brawl at one of Boston's taverns; he'd been revenated in the depths of winter. The demon that Swaine had chosen for him had turned out to be particularly virulent—a problem with using a demon that had no recorded history, as it had been one we'd caught in a planar clock and thought suitable—and we'd had to relegate the revenant to patrolling the wilderness in endless circles, day and night. Any closer, and it had never failed to attack another revenant.

"Doctor," I whispered.

The revenant scanned the crowd and pushed his way inside.

"Who is that?" Grayson said, following my gaze.

One of the soldiers didn't take kindly to being shouldered aside, but when he grabbed the revenant by the shoulder, he had his wrist twisted and shattered in an instant, the revenant spinning him to the ground without breaking stride. He continued straight for me. A demonic awareness brushed my thought. Knowing that a single determined revenant could kill most of the men in the public room few with ways to stop it, I stepped to the stairs.

Here, fiend. That was all it took. My face and scalp tingled.

"Mary—get everyone away from me," I said, not taking my eye from the approaching revenant. Before I could speak a ward, a shattering crash came from the kitchen behind us and I felt yet another infernal presence. "Keep away from him."

Wrapping my fingers around the well-worn key to command the revenants I wore on my wrist, I turned. The revenant came at me. Another pair of soldiers tried to stop him, but he flung them off as though they were no more than kittens. Confusion spread through the room.

"Not a step farther!" I commanded. The revenant didn't slow. Swaine had neutralized the magic of my key, cancelling my power over his demons. I tossed aside the useless key.

From the kitchen came the female revenant I'd long detested. Her eyes glittered.

Doctor Rush raised one hand and spoke a ward of some kind, but the magic went sideways on him, blue flames climbing the posts and walls, riding up across the ceiling to snap and cling to the joints between beams.

I spoke Hume's Twenty-Third Ward. "*Her on þysum geare for se micla here. We gefyrn ymbe spræcon, eft of þæm eastric westweard þær wurdon gescipode, swa þæt hie asettan him on anne siþ ofer mid horsum mid ealle!*"

The air behind me shifted and wavered as though a thick sheen of falling water separated me from the stairs. A tremendous flare of light drew every face, every mug, plate, and table in bright relief, driving back the dim half-light of the public room. A thunderclap exploded overhead as the lightning split a massive maple not twenty paces from the door of the tavern. I stumbled forward, landing on my hands and knees. And then the revenant lunged, a dark silhouette passing between two tables. I bided my time, letting him draw closer. Just as he reached me, I let loose yet another spell, whispering the incanting phrases.

A furrow appeared in the floorboards, rising and racing forward, splitting the wood open in a jagged line that headed straight for him. The revenant charged, and as it reached the churning floorboards, a blinding line of lightning—the energy of it drawn from the storm—leapt up and wrapped around the revenant in blazing chains.

The revenant wrenched its arms this way and that, but the wraps of lightning sank further into its flesh. Shadows rose, twisting and coiling. It staggered and loosed darkness that flew like smoky darts, trailing soot and haze. I concentrated my energy before me, as a shield. As the bolts reached me, they burst into fiery embers, knocking me back with a searing heat and a sulfurous stench. Shattered bits of flaming sparks few, landing on me, burning my hands and setting my clothes to smolder. I batted away the embers from my hair and cloak and shouted another spell. Wind spun up around me, strong enough to prevent any such flames from reaching me a second time.

Voices raised, the crowd staggered back from the revenant. The windings of lightning blazed and contracted, sending him to his knees. His flesh seared—and then sliced into pieces, falling to the floor in chunks that sizzled. His head fell away from his torso, his chest and abdomen seared into two, his limbs divided into segments. The demon raged, and the pieces clenched and twitched, but he couldn't reach me.

Just as I turned, the female revenant grabbed a chair and hurled it at me—as the wood flew, flames sprang out of it. I spun and shouted a phrase. The burning chair crashed into the unseen barrier, embers and fire exploding in a shower of sparks. A vast web of shadows trailed from the revenant's limbs, gathering up darkness, filling the room with a restless dark, black as a raven. As it reached my feet, the shadows whipped around and rushed in my direction. The horrendous magic of this new demon pressed against me, setting my skin and muscles to prickling. Lanterns swayed, tables creaked and snapped, chairs slid across the floor to crash into walls, all of it rising in a cacophony unlike anything I'd ever heard.

I lifted my hand high and shouted. Whorls of blue light spun around me, a brilliant cage that deflected the shadows that the demon had unleashed at me. The tavern rumbled. My witchcraft strained, gaining energy from the real storm overhead, while I pushed back at the demon. The revenant charged at me, a crown of flames erupting over her head, fire running along her arms and torso. It crashed against my magic in a flaming brand, and I flew back, losing my footing once again. The revenant cried out, and for a moment I was smothered beneath a crashing wave of shadow and flame.

The soldiers tried to help, aiming musket and pistol. Two shots barked, filling the air with gun-smoke.

I pushed myself upright and let the power inside me well up and burst, a geyser. I lifted my hands, and the air shimmered. A foul magic pressed in on me, strands of it in my face, my nose and mouth, my ears. I cried out and drove the revenant back toward the kitchen, my witchcraft roaring from my palms. The air went strange, blurring the room, the ceiling, the windows, distorting the revenant and the shadows that closed in on me. The power that flowed through me exploded—if what I'd done to the first revenant had been a stream of magic, this was the Atlantic during a fearsome storm, massive, unyielding, sweeping all before it beyond any control. Still, I pushed harder, willing the energy to the furthest heights. Wild lines of lightning pulled through the ceiling, a thousand delicate cracks in a glass bowl, snapping from table to hearth to floor to doorway. Plates exploded into fragments. Windowpanes snapped and shattered.

The revenant lifted off her feet and hovered for a few moments in the maelstrom before being hurled back against the bricks of the hearth. I focused my concentration on the demon and watched as the lightning found her, coiling around her in bright loops, head to toe, a poisonous insect rendered harmless, wrapped in spider silk. As the revenant struggled, I got to my feet and neared her, my hand extended. Unlike magic or sorcery, there were no words I needed to speak with this witchcraft—only images I needed to keep in my mind, and in this case, I thought of the strangling of vines, twining, convoluted spirals, the strength of such forces.

"Be gone," I whispered.

The light around the revenant blazed, and in an instant the shadows fled, darting off through the trees into the storm. With a heavy thump, the body landed on the floor, still. I knew the corpse was once again a corpse, and no more. Just the sad body of a young woman, twisted on the flagstones while the rainwater soaked into her dress dampened them.

I'd severed the demon.

I stood looking at the body, breathing hard, the pounding of my heartbeat in my ears competing with the chaos of the tavern around me. Had I neutralized the revenation? Or had I severed the bonds that kept the demon under the will of my master? Swaine knew where I was, without question. His demons had told him by now.

"We're not safe here," I said.

"Whatever gives you that idea?" Grayson said, dusting shards of glass from his chest.

I knelt by the revenant. "Mary—have the men gather the horses. Bertram—go with her, then get back to Clara. I think—"

The revenant's hand twitched. I paused. Before I could do anything more, a jolt exploded across my back, filling my ears with a loud buzzing and sending my muscles into contractions. I jerked and collapsed, cracking my head on the floor. I couldn't move.

Rush was at my side a moment later. With his middle fingers curled in toward his palms, he traced a pattern in the air. "*Primae autem quartaeque intervallum, quod habet duplam portionem, diastema facere,*" he said. A multi-hued shimmer rolled in waves above my chest and arms, up over my face. It crackled, forcing Rush to lean back away from it, a look of alarm on his face as the illumination faded. He whispered as he placed his palm on my forehead, my chin, my throat, the middle of my chest, stomach, then thighs. The life returned to my limbs in an instant.

"What was that?" I gasped.

Rush eyed the revenant. "Potent counter-magic."

"Swaine knows where we are."

The floor shuddered. The air grew chill and filled with a rank smell. Wood splintered as the ceiling tore apart. Rush attempted a spell, but as he spoke the words, the table we'd gathered around earlier lurched sideways, the legs scraping the floor, one of them breaking. Still the table slid with a wooden roar until it collided with the stairs—sending the haversack, along with the *Occul-*

tatum Ostium careening off the top, straight onto the stairs. I sensed a demon, too late. The haversack spun up into the air, hints of shadow surrounding it. Rush and I both called out as the book disappeared through the hole in the ceiling, out into the storm above.

The air around the stairs remained uncanny, as though the rain and drips from the broken beams, boards, and slate overhead slowed to a quarter of their normal speed. Mary helped me to my feet. Sounds were distorted as we staggered through into the broken glass, tables, chairs. We hurried, Rush, Grayson, Mary, Bertram, and the rest of the company, picking our way to the door through a shifting mutation of residual sorcery.

"There will be more," I said. "More demons. More revenants. Hunting me. We can't stay."

17

WILL AND DETERMINATION

The edge of the forest held the light of sunset, brilliant along the highest branch, trunk, and leaf, everything washed clean by the storm, gleaming with ten thousand clinging drops of rain. Tattered scraps of clouds sped toward the west. We gathered at a muddy crossroads, preparing to part ways. Francis and Grayson sat astride a pair of stallions at the head of a column of mounted men, a score in all. Only two men had fled after the mayhem at the tavern. The rest eyed me with a flinty reserve. I took no offense. They'd remained, whether out of loyalty to Grayson, to Mary, to Francis, or to some other principle. Mary herself had reluctantly—and snidely—agreed to remain with Bertram, offering him and Clara what protection she could. She'd behaved as though I'd betrayed her. With no time to quibble, I let the matter be.

Doctor Rush rode a smaller horse alongside mine. We each bore a haversack stuffed with magical equipment and supplies. Mine weighed me down, largely due to multiple coils of chain. Rush's wasn't much lighter, but when I'd urged him to let me take more, he'd declined.

"I don't like the two of you heading off on your own." Francis

looked the worse for wear after forty hours without sleep, dozens
of miles of riding, scouting each route and doubling back to make
sure the governor's men hadn't caught our trail.

"If you'd seen what followed Finch to the tavern, you might
change your tune," Grayson said.

"We have a plan," I said. "This is the key to it. It has to be
quiet."

"Tell that to those hideous demon corpses."

"We're better prepared." Rush and I had fashioned a pair of
glamoured rings designed to cloak us from the unseen realms.
The principles and techniques were sound—and, as yet, we'd
seen no sign of infernal stalking. I suspected, however, that
without the *Occultum Ostium* in my possession, I'd grown less
interesting to the demons serving my master. Or so I hoped.

"I still don't like it," Francis said.

"None of us like it," I said. "We just have to do it."

"Finch is right," Grayson said. "I don't like damp clothes,
muddy lanes, being shackled, shot at, hounded. Briars, braggarts,
or street brawls. None of it—yet here I am, enduring all of them
for the sake of—sorry, what was it for the sake of, Finch?"

"The safety of everyone in the colony," I said.

"And beyond," Rush added.

"Ah, yes. All that. So buck up, my good Rattlesnake—and
know that our sacrifices will actually mean something for once."

"Braggarts?" Francis said.

"You've a good ear, lad."

"You've both done well," I said. "You both wanted respect.
Glory. Purpose. Now you're getting it—so stop bickering. And you
may thank me later."

"I might not be the only braggart here," Francis said.

Grayson tugged the reins of his horse, turning it to leave. "Our
humble little Finch might not be so humble after all. Would you
look at that."

"Just keep everyone away," I said.

"Spoken like a bloody officer in the Governor's Own," Grayson said. He spurred his mount and started off down the southern road.

Francis nodded at me with a smile. "Stay safe," he said, giving his horse his heels.

Rush and I watched as the motley line of horsemen sprang into action, filling the lane two abreast in a long line, soon disappearing around a bend thick with maple trees, leaving us alone at the crossroads.

The Doctor clenched an unlit pipe in his teeth. "I hope you've saved a few encouraging remarks for me, Miss Finch."

"I could make some up, sir." I stared down the faded route leading into the forest, the one that would take us into Salem. "I think."

We exchanged a glance, then started our horses forward without another word.

By the time we reached the edge of Salem, the night was deep beneath a bright moon. I slowed, drawing my horse to a stop. The surrounding countryside held its breath. After even a short time away, I'd forgotten how deep the silence around Salem could get. No roll of wheel, clomp of hoof. No chatter of bird, no trill of cricket. The sigh of the sea and the lonesome wind were the only sounds beyond our own passage, and the nearer we drew to the town, the more sullen and brooding the silence grew. Off to our right, the road—unkempt and grown over with riotous spring grass—ran to a wooden bridge stretching over slowly moving water.

"We can see more past this rise," I said. "But we should go on foot."

We hitched the horses to a young tree. Adjusting our packs, we kept to the thicketed stretches of woodlands. Slow going, but hidden. I led Rush up a gentle slope, moving through saplings and ferns that cropped up between older pines. Granite tufted with soft moss broke through the soil. Toward the top of the hillock, the pines were joined by ghostly birches, seeming to shine in the moonlight.

I motioned with my hand, *stop*, and crouched. Rush did likewise, with a grunt. I pointed. Where the road wound up from the bridge, four figures stood watch, shadowed in the blue. I didn't need to see their features to recognize them as revenants. I scanned the overgrown meadows to either side of the road, and spotted others. Worse, I detected a heavy presence of demons. I concentrated, playing a careful game with my cloak. As I was familiar with most of Swaine's demons, I tried to figure out which ones they were—and was shocked to realize that while I recognized a few of them, there were more that I didn't. A few I had a passing familiarity with, and it became clear that he'd released them from the planar clocks we'd stored in the barn.

It was insanity.

"How many more do you think are out there?" Rush whispered. His eyes were sharp, and his color hale—he showed the vigor of a man two decades his junior, rising to the challenge we faced.

"Too many. He knows we're coming—or at least he's prepared for that possibility." I chewed at the corner of my lip. The growing worry had gnawed away at me that Swaine would make it impossible for us to approach. Seeing I'd been right gave me no satisfaction. "We may have come too close already." I didn't yet detect an infernal awareness, but feared that my master had more in store for us than I suspected.

"Is there a way past them?"

"This would be the way he'd least expect," I said. "So the other approaches will be even more heavily watched."

"The boundaries in between?"

"Patrolled by more demons. As ever." My knees pressed into the cool earth.

Random demons. Stealing back the cursed book. Whatever

he'd done at the sorcerium to instigate the planar breach. The energies involved were tremendous, so great as to effect a radical shift in the planes. Such folly. As I stared out beyond the edge of the woods, I wanted to march into Salem and find my master, grab him by his lapel, shake sense into him. Calm his fevered delirium. Cast the demon from his mind. Embrace him and assure him that all would be well. Rescue him. Rescue us. Every emotion I'd ever known seemed to rise to the surface, colliding with the force of the planes. My heart ached.

"We have to get to him," I whispered.

The good Doctor put a hand on my shoulder. He knew how strong my feelings ran. As we'd discussed our plans, my top concern—doing whatever was necessary to pry Swaine loose from the grip of possession—didn't align with Rush's priority, the risky, uncertain, but critical sealing of the planar breach at the point closest to the subduction he'd detected. Without disagreeing, we'd settled for a policy of *wait and see* as the specifics of circumstance grew clearer.

"There must be a way in," Rush said. "One he won't be aware of."

"Such a route doesn't exist, Doctor." I spoke more curtly than I'd intended. "The woods are full of revenants. The roads surely watched, as well. Every path to the manse is guarded. If we can even get past the demons—well, we will not do so without Swaine knowing."

Magic, too, was out of the question. No mirror or portal magic could be relied upon to teleport us to the manse—not with the surges of planar energy battering it. Such techniques were risky under the best of circumstances, and suicidal under the present ones. We'd run through idea after idea: cloaking, shadow manipulation, decoys. Every spell, every enchantment, every ward or glamour—each carried enough risk to cast the entire effort into doubt, and we'd crossed off every one, leaving us with nothing more than a paper filled with disappointment, and a growing sense of desperation.

"Then I don't see that we have a choice but to attempt your other suggestion," Rush said.

I shook my head. "I should never have said a word about it."

"Be glad you did. It is an option where no others exist."

As we'd scoured maps and bandied about one unworkable idea after another, I'd mentioned the opening into the demon-mere behind the Rogers' house, where I'd found a witch-well and seen my skin erupt into symbols of ravens, keys, and coffins. I hadn't been serious, instead tossing out what I'd thought to be an appropriate dose of gallows humor. Rush's prolonged silence after I'd said the words had scraped the mirth from my tongue. For every argument against it—and that list grew rapidly—there remained one unassailable argument for it: if successfully traversed, such a passage could bring us to the heart of Salem undetected, with no expenditure of magic required.

Of course, we could also find ourselves lost for eternity.

Or swallowed up by the strange planar darkness that seeped in from all angles in the Hollowing.

Or mad, as many would-be explorers of that infamous realm had discovered.

Or any one of a hundred other terrible fates that could come from delving into the strange detritus of centuries' worth of magic and sorcery.

"I have no encouraging remarks," I said, staring at the strange lights over Salem.

"We need none. Only will and determination—and all the luck Fate thinks we deserve."

Rush squeezed my shoulder in a gesture meant to reassure me.

It didn't.

18

WHERE WISDOM FAILS

A month of abandonment hadn't been kind to the gardens belonging to the widow Rogers, fled with her children to escape the terrors stalking the stretch of land between two wooded rises. Faded meadow rue drooped in patches amongst the overgrown bittersweet curled around the hinges and latch of the gate we passed through. The windows of the empty house stared mutely into the night. I led the way, a lantern held aloft.

Past the corner of the house, moonlight revealed the edges of the stone wall leading to the witch-well and the entrance to the demonmere. The huff of the lantern's flame filled the silence. We both frowned as we approached the stones, lost in our own thoughts. Tracing the line of fieldstones, we came at last to the witch-well. Fresh boards covered the opening.

"The opening is also glamoured beneath the wood," Rush said. "I didn't want anyone to bumble their way into the infernal realm."

"Save for us," I added.

"We're not bumbling. Not quite." Rush shrugged off his haversack with a grunt. "In fact, I believe we stand as good a chance of finding our way as any two who have ever ventured into the demonmere. I've studied the topography and topology of the planar realms intersecting this area for over fifty years. The seams. The fault lines. The energies. And you, I need not remind, are a witch. As such, you bear a unique relationship to this realm. It responds to you directly, as you've seen yourself—iconography and images appearing from one visit to the next. An interplay, as seen on your own skin. How you found that woman, Clara. It clearly reacts to you as to no other. If my theory is correct, the nearer we draw to Salem, the more we shall see indications of your influence. Signs of the magic you practiced. The sorcery. Your witchcraft."

I recalled all of the books on witches and witchcraft I'd seen in his library, the pages of notes. "And if we don't?"

"Then we shall rely on our precautions and find our way back out." He opened his pack. "Now. We'd best ready ourselves."

I nodded and placed the lantern on the ground near the opening. "I'll pry the boards up."

"Very good." He spoke the words not as a man being encouraging, nor as one satisfied—but rather as one condemned, ready to meet his fate.

Within the hour, we were ready. I bore the larger pack, weighted with six 10-foot lengths of chain forged from six different metals, clips and rings of steel, and a carrying case lined with small glass bottles of tinctures and powders. I also carried a six foot pole of iron, a spiked end on the bottom, a ring at the top, buzzing with a complicated series of enchantments.

Rush adjusted his pack on his shoulders, this one filled with ropes, notes, maps, the more delicate instruments, spare food, water, and a box filled with those magical ingredients he'd thought suitable to face a spectrum of contingencies. While his pack weighed half of what mine did, the effort to keep it steady would be a trial for the old gentleman. Still, he'd brooked no more offers to add more to my pack. His pride remained intact, so I let the matter go.

As Rush rechecked the contents of his pack, I fastened a glamoured spike into the ground, setting it in with a hammer. Around the spike, I wrapped the end of a fifty foot length of thin rope. The spells we'd imbued it with would extend a shining blue line from the other end, keeping pace with us as we went, always leaving a trail we might follow back to the entrance if we became lost, one of the most treacherous aspects of the demonmere. I pulled at the rope, making certain it held fast.

Rush cleared his throat. "If you're all set, I say we begin, lest I feel tempted to recheck my equipment for a fourth consecutive time."

"Such preparation is wise, sir." I got to my feet and brushed the dirt from the front of my skirts.

"Given what we're about to do, Miss Finch, I'm not altogether certain we may count wisdom amongst our travelling companions." He adjusted the straps of his pack and straightened his back. I noticed his knuckles grew whiter than normal as he gripped his cane. "But where wisdom fails, desperation must suffice."

"Well said, sir." I hefted my pack again, settling the weight to the center of my back.

Rush approached the well and raised his free hand to the glamoured opening. "*Recludam magica.*" A brief flare of light traced the edges of the stones and then disappeared. Rush leaned forward and looked down. A gust of strange air flowed from the opening, where a set of narrow stairs disappeared down into the darkness. The flames in both lanterns we'd lit fluttered. Rush met my gaze. "Are you ready, Miss Finch?"

I lifted the spike from where I'd leaned it against the stone wall and nodded. "I'm ready."

Was I ready? My heart told me it was a terrible idea. My knees shook and my chest tightened.

The Doctor nodded, his expression unreadable. "Then we bid a fond adieu to wisdom and begin."

"I'll lead the way, sir." I gave one last look around the Rogers' overgrown fields and straddled the lip of the well, taking the end of the glamoured rope with me. Patches of dirt and fieldstones marked the opening, but from these extended yellowed plaster walls that formed a landing above wooden stairs leading down, angling to the left. The layout of the space was familiar from my earlier journeys into the demonmere. As before, my senses rioted, reacting to the energies that pressed in from every direction. I helped Rush onto the landing, then started down the stairs. My skin rippled; my scalp tingled. The walls leaned in with the pressure of a thousand other worlds. We soon reached the limit of the rope. "Fifty yards."

Rush paused. He rested his pack against the wall, his shadow angling up behind him like a shifting gargoyle.

"Has it narrowed, sir?"

"Yes—and steepened." He spoke an eight-line incantation. Fine dust feathered down from the slanted ceiling, and the surrounding angles changed, as though the stairwell itself were a massive serpent, not liking the magic being performed in its belly. Deep rasping sounds and the screech of nails pulled from wood rose from behind the walls. When the spell was complete, a deep blue line, thinner than the rope itself, extended from the frayed end to Rush's heels.

Rush steadied himself. "This line will pace us."

I nodded and set off again. The line of magic followed along with me. Time took on a peculiar quality, one step after another, ten, twenty, scores, more, our passage the only illumination. An airless chill seeped from the walls. After another half an hour, the stairwell narrowed such that I could touch both walls at once. Still curving to the left, the steps lengthened, and the wood creaked with our steps. "I feel as though it's tilting, sir—is it just me?"

"It may be reacting to our presence in some way."

"The *aberrant intelligence* that Summerfield wrote of."

"Exactly."

I found the idea disconcerting: a construction built out of a nightmare, somehow alive. I inhaled, clearing my thoughts. "Well I don't care for it."

"A strong second here, Miss Finch."

Already, we'd descended more stairs than I'd ever traversed at one go, still with no end in sight. "What if it keeps going?"

"I've counted eleven hundred and sixty-six steps."

In the absence of any other features, my balance was off, and I banged the iron pole against the ceiling. Looking over my shoulder, I said, "I think the ceiling is lower."

More stairs disappeared into the darkness ahead of us. The thought of the lanterns snuffing out leapt into my mind—forcing me to push back at the terror that such an image conjured. Pure darkness. I imagined descending so forever. The soles of my shoes slid on the wood, and it became difficult to keep my balance, not least because I bore a sack full of chains on my back. I stumbled and nearly pitched forward. The stairs assumed an undeniable roll leftward. Worse, they steepened even more. I found myself dizzy and paused. By this point, I had to tilt the iron pole backward to make room for it.

Rush paused, leaning on his cane, winded from our descent.

"Are you all right, sir?" I said.

"Well enough. Let's keep going."

And so we went, deeper. The sounds of our descent echoed off in both directions—the tread of our feet, the clang of the iron pole, the knock of Rush's cane, the muffled shifting of chains in my pack, our own labored breathing. After another half hour, the stairwell became nearly impassable, canted forty-five degrees to the left, the ceiling now so low as to force us both into crouches from which we half-slid, half-climbed. Sweat ran along the sides of my torso and trickled along my temples in spite of the chill that gripped the air. Our shadows loomed up in crazed distortions as the lanterns tilted and bumped along with us.

I slipped at one point and tumbled forward seven or eight steps. My pack stopped me from going farther—and just as well, for the stairwell bent in a precipitous curve just in front of me. The sight of it made my stomach drop, for not only was it steeper than we could traverse, but the passage narrowed to a chute, barely wide enough for even my pack. And that was only the section I saw. Beyond was anyone's guess.

"Miss Finch?" Rush called after me.

"I'm fine—but be careful, sir. It's terribly steep, and it—well, you'll have to come and see."

I watched the Doctor slide on his backside, cane and lantern banging along next to him. This was no good. As he came to a rest next to me, it was clear how much the efforts had already taxed him—his cheeks were flushed, his breathing ragged. He looked past me into the darkness, holding out his lantern with a shaking arm.

"Do we turn back?" I said.

"An unpleasant prospect." Rush closed his eyes in thought. He opened them after a minute. "I think we must risk another small amount of magic. Giving up at this point is not a decision to be made lightly. We would have to find a different approach into the demonmere—and even then we would have no guarantee that our route would be any easier. And the only other entrance I'm familiar with is in the Whitelocke crypt, with all the difficulties that would entail."

"Surely there are others? Near some of the seals."

"Almost certainly—though we would have to locate them, which would take days. We don't have the luxury of such time, I fear." He wedged his cane and lantern alongside him as he slipped the pack from his shoulders. He untied the top of his pack and rooted inside it. He pulled out a glass marble, and a palm-sized mirror. "No. We've come this far. Let's see what lies before us. Or, more precisely, *below* us." He placed the marble atop the surfaces of the mirror, balancing it just so, then passed his other hand over both, saying, "*Wigcræftigne, nales wordum log. Searwum gearwe, wigend wæron.*"

A glare erupted from the glass of the marble, brighter even than the lanterns. I squinted at it. Rush repeated the phrase, reversing the order of the words, entraining the mirror to the marble. As he lifted the marble, I glimpsed both our faces, stretched and strange, projected into the mirror glass.

He held the marble out past the drop-off. "Let's hope no one's listening." With that, he let the marble go. It dropped from his fingers, and knocked off one step that fell away, then another. *Bang, bang, bang* it went, taking the light with it, filling the stairwell with its racket. I half-expected it to keep going forever, or to take to a steeper fall, where it might descend in silence to who knew where. Instead, it banged, and bounced, and knocked back and forth, coming to a rest with a diminishing paradiddle no more than twenty feet below us. The curve of the stairwell made it impossible to see the marble itself, but the light was clear. Rush and I both leaned over the mirror. In the glass, we saw a close look at wooden floorboards, the brethren of the ones we crouched on. Rush moved his finger along the surface of the mirror, and the view shifted with his swipe. Walls, more narrow steps. A small landing—and a door.

"There," he said. He adjusted the view.

"How distorted is that view, sir?" I said.

"Somewhat."

"Then doesn't that door look—small?"

"It does." He shifted the view.

"How big is it?"

"It appears—" he waved his fingers over the glass, and the view grew closer to the door, "—large enough to accommodate a dog."

"Not a large one," I said.

He looked at me. "I fear that we have come to the first of many such moments when the demonmere will test us. This isn't a realm meant for people. Any resemblance is coincidental, being the byproduct as it is of magic created in this world. There may be nothing at all beyond that door. Or, there may be a way forward."

"And the passage may continue to shrink," I said, staring into the narrow, bent stairwell.

I could immediately think of a dozen reasons to turn back around. Possibilities. Limits. Caution. Yes, they went through my mind—but I hadn't the better part of a year as August Swaine's apprentice for nothing. Possibilities were meant to be chased, not eliminated in the face of challenge. Limits were often only the point where others' will had failed. Caution was to be doled out in pungent, concentrated spoonfuls, not tossed by the bucketful, as so often done by those who valued their comfort above all else.

I turned to Rush. "I'll go down there and look."

"You're sure?"

"I'm sure."

With that, I slid my pack from my shoulders, and looked into the semi-darkness. Judging from the light at the bottom, the overall width at the bend left little room for turning. I thought for a few moments about attempting it head-first—but being stuck upside-down at the bottom was too much to risk. No, feet-first it would be, allowing me the option that should the door prove impassable, I might still climb free using a rope from Rush's pack. We took out a coil of rope and spent several minutes securing it to one runner with the help of a steel spike and the hammer. The silence after the bangs had echoed back the way we'd come grew sinister.

"That should let them know we're here," Rush said.

I tested the rope. It held fast. "Just a magician and a witch, passing through."

Rush gave me a thin smile. "I shall admit I often fancied that, were I to chance to meet a living witch, I would find myself in the company of a kindred spirit. A suspicion you have quite confirmed, Miss Finch."

I reached out and squeezed his hand. After a moment, I took a firm grip on the rope. "Here I go, then."

With both arms holding tight to the rope, I edged past the dip. The stairwell continued its twist to the left, and I found it easier to slide along the wall, rather than the steps themselves. I fought to grab hold with my feet, but it wasn't much good—every angle conspired to push me into a free-fall, and I dangled from the rope, banging against the sideways wall. The effect was disconcerting. While the Doctor was good enough to extend a lantern out over the drop, much of my passage was into darkness, and while gravity knew which way to pull me, my eyes kept insisting that all was sideways, or that I was floating backwards down the stairwell. Worse, the walls narrowed more than I'd thought, for my heels and elbows and hips met one side, then the other, and finally both. I paused just over halfway, breathing hard. My arms shook—but I jammed my back against one wall, my knees against the other, and held my place. One small consolation of the diminishing space.

"Can you continue?" Rush called.

"So far." I opened and closed my hands, which complained about exerting themselves on the rope. "It's getting tight."

I looked past my chest, between my knees. Below me, the light from the glass marble shone.

"Don't get yourself stuck."

"I shall try not to," I said, understating my feelings on the matter. A trembling took my arms and legs. Was there enough air? What if I wedged myself in? Could the Doctor pull me free? I closed my eye. My knees banged against the small steps as I wriggled lower, yard by yard. My dress bunched up around my waist, and I was about to call a halt to the entire effort, sure it was too narrow to go any farther—when my feet touched bottom.

"I'm down," I called out. I had just enough room to turn, finding myself seated in the corner of a tiny landing. The floorboards beneath me were doll-sized, compared to what we'd seen above. The door itself was ridiculously small: only fourteen inches high, ten wide.

"How does it look?" Rush's voice floated down.

"Not encouraging—but there's room."

"Lift the marble so I might see it."

I picked up the glowing sphere of glass and held it out. "Yes?"

"Yes," came his reply after a moment.

"I'll try it." I placed the marble in front of the door. Grabbing the latch was absurd, it was so small. Not for the first time, the thought crossed my mind that I was in the midst of a strange dream, rather than the demonmere—that I might any moment wake to find myself in my bed in Salem, or even in Andover. Still, the iron of the handle was solid. The chilly air around me did nothing to stave off the stuffiness. My palms were sore from the rope. No dream—only a waking nightmare of sorts. The latch moved. I pushed the door open. The air in the small landing whooshed out, pulled along into a wider current of air.

To peer through the door, I had to contort myself onto my hands and knees. I grabbed the marble for the sake of its light and poked my head in through the tiny doorway. My first reaction: *Thank God.* It wasn't another corridor, diminishing in size, impossible to traverse. Rather, it was a large space, much larger. The wooden floor ended at the doorway, and beyond stretched a large slab of stone.

I didn't need the light from the marble, for what appeared to be daylight—albeit the palest of light, gray as the first hint of dawn—fell in from the left side of a massive chamber. Stone slabs, flattened, fitted together, extended out before me. One hundred or more yards ahead, a wide staircase occupied at the opposite side. Both lengths of the chamber rose in stone walls. Atop those walls, great pillars of stone spaced every ten feet lifted eighty feet, connecting to the underside of a great vaulted ceiling that arched over the entire chamber. Beyond the columns, there appeared to be nothing but sky, dawn to the left, stars to the right. In the corner, rose vines ran rampant, climbing the stone, the blooms a deep scarlet that glowed like velvet in candlelight. The air itself smelled fresh, and I heard the sound of running water.

I worked my shoulder and head through. Satisfied it was passable, I pulled myself back into the tiny landing. "It's a chamber. Columns. Sky."

"Did you say *sky*?" Rush called back down.

"Yes. Sky. And there are stairs on the opposite side. Shall I explore and let you know?" The thought occurred that if that chamber were a dead end, getting the good Doctor back up through the vertical stairwell might prove impossible.

"No, no—I shall join you. I already worry about the time we've lost."

He sent my pack first, and it landed with a thud that knocked a section of plaster from the wall. The iron spike was more difficult, for it couldn't afford to be damaged, forcing me to climb back up part of the way, and then grab it from his dangling hand —the process of which nearly pitched him head-first down the stairwell. I shimmied back, one-handed, only to find that the angles prevented me from getting the pole into the landing. I dodged the hammer when Rush dropped it to help me, and then banged away at the corner of the stairwell, knocking loose plaster and slats, ignoring the freezing darkness and the fear I was drawing the attention of every planar entity connected to the demonmere. It took well over half an hour to demolish enough to slide the iron pole through. After that, we lowered Rush's more delicate pack on the rope.

Getting Rush down was harrowing. His grip was poor, and as much as I tried to explain how he might brace himself along opposing sides, he couldn't get the knack of it. A running stream of commentary on his difficulties and deficiencies accompanied him, painful inch by inch. I ended up climbing beneath him as he neared the mid-point, allowing him to put his feet on my shoulders, his shoes digging into my flesh, pulling my hair. With the extra weight on me, it was difficult not to slip. It was only during the last few yards where Rush collapsed on top of me, sending us both to the bottom with a pair of grunts. After disentangling ourselves—fortunately no sprains, knocks, or breaks of concern —we navigated the doorway, working both packs, lanterns, the pole, myself, and finally the bruised, rumpled Doctor through to the other side.

After such confined difficulties, the simple opportunity to stand upright was a gift. The glowing blue line followed us from the door. "Should we wedge it open with something?"

Rush nodded, smoothing out his hair. "That would be prudent, yes. Doors, locks, and latches are not to be trusted here."

I looked for something I might jam the door open with, but everything around us was immense, and smooth. Dust filmed the stones and even the roses, lifeless as though made of fabric. I settled for crawling back into the entryway and sweeping out the larger pieces of plaster and slat I'd smashed free to fit the iron pole. One piece of wood, crisp and stone-like, was large enough, so I set it between the door and the jamb. I wiped my hands on my skirts. "This daylight is strange."

"Indeed," Rush said, craning his neck and looking up between two of the columns to our left. "Samuel Blackburne posited that sections of the demonmere branched into other worlds altogether—*beyond the dreams of summoners*, was his phrase, I believe."

I shouldered my pack again, not happy to be bearing the weight of it again. "My master hated Blackburne." I frowned. "Hates."

"With good reason. The man was despicable. Nearly the entirety of what he claimed credit for he stole during several trips he took to Venice and Naples. Worse, he paid enormous sums to have the magicians he'd stolen from disparaged in print. Then he had the nerve to spend the following years railing from his estate about the pathetic shortcomings of Italian magic."

I helped Rush get his pack back on, then handed him one lantern. "The stairs?"

"Yes," Rush said. "The space beyond the columns looks unwholesome."

We crossed the long chamber. I gazed to the right where a starlit sky peered between the columns. I recognized none of the constellations. The sight of it filled me with a peculiar mixture of wonder and dread. What world was this a glimpse of? Or from? Part of me would have liked nothing better than to sit and stare, to chart the positions of the stars in that strange firmament, to drink in their beauty. Something about it stirred a recollection in me of Swaine, shortly after I'd met him, telling me in reverent tones of the final words of Gustav Koeffler, the Great Man, the father of planar theory, spoken by him on his deathbed: *So many rooms within the heavenly mansion—I look forward to exploring each one.* In that moment, I missed my master fiercely. I wished he could share the sight of a thousand strange stars. Driven as he was, unconcerned with the niceties of social intercourse, dismissive of the tiny dreams of most of humanity—well, his heart ran deeper than even he admitted to. Such a sight would have surely given him a moment of awe.

I tore my gaze away from the numinous heavens, focusing instead on the stairs ahead of us and the darkness of the demonmere beyond, ready to face anything to save my master.

19

A MADWOMAN'S NIGHTMARE

Time is peculiar. An arrow that points but one direction.

I thought of Swaine's note as we crossed through the strange landscape of the demonmere. With each passing hour, I at least had the comfort of knowing that time would only carry us forward, leaving each terrified step in the past. Eventually. Yet aching under the weight of a pack full of chains, lugging an iron pole, gazing beyond the edge of my lantern's light, I was all too aware of each sweep of the second hand.

The curious spans, stairs, ever-changing maze of hallways. No angle ever quite right, walls and floors stretched or warped as from a madwoman's nightmares. Each new turn brought us more puzzles. Shadowed doorways. Elaborate cracks in plaster walls looking like hideous faces. The sound of a plunging bucket in an unseen well; a stone clacking against another like a signal of some sort; distant wind knocking a shutter, the clangs pacing us. Iron railings on narrow bridges. Cold breezes grabbing at the back of my neck. Stone steps. The murmur of rushing water. Stray echoes of our footsteps, seeming to trail us. At various points, we saw—or thought we saw—the shining eyes of an animal. We heard—or thought we heard—distant screams, whispers, chimes, bells, scraping. We came upon openings with broken brass hinges, guttered ends of candles, dark ropes extending into narrow holes, stretches of rotted wood, water-damaged papers scrawled with nonsense. One hallway held walls of carved faces, each in despair. Another rows of paintings, each with figures in finery with black eyes staring out as we passed. Glass windows shone with queer moonlight. And darkness, always darkness.

Confusion pressed in on us, a constant enemy. We fought to stave off the fear we'd taken the wrong route, over and over again. We hadn't seen a single sign of my magic or witchcraft, no hint of ravens, keys, coffins, or the like. Rush's face grew ever more haggard as he crouched over one of his maps in the shifting light of our lanterns, muttering, tracing this line or that, glancing up without comfort at our surroundings. We made frequent readings with his planar compass, uneasy with the application of such magic within the demonmere, but unable to otherwise calibrate our progress within the known intersections of planes, so crucial to deciphering the way forward.

We came to feel we weren't alone. At one point, we came upon a tiny table in a dark purple sitting room, set with three cups of tea from which steam rose, one chair tipped onto its back. At another, we stumbled into the scent of tobacco smoke, clouds of it hovering dune-shaped in the air in a circular library, the shelves lined with the same book, the terrible name of which I will not set to paper. Shadows slipped past the other side of keyholes. Tiny doors slid shut. From far off along a slanting hallway with polished marble floors and a row of velvet bell-ropes hanging from a ceiling came the crying of an infant—hushed, then spirited off with the clack of hard shoes that trailed off down a staircase. We followed one rickety set of stairs into what appeared to be servants' quarters and kitchen, to another set of stairs leading into an identical—or nearly so—quarters and kitchen, repeated three more times, and each time we heard the clang of pot, the chop of knife on cutting board, the indecipherable hum of chatter, each time falling silent the moment we set foot on the middle step of the stairs.

As for demons, they were ever-present. They passed beyond walls. They lurked around in the areas we'd traversed, drawn to our passing. The entities didn't trouble us much. Still, the sharks were being drawn, and there we were, floating deeper and deeper in the dark sea of the demonmere. As we went farther, crashing noises erupted back in the direction we'd come—the shattering of glass, the bang of heavy furniture tipped over, a collapse of marble stairs, the sound of a hundred books taking flight into an opposite wall. Each time, we jumped, listening as the disruption echoed through the endless halls and stairwells, fading in the distance, giving the silence afterwards an even heavier air of brooding. At one point, we both heard a delicate *clack-clack-clack* trailing us, as of small, wooden feet. As I looked at Rush, he shook his head, his mouth a thin line. "Impossible," he whispered, no doubt hoping the word might banish the image of a marionette puppet from both our minds.

Nothing about the time we spent in the demonmere seemed more than an arm's length from nightmare.

Some fourteen hours into our journey—we'd allowed ourselves only a few short rests, never comfortable enough to sleep, but trading off brief naps—we followed a spiraling corridor that wound upward, the walls deep scarlet, floorboards the color of bleached bones, waxed and polished. A row of fine teeth ran along the walls, a disturbing moulding. After several turns around the center, we found a door of wrought iron, patterned as eyes, large and small. I pushed the door open. It squealed, and beyond it was darkness. Wind ruffled my sleeves and skirt. A tremendous space opened beneath us and the air smelled of water and slate.

Outside the door, the floor was replaced with iron runners

three feet long and only eight inches wide, one after another with a gap of a foot, extending out over the emptiness. I held my lantern aloft, unhappy to note that the runners continued out beyond my light, rising in an arch. Not too steep—but there was no railing. I turned back to the Doctor.

"I don't think it's possible," I said. My words echoed off into the massive darkness.

Rush nodded, and retrieved the map from his coat pocket. Unfolding it, he didn't look pleased by what he saw. "Not good. The last plausible alternative was before that series of rooms with the glass walls. In that little corridor—that smaller passage heading downward."

I hung my head, exhausted. That had been over three hours earlier. Our reading had shown a stronger planar connection along this route, while the other had shown uncertain numbers. Worse, the other route had reeked of decay. Retracing our steps that far was terrible, a crushing prospect. I lifted my head. "Let me at least take a look."

"No, it's far too dangerous. One slip—that's all it will take."

"We don't know. It might change, or mightn't be as far as it seems. It's worth a quick—and very careful—look."

Rush straightened. "I don't like this at all. We're tired. We want to leave. The fear that's gnawing at us is having its way with our judgment."

"But the readings were definitive."

"Suggestive, not definitive."

"No less so than every other reading we've made." I had a point, and he knew it. The reverse was also true—for he had a point. Poor judgment was yet another enemy, and if either of us fell, that would be it.

Rush fixed me with his stare. "Not far, Miss Finch. And you will secure yourself with a rope."

"Fair enough."

I set aside my pack and the pole and risked a touch of rope

magic to make sure that the knots I tied to the iron of the door and the one I cinched around my waist wouldn't slip apart under strain. I had forty feet of slender line, glamoured for strength as part of our preparations. Taking the lantern in one hand, I stepped out onto the runners, one after another, taking my time. The trick was looking at my feet without looking *beyond* them. Not an easy trick, I may report.

When the air gusted, which was far more frequently than I'd hoped, I paused, one foot on adjacent runners, my arms out for balance. Six, ten, fifteen, twenty runners. The circle of light from my lantern illuminated the next few runners, while those beyond were lost in shadow. I neared the end of the rope. All seemed unchanged—and therefore a poor possibility. I was about to say as much before turning back, when I glimpsed a shape in the darkness ahead of me, at the far edge of my light. I raised the lantern. There. The light shone off something higher than the runners, only ten feet ahead of me.

"I have to take off the rope," I called out.

"Off? No, no, no." The panic in Rush's voice was clear as it echoed out around me. "Leave that rope on, whatever you do."

"I've found the end, I believe—but I won't know if I can't reach it."

"Then *do not* try."

I understood his caution. I also understood the cost of doubling back the way we'd come. The hours lost. The uncertainty it was even the right decision. So I ignored the old gentleman and held my hands above the knot at my hip and whispered, "*Loslassen selbst.*" A flare of light zipped along the hemp fibers, and the rope fell away. I ignored the doom should I stumble, concentrating only on taking one step after another after another, eyes forward as soon as I had my foot settled each time.

Seven steps and I reached firm footing. A length of elaborate ironwork rose on either side, the metal underfoot replaced with solid planks, no gaps. A railing lifted on both sides. "I'm safe," I yelled out. My heartbeat slowed from racing to merely galloping. I leaned forward, grasping the railings. "Thirty-three steps, Doctor. After that a respectable bridge." Rush stood on the far side, holding out his lantern. After a moment of pure relief, I straightened and lifted the lantern. "Let me take a look where it leads." The bridge continued forward, iron rising on both sides in a complex webbing, and soon came to a door of wood, inset into a wall of stone. "A door," I called back.

Turning to the door, I found a handle made of pearl. Holding my breath—for we'd encountered many false or locked doors—I tried the handle. It gave way as though it hadn't been opened in a century, but it gave way. Hinges squealed, flecks of rust grinding and falling, but I got it open. Faint light flooded into the space, torches burning along the walls of a slanting corridor. It looked promising.

"There's a way through," I shouted. I turned and headed back to the edge of the bridge. "I think we can make it, sir."

"Good thing I'm far more graceful than you, Miss Finch. Otherwise, I'd be quite terrified."

...terrified...terrified...terrified... His words echoed down into emptiness like bats in flight.

Crossing the railless section of the bridge proved every bit the ordeal we feared. I did it three more times in each direction: with my pack (every step a fright, top-heavy as I was); with Rush's pack and cane (my heel slipped on one runner and I nearly stumbled); with the pole, held sideways for balance. Doctor Rush couldn't manage over two runners before being overcome with vertigo, a difficulty with his balance that had plagued him for several decades, he informed me. He tried, once, twice, thrice—but each attempt ended as the others had, with his arms flailing, my heart in my throat, and his return to the iron outcropping behind him.

We used every rope we'd brought along, plus several more spells on said ropes, plus one more set of crossings on my part to string together railings of sorts, binding the ends of the ropes to the iron on both sides of the railless section, one to the left, the other to the right. Taut and sturdy, they gave the good Doctor enough stability to slowly and with much fretting take each of the thirty-three steps required. He'd been forced to leave the second lantern back on the landing behind him, requiring both hands to hold the ropes. There it remained, burning fitfully.

Once safe on the other side—if any location in the demon-mere might ever be said to be *safe*—I gave him a reassuring hug before manipulating the magic I'd imbued into the rope to loosen the far ends and reeled it in. Rush peered in through the doorway as I put the rope back into his pack, being careful to keep the delicate instruments from being knocked about.

"It looks promising," he said.

I tightened the drawstrings on the top of his pack. "I agree. If our calculations are correct, we may be getting close."

Shrugging my pack back on, I hefted our remaining lantern, the iron pole, and Rush's pack. He took both the lantern and his pack, and we stepped toward the doorway. I gave one final look back at the lone lantern burning across the way, wondering how far off the moment was when it would flicker and extinguish, out of oil, darkness claiming the chasm once more. Rush stepped into the wide corridor, and I followed. We hadn't gotten fifteen or twenty paces from the door when a screeching and howling of metal burst from where we'd stood—groaning, bending, ripping iron. We froze, looking back. After a moment, the sound changed with a final wrenching shriek of metal falling away.

"The bridge," Rush whispered, the lantern held shoulder height.

There was nothing after that, until we heard one distant knell, followed by another, then another, deeper, deeper, and deeper.

"Demons?" I said.

"They're growing more brazen."

"We're liable to find more as we near Salem," I said. "And Salem itself is certainly swarming with them."

The Doctor paused, leaning on his cane. "Yet another obstacle. That said, I'm not inclined to stroll about the town. With such forces lashing the area, we'll have one advantage—the *occulta proluo*. The more that we can take advantage of such passages, the more hidden we'll be."

"But how workable is that?"

"I've taken advantage of them for years. Primarily to avoid various social encounters, if you must know the truth. There's skill and familiarity involved, but I trust that with your senses, you'll be able to keep up." Rush turned and started off away from the clamor that still whispered from that direction. "We'd best not dawdle."

We descended the length of a torch-lit corridor. There were many such unnatural illuminations throughout the demonmere, whether in the form of torch, candle, lantern, or peculiar glass globes lit from within. They gave off no heat, and couldn't be moved from one room or chamber to the other without crumbling into ashes in one's hand. Even the light they spilled didn't seem to be all that bright. The Doctor theorized that, like the rest of the details found within the space, they were no more than symbols, a sort of visual iconography derived from the same dark materials that resided in the minds of the practitioners whose work seeded the entire realm.

In the weak light, the stones overhead formed an arched ceiling that played tricks with my ears, turning our pair of footsteps into a marching troop of them. There was something serpentine about the corridor as it meandered downward, curving, dipping, as though we'd become a strange version of Jonah, save we found ourselves in the belly of a monstrous snake. Rush paused a few times to catch his breath, claiming that he was still doing fine when I asked him. I took the lead and was the first to enter a curious foyer. Wood-paneled walls rose to a frescoed ceiling, decorated with images of winged fiends. A dozen black high-backed chairs stood along the walls. Another corridor passed through the foyer, with openings on the far ends. A thin line of blue stretched from one doorway to the other.

I halted, the bottom dropping out of my stomach.

The Doctor came up beside me. "I fear I've been too stingy with the water, and I'm—" His words ceased as his gaze settled on the blue line, the same blue line that trailed us at that moment, the spell that marked our passage. We both stared at it, silent. We'd passed through that foyer hours earlier. Seven, nine hours, untold miles—meaning we'd gone in a massive circle, and crossed our own trail. After a moment, Rush put his hand to his face, took off his spectacles, and rubbed his brow with thumb and forefinger. The sigh that escaped him said all there was to say.

"I don't understand," I whispered. I strode into the foyer and stood next to the faint blue line of magic, sighting down it in both directions. We'd done a reading inside the far doorway.

Rush lowered his hand. "Ruinous."

"Well—we'll have to find the right way forward."

"I'm at a loss as to how we might do that. The one fear that has nagged at my mind since we prepared for this has proven true: readings from within here are inaccurate. We may have no confidence we can find our way to Salem. None." He set his pack on a chair, and put his fists to his hips, gazing along the line. "I fear that we must abandon this attempt, lest we waste any more time, or even our lives. We might wander past the point where our supplies could guarantee our return. And then what? No, it's too dangerous."

I didn't like giving up, and frowned at the suggestion. "Another day will be lost just finding our way back, maybe more," I said.

"Better such time lost than everything lost."

"But everything *is* lost if we can't make this work. How else are we getting into Salem? We don't have an army. We have nothing else that might give us an edge—he'll know we're coming, and he has an army."

Doctor Rush, to his credit, didn't let my raised voice nor my stubborn insistence on spelling out what he was well aware of ruffle him. He knew the strains that tugged at my heart. Even after such a disastrous turn of events, he was a gentleman. "We must find another way. A distraction of some kind. It will add a worrisome element of time to what we need to do—but I don't see that we have a choice. Surely you agree, Miss Finch."

I raised my hands. "You're right. Fine." In that moment, I hated that place—with its loathsome, absurd turns and twists and idiocy—with an intensity I'd never known.

"We ought be glad we didn't push beyond the point of no return. Fate may have been kind to us, returning us to this spot."

I refused to see kindness in the giant circle we'd traced—only defeat. My pack felt twice as heavy on my shoulders at the thought of bearing it back along the route we'd come. The inclines, the crawlspaces, the steep stairs. All of it—to bring us right back where we'd started, nothing to show for it.

As the good Doctor put aside his cane and spread out his map to refresh himself as to our position, I wandered to the far end of the foyer. It seemed ages earlier, and my mood further soured. I shook my head, frustration forcing me to knead my neck muscles, wanting to yell, scream. The fiend on the ceiling stared at me, winking. I stared at the grotesque fresco, one fiend to the next—and noticed that all were winking. One eye closed, as if in pure mockery. I lowered my gaze to the doorway and sighed, about to turn back to Doctor Rush, but stopped as I spotted a trio of words carved into the wood above the doorway: *Never. Ever. Ever.* I stared at them—they were in perfect English. It struck me as more than a little strange... but also brought a wash of sadness to me. Why?

A moment later, I realized with a shock that those were the

words that Swaine had spat at me as he'd beaten me with the riding crop. What were they doing in the doorway?

I leaned in closer, scanning for other words. Down along one side, I found *Grenfell Glamour*. My pulse quickened. Along the other side: *iron-breaker*. Iron-breaker? My mind filled with an image of the door to Swaine's bedroom falling away after the first spell I'd ever cast, a spell of iron-breaking from Neile's book, which I'd read.

What on earth was going on?

I stepped back and looked at the ceiling again. All the fiends, all with but one eye showing. Frowning, I poked my head through the doorway. The blue line marking our earlier passage ran up a set of stairs. I remembered the bannister having been loose and not trusting it to keep us from tumbling over the side. I ducked back into the foyer, about to look at the words again, when my eye caught a hint of light in the darkness beyond. I paused. Off to the right, a wider set of stairs opened out downward, and at the bottom ran a floor in a curious pattern of light and dark wood.

Rush muttered to himself, still hunched over his map.

I left the doorway and stood at the top of the stairs. In the light that came from some unseen distance away, I made out the intricate parquet of the boards. For a moment, I felt a nag of worry I couldn't place—and my breath stopped. "Doctor."

"I'm—Miss Finch?"

"Over here, through the doorway." I stepped back from the shadows into the foyer, waving for him to follow.

"You're all right?"

"Yes. Yes. Come here, sir." My pulse, fast as it was, failed to keep even with my thoughts, which raced ahead. When the Doctor came through the doorway, he gazed at me, then at the line of magic leading up the stairs.

"No, not that way," I said. I went to the stairs. "This way."

"We went *that* way." He pointed at the magic. "I recall those stairs."

"As do I, sir. But do you recall *these* stairs?"

He turned and approached me. "Well we didn't go this way."

"And do you remember why not?" I said.

"Well—we'd done a reading. The way to the right was indicated."

"No, no—that's not what I'm saying, sir. Do you even remember these stairs being here?"

He still clutched the map and glanced at it. "I don't recall them being here—or not being here. Either way—we've seen many stairwells, haven't we?"

I touched his arm. "But we would have remembered these, sir."

"Pray, why?"

"Because they lead down into the ballroom of the Whitelocke manse," I said.

"I don't understand." He stared past me, into the space below.

"The floor. The pattern."

"Yes," he said after a few moments. "I see the familiarity, but—"

"It's not a familiarity. Or similarity. It's the actual pattern. Look." I started down the steps. The floor stretched out into the rest of the room. Chandeliers, dried flower arrangements, glass doors. There were even stringed instruments arranged off in one corner: two violins, a viola, a cello. Nothing was quite at the same dimensions as the actual Whitelocke ballroom, but even the exaggerated scale of the space resonated with me.

Because I'd created it.

Rush followed me, gasping as he got a full vantage of the room. "How did we not notice this before?"

"We didn't notice it because it wasn't *here* before," I said. I turned, spinning my skirts. "That's why. We never passed by here.

We haven't circled back on our route, sir. And I think we're getting closer."

He gazed around the room and looked back over his shoulder.

"It's the magic, Doctor," I said. "The magic we used to take the readings."

"I don't follow."

"Do you remember that I spoke the incantation over the device back in the foyer?"

"You did?"

"I did." We'd alternated the spell-casting to minimize any depletion or other side-effects. "I'm certain of it. And in doing so —my magic added to the demonmere."

Rush put a knuckle to his chin.

"What's back there is a *re-creation*—or whatever we want to call what the demonmere is—of the passage we'd made, rippling from that spot." I paced back and forth, my shoes tapping on the hardwood floor. "Because of my magic. And it's different—subtly so, but different."

I explained to him the fiends on the ceiling which hadn't been winking when we'd gone through the original foyer. I described the words, and their meaning. "And this—" I raised my arms to the wide ballroom we stood in, "—wasn't here when we went through the first space, but it's here now because I did magic here, last year. Not *here*, but in the Whitelocke manse. The night that General Whitelocke died."

"Which instantiated this space in the demonmere," Rush continued, grasping the implication of my words. "When it happened."

"I think so. It feels—I don't know—more *right* than any of the other spaces we passed through. Familiar. Not only the details, but the texture of it. As my own dreams are familiar. I *know* it because it came from me. There's no question." I pointed at the rest of the ballroom. "All of it is connected. The magic I did back in the foyer recreated that portion of our path. And it connected to this."

Rush folded the map. "This would then be connected to other magic you've executed—which would mean that we are likely nearing Salem. Where else would your magic lead us? That's where you did the most, so one would assume that it becomes concentrated in some fashion." He looked up at me. "Our readings were right. My goodness, Miss Finch."

"We may have done it, sir," I said. Hope surged in me for the first time since we'd entered the strange realm.

Rush nodded. "Time may still be on our side."

Time, an arrow indeed.

20

TRIFLING FLITCH

O f all my memories from the demonmere, the strangest are those of burning shame. Imagine, if you will, inviting another person into your dreams, where they might witness firsthand the way that your mind works—the distortions, the raw emotions, your deepest fears, desires, and fixations on display. No scrim of manners or censorship to soften the hard edges of any of it.

Mortifying, no?

So I felt as Doctor Rush and I made our way through the sections of the demonmere that had sprung from *my* magic, *my* mind. The alternate Whitelocke ballroom where we started our final sprint was immense and intimidating, as though observed by a small child. Worse, the light from the chandeliers danced prettily, and flowers lined the walls. The work of a serious practitioner? No, more like that of a young woman who thought the romance of dancing the height of marvel. The hallways that extended from the far side resembled those further into the manse, with high ceilings, polished floors, and a ridiculous amount of gilding. As we passed along their lengths, I bit back on the urge to insist to the good Doctor that I wasn't as dazzled by wealth and finery as my magic made it seem. Secretly, I wondered if I was.

The corridor narrowed to a tall door beneath a luxurious set of stairs—the rails and balustrade of gold—leading to the wine cellar wherein I'd been attacked by the possessed General John Whitelocke. Down rickety stairs into the dimness. The air of the tomb hung about the space. At the bottom, enormous casks stretched off beneath a low ceiling, row after row. Interspersed between them stood upright coffins, each with a pair of well-shined boots set out before them. Scarlet uniforms decorated hooks next to them. While I knew Rush had heard, from my own lips, the true events that had led to the death of John Whitelocke, I wondered if he thought it a lie, revealed by the profusion of coffins and uniforms which my magic confessed. Rush said nothing, facing it with the same determination with which we'd navigated earlier miles of the journey.

After crossing the faux wine cellar, we found a rough wooden door that opened into a series of rooms filled with dresses of every imaginable hue and cut, each upon a stand beneath a chandelier. Lace, silk, brocade, velvet. Tassels, embroidery, herringbone. Bodice and petticoat. Stocking and ribbon. Shoes, stretching off like footprints, pair after pair. A wall covered in eyepatches of mauve, peach, coral, violet, silver, autumn yellow, decorated with jewels, sewn with patterns of butterflies and fleur-de-lis. Oh, and mirrors, dozens of them. My face went scarlet as we passed among the vain frippery. He was kind enough not to make note of it...aloud.

It was my acute chagrin that kept me from noticing sooner that something was amiss. To be fair, the environs had a different texture to them than what we'd already passed through: the colors more vibrant, the light brighter. Flecks of illumination danced in corners, in the detailing of decoration or dress. When I pointed it out to Rush, he nodded.

"Your witchcraft," he said.

We passed through the public room of an abandoned tavern, fires burning in smudged lanterns and a wide hearth.

"But I used no witchcraft when I did any of this," I said. "Wouldn't it be limited to the magic I'd performed?"

"Not necessarily. I suspect your witchcraft had long imbued your magic. Imbues it even now. It's at the core of your abilities."

We pushed through a snarl of narrow, winding alleyways under a low sky. We caught glimpses of sea-stained pilings just past them, looking over an expanse of black water that tugged at the piers.

"Wait," I said, coming to a stop. "Do you feel that?"

"What?"

"The ground. It shifted."

Rush paused. I ran to the side of the alleyway and lifted myself up to peer over the top of a wooden wall. Water danced up into the sky, above which turned a massive thunderhead, the largest I'd ever seen. In the depths of the mountainous crests and whorls, strange light seeped out, flashing here and there like a fierce storm. The air blurred and shook. As I looked, other structures nearer the water's edge appeared to snap in and out of existence, flickering. In their place, I saw strange distortions—dark hallways, halves of chambers, vertical stairways. A current of energy passed over me and set my skin to prickling, my hair to standing on end.

"Doctor, come see."

I assisted Rush in getting a view. He grunted as I held him steady. After a minute, he said, "Fine, fine. Let me down."

Back on steady ground, he shook his head. "This is what we've feared. The planes are breaching one another. Bleeding worlds together. And from the looks of it, warping even the demonmere itself—this may be the beginning of a massive collapse. We have to hurry."

The alleyway brought us to the entrance to a stonework tunnel. The opening was blocked with wagons, a dozen or more of them, some of them normal-sized, others half that. Of course I recognized the wagon, for it was Swaine's, the one I'd been driving when I'd been waylaid by Francis and the other Rattlesnakes, using my magic to fend them off. I searched for a way around or through them, but they formed a perfect barrier.

"Is there some other way we missed?" Rush said. The winds whipped his coat and hair.

"No—it's this way. It has to be." As I tried to squeeze my way past the wagons, the brick wall of the alleyway next to us disappeared, then reappeared. Again, it shifted, flickering, revealing a stone balcony with the low light of sunset painting everything the color of rust. "Doctor."

"I see."

Neither of us spoke, watching as we saw *ourselves* passing next to us. We'd been only four hours into our passage when we'd reached that balcony. Past the stone railing, a mountainside looked over a mist-shrouded vale, shadowed in eternal twilight. Strangely, both of us—looking bent beneath our packs, unease stamped on our faces—glanced into the wagon-strewn alleyway, and I had the unnerving experience of catching my own eye. A series of stained glass windows had caught the dying light, a tableau of executions: gallows, the axe, the fiery stake, pressing— I recalled staring at them with a strange fascination as we'd passed them. I didn't recall having seen any images of myself staring back from a stormy alleyway. Still, for a moment, I considered stepping forward, to better watch myself. Rush laid a hand on my upper arm. The brick wall snapped back into place. A moment of vertigo took me.

"We mustn't cross our path," he said.

"I—" I shook my head. "Sorry. Confusing."

"I quite agree," he said. "But if we get tangled up with our earlier timelines, we risk never getting out. We'll be stuck in a loop."

I nodded, and turned back to the wagons, ignoring the drift

and blink of the walls next to us. I crouched, resting a hand on the nearest wagon, trying to see if it were possible to crawl our way underneath them—knowing Rush would have difficulty with such a challenge, and I'd end up having to drag both packs, and likely him for part of the way. Unappealing as that might have been, it also looked impossible. The way through was blocked at every angle. Some of the wagons rested on their sides, others upside down.

I got up, shaking my head. "We need to use magic."

"I don't like it," Rush said.

"Neither do I—but this is the way forward, and we're fresh out of horses and strong men."

Rush sighed, then nodded. "Then you'd best cast it. Given we're in the thick of the effects of your own magic, introducing my own into the situation might well alter matters in unhelpful ways."

"Any suggestions?"

He pursed his lips. "Basic elemental energies and a touch of tranferrent adaptation ought to work."

Turning to the wagons, I readied a variation of Summerfield's *Trifling Flitch*, which would allow wood to assume the weight of feathers. Tired as I was, I had a difficult time reaching the proper level of concentration, and stood in silence as the winds and unseen energies from the planar breach whipped over me. When I at last recited the proper incantation, the words echoed. "*Brittun wood and downe bringe, wythoute any helpinge, hen till tomorne atte day, I cummaunde yo—*"

Flashes of energy grabbed at me from the tamped soil, straight from the bricks and stones. Everything tilted sideways, and the barriers between where we stood and where we'd been earlier rumbled, tearing apart. Rush ducked his head as jagged bursts of light filled the air. He lifted his hands.

"Stop, stop!" he cried.

I broke off the incantation mid-stream, always an unpleasant sensation, energies gathered and building up within me, half-realized. I shook out my hands and arms. Still, waves of force rolled across me. "What was that—what happened?" I said. My arms ran with the sensation of being a pincushion and the muscles in my neck and shoulders cramped.

"We're too near to the breach." Rush watched as the walls wavered, solid one moment, translucent the next, and open to an altogether different view. "It's interfering with the magic. Koeffler wrote of this. The proximity will continue to deflect the energies."

A streak of pale fire tore across the sky overhead and a rumble shook everything around us. "What about my witch-craft?" I said.

"Far too many demons have lurked behind us," Rush said. "And with the planes colliding so, there may well be worse, closer than we realize. No, that's far too dangerous."

"If I cloak us at the same time?"

"Can you?"

Another fireball ripped through the sky. More light poured from the thunderhead over the false harbor. I gathered my witch-craft, pushing aside the fear and pressure, the quaking that surrounded us. "Stand near me, Doctor—it shall make you less visible to any demons."

The ground rocked with tremors. I laid aside my pack and readied myself. My strength rose to the surface, heightened by so much planar energy, responding to the particular fingerprint of my magic. Rush stood next to me, keeping an eye out for encroaching demons. I cleared my thoughts and focused on the blockade of wagons before us. My plan wasn't to stretch and bend the wood to the breaking point. There was too much of it. Rather, I needed to be in touch with the wood, achieving a sympathetic concordance to allow me to replicate what I'd been attempting to do with the *Trifling Flitch*.

And keep myself and Doctor Rush cloaked, at the same time.

There's no secret, only practice. So Swaine had told me, month after month, until the truth of it became inarguable. Concentration in the face of fear, of danger, of peril: the heart of sorcery. With one last look at Rush, I closed my eye, and let my senses well up. Behind my forehead. At my sternum. An inch beneath my bellybutton. A well-spring of the currents that moved through me. When I registered the force of it, I extended them past the surface of my skin, down my limbs in rushing brooks and streams. Out and around. Out and forward. One circle turning one way, one turning the other. Both spinning, both even. I registered that Rush gasped, but kept my attention where it needed to be. Out and around, out and forward.

I raised my hands. As I allowed the energy to extend to the wagons, the current within me strengthened: no longer a meandering stream, but a roaring waterfall. The tumble of wagons shifted a yard, shuddering, scraping, banging into one another. *Not that way*, I directed. *Come.* With the unseen tendrils that gushed from my outstretched hands, I lured the wood in my direction, and it responded, the memories of life awakening within it, drawing it into harmony with my witchcraft. I wrapped Rush and myself in a powerful cloak.

The pile of wagons shifted forward. I pulled at it, straining. Concentrating more deeply, I reminded the wood that it had once been slender, light, buffeted by the lightest breeze. The lightest of saplings. The wagons slide forward much farther, shimmying, skidding, bumping. A few tipped. Some of the smaller ones fell, freed from where they'd been wedged. Closer and closer they came, until most were outside the entrance to the tunnel—at which point I whipped both hands sideways, and send them crashing and careening over and against the wall that fronted the angry waters beyond.

I relaxed my arms, my senses still roiling out, and shook my hands as though flinging off drops of water. "There," I said.

Rush nodded in admiration. I had little time to bask, however, for my display had caught the attention of the demons. Entities circled, scraps of shadow and flaws in glass. Worse, every time the planar breach next to us flickered, I saw more and more hideous forms, swarming. I worried that they might begin to frenzy—a rare occurrence recorded but a handful of times in the history of sorcery.

"Let's hurry," I said. I grabbed up my pack and the iron pole, redirecting my entire focus on keeping my cloak as potent as possible. The ground rumbled, and lengths of the brick wall collapsed. Cracks appeared in the others, and in the earth beneath us. Winds howled off the water and in from the breach. Amongst it all, demons. Rush stared at the planar breach. I grabbed up his pack and thrust it into his arms. "Doctor." Still, he stared into the breach.

Following his gaze, I saw the pair of us, standing in the other plane, me pressing his pack against him, him staring back at us. Beyond that, I saw us yet again, this time shifting and semi-transparent. A planar eddy had us in its current.

"Doctor!" I didn't wait, just grabbed him by the arm and pulled. Blinding streams of light flared out over the harbor. "Run!"

Rush blinked and looked away. Without another word, we sprinted into the tunnel opening, skirting the few wagons that remained near the entrance. As we ran, our doppelgängers paced us on the other side of the breach. The sensation was terrible—for as we ran, I also saw us running into the tunnel, as though some part of my consciousness had slipped across the breach itself, and was in the other plane.

I pulled Rush along with me, ignoring the dual—triple—awareness that threatened to swamp my attention. *The sorcerous mind has but one point of focus.* The tunnel shrank and ended at the closed door of my bedchamber in the Salem manse. I lifted the latch, and burst through. Rush staggered in behind me. I slammed the door shut behind us.

We stood in a replica of my bedroom. Books stacked high. Ingredients stashed into every available nook, on every surface. Candles burning, reflecting on the windowpanes where night pressed in. Clothing scattered here and there, some fit for a child, others for a grown woman. Strange as I found it, it brought me a sense of comfort I hadn't known since we'd set foot in the demonmere, nearly a full day before. Everything rumbled, shaking.

"The instability is growing," Rush said.

"We're almost there," I said. I opened the door to the hallway —and was confronted with another version of my room. The candles weren't lit, and pale dawn seeped in through the curtains. Different books sat open upon the writing desk. Two doors opened from there, one where it should have been, and a second on the wall opposite my closet. I slowed, looking back and forth between them. The terrible thought came that every instance of magic I'd done in my room had created a separate version of it in the demonmere. Hundreds of them.

Behind us, the walls shook.

"Which way?" Rush asked.

I hurried to the proper door out and pulled it open. Another version of my room. I leapt over to the second door and opened that one. A pair of steps led up—into yet another version of my bedroom, this one somewhat smaller, everything in it scaled to seventy percent of its normal size. More candles burned away. "This one," I said, not sure why I'd said it. Something drew me.

Rush made no argument, and we ran up the steps and into the smaller room. Another room greeted us, this time the floor about halfway up the doorway, while the underside opened into a treacherous fall into darkness. The bang of doors slamming followed us. I helped Rush to belly his way onto the floor, and then followed him. A tearing sound came from the way we'd come—and I didn't want to find out what was causing it. Up in the new room, we were confronted not by two but three doors. I flung them each open, and opted for the one in the middle, which led into a normal-sized instance of my bedroom, this time hung with the stink of burned wolf's bane.

And so we sped, doorway after doorway, guess after guess, hurrying through my room, again, and again, and again. The tremors grew as the planes resounded with their massive collision. Some rooms were larger than normal, more than a few smaller, and one was normal-sized, but with the ceiling only three feet off the floor, which forced us to crawl. One was full of rings—silver, brass, steel—that vibrated and danced, making me think of Inverressayte.

Even as we hurried, sections of the walls blinked in and out, items vanishing, the structural integrity of the rooms groaning against the lashings of planar disruption. One door, another, another, all of it shaking apart.

We pushed into my room yet again. Confronted again with the sight of my studies, of the place where I'd passed from being a child to being a woman, a sadness came over me—it was the inevitable feeling of loss, I suppose; for everything, no matter how cherished or valued, eventually changes, and disappears. Moments, memories, all of it. The time I'd spent in my room had been more precious than I'd realized, and it was only then, spurred on by fear and desperation, that it came home.

So much of Swaine's hand was behind it. His encouragement, his sense of purpose, his drive—I saw that in the heaps of books, pages and pages of notes I'd made, the residue of spells both successful and spectacularly not. The care he'd extended toward me. I'd appeared in the dark of night, unasked for, unexpected, and altogether rather hopeless, yet he'd taken me in. Perhaps it had been the lack of a convenient way to get rid of me, at first—but he'd seen something in me, and given me a chance to be more than I'd ever imagined, in a role he'd never considered himself as having needed. That was kindness, even if Swaine himself mightn't have put it so. And while he wasn't the man to voice the trite clichés of affection, the heart had other languages that spoke of love—the sharing of enthusiasm, the challenge to excel, gestures of honesty and trust, respect earned. And the greatest love of all: he let me become my own person. Given everything that had befallen me prior to my appearance beneath a stack of corpses, I could neither describe nor even imagine an alternate set of circumstances that would have been such a gift. So if you must know what drove me onward, past any consideration of exhaustion, doubt, or terror, there you have it. I owed all I had to August Swaine, and if it took my last breath to save him from the abyss of possession, I would gladly give it.

My last breath appeared imminent, unfortunately.

A violent tremor yanked me back from my thoughts. As I turned to hurry through yet another of my doors, my gaze flicked to the corner of the room, down to the floor. A hint of light seeped through the boards. I'd noticed an oddness to that corner throughout the last several versions of my room, though in our desperation, I'd paid it little heed. I stared at it.

"Miss Finch," Rush implored.

"A moment," I said. The air around the section of board I'd cut and then disguised shimmied, pulsing with energy, out of focus and warping. I sped to the corner and knelt. A peculiar force washed against my skin.

"We don't have time," Rush said.

"It's the burial silver, sir. This is where I hid it. I mean—not in this version of my room. But in my real room." I held my palms to the queer light. "Can it be?"

"Argentum inferi maintains a transplanar presence—one reason for its potency. Given the method behind its creation, we shouldn't—"

I didn't give him time to finish, instead holding my hands above the floorboard and whispering the phrases releasing the glamours I'd put in place. As they sundered, the wood crumbled away, turned to fragile cinder. I swept aside the remaining edges and reached inside, grabbing the box of burial silver. It thrummed in my hands, still bound by the containment spells I'd woven around it. Solid. Real. Beneath it, an endless line of wooden openings, a hall of mirrors extending throughout the demonmere—one of which must have been my actual room in the manse.

I leapt to my feet. "It means we must be close. And we have it. Turn around, sir." As he did, I slid the box into the Doctor's pack, my fingers trembling as I worked the buckles. "I don't know how we'd have made it into the manse, to tell you the truth."

"A boon of the demonmere, Miss Finch," he said. "Though I daresay quite outweighed by its less attractive traits."

"Amen. Let's hurry, sir."

Rush and I barely made it through the last room, the walls disintegrating behind us even as we raced ahead. Crashing through the next door, I stopped in my tracks, for the room beyond no longer held the familiar trappings we'd passed through. Instead, the walls were plain, and the ceiling slanted. A small bed stood beneath the eave, a narrow window next to it. Three books stood spine out on the floor. Doctor Rush stumbled into me.

A small door stood across from me, but my eye was drawn to the little bed. "It's my room from childhood. In Mayfair. I never used witchcraft there."

As I spoke the words, flecks of light danced over the ceiling and window. Gold, ruby red, violet. I put a hand to my mouth as the memory came back, both as familiar and strange as though someone had thrust a toy I'd had as a babe into my face. I recalled, like a dream, lying on my bed, happy to watch the pretty lights chasing each other around the room, out the window, laughing and pleased. And I remembered my mother scolding me, as though I'd done a terrible thing. How had I forgotten that?

"It would appear that you did," Rush said. "But we have no time to wonder."

"Yes—yes, of course." Could I have done such a thing? And what had that meant to my mother? What had she known? I followed Rush to the other door, my head ringing with thoughts, the floor heaving beneath my feet. Had she known more than I'd imagined? Had she perhaps related it to something she herself had done as a young child, left abandoned and raised in an orphanage? What had she thought when she realized the strange gift—or curse—we shared? Her last child, her only daughter. More than once, I glanced back, catching just a glimpse of the lonely, forgotten bed.

"Here!" Rush said. He pulled open a short door. I recognized the corridor on the other side. Cracked marble tiles on the floor, an off-yellow plaster on the walls, unusual columns every thirteen feet. A chamber on either side.

"I know where we are," I said, flicking away the last of the tears with my thumb. "We're almost there. Come."

"You've been here?"

"Yes, with Swaine. This is the furthest we got." We stepped into the corridor, and I turned to examine the doorway we'd just come through. "There'd been no sign of a door, though." The back of the doors looked to be of the same plaster as the other walls, explaining why we'd not seen it upon first discovering it.

Behind us, the walls fell away into emptiness. I led the way, dragging Rush by his sleeve. We sprinted through a large room of rounded stone walls, past the room with miniature chairs and tables set with tiny forks and knives, now bouncing wildly about. A corridor of wooden walls and stone floor that ran for twenty-six feet with a metal wall that opened into a larger space. The wall flickered, there one instant, a fiery light filling the spot the next. We raced through a pair of stone doors and up an inclining corridor that ran for over three hundred feet. All around us, the demonmere distorted, massive energies buffeting us. We reached the bottom of a set of stairs, the first of two flights.

I went first, pounding two steps at a time, hurrying the Doctor along. At the top, I slammed my hands against the wooden doors Mr. Twelves had installed over the opening in the floor of the Rivers house. They flew open with loud bangs, and I turned and pulled Rush out.

We'd made it into Salem.

21

HELL UNBOUND

S tanding in the canted doorway of the Rivers house, battered, aching, and exhausted, I looked out at the nightmare of Salem spreading out before us. Eldritch light poured from the breach in the sky in great falls, crashing upon roof, lane, and field. Trees swayed from the howling winds. Ice hung sideways from the edges of roofs, stretched out like fangs from the corners of abandoned houses. A low rumble shook everything, rattling the remaining glass panes, the shutters, the loose hinges.

I stepped outside, steadying myself against the bracing wind, and looked towards the manse. No lights shone. So far, I couldn't see signs of any revenants or demons, nor did I sense their attention in any fashion. In the other direction, I saw the sorcerium, alight from within. The roof had collapsed. Over it spun a planar disruption that extended up hundreds of feet, narrow and bright, twisted like a length of molten glass. From that glaring point stretched tendrils of light that filled the sky. Off to the north and east, massive glares flickered, great streams of energy connecting down to the location of multiple shattered seals. The worst had happened—the seals and bindings and glamours throughout the town had been breached.

What had the demon who possessed Swaine done?

Rush looked this way and that. He hesitated, staring out at the depths of Salem, the place he'd wrestled with for so long, a place that held a special terror in his heart. His voice didn't quaver, but his cheeks hung and his skin grew ashen. "We have to find a place to set up the Koeffler Tap, somewhere near the primary breach."

"Do we still have a chance?" I yelled over the wind.

"I don't know," he said, seeming to snap out of his thoughts. "But I for one am not willing to concede anything until we're certain. Not a moment to spare, however. Come."

We raced through the overgrown fields around the Rivers house. Swells of wild magic rose around us, grabbing at the gear we carried, snapping and stinging exposed skin. I caught sight of demons flying about in the maelstrom. Rush consulted his planar compass as we ran, identifying a nearby rise as a potential site from which to activate the Koeffler Tap. Cutting across one of the deserted lanes, now flashing with pale green and white planar energy erupted from the torn sky above, we headed for the rise.

A shadow swept from the sky, nearly taking off Rush's head. With a massive expulsion of witchcraft, I sent the demon careening off into the trees. Another demon whirled up from the earth in front of me. I shouted a ward and watched it coil into a knot of shadows, vanishing. In the commotion, I grabbed Rush by the arm and together we spun, ducked, and dodged our way through the swarm of infernal entities. Shoving him over the remains of a split-rail fence, I helped him up the hill, steadying him until I was sure we weren't going to be mauled or flayed. At the top, I continued the fierce brawl, hurling witchcraft out along the hillside, sending more demons flying.

"This way," Rush said. He'd found a level spot on the open ground suitable for the Koeffler Tap. A frigid wind swept through

the trees next to us. We slipped off our packs, and Rush instructed
me to enchant a glamoured circle and ready the materials. As soon
as the glamour activated, the demons swarmed, but could get no
closer. I gasped for breath, my hands on my knees. In the light of the
planar breach overhead, Rush consulted several diagrams he'd kept
folded inside his coat. I could make out sinuous lines that traced
strange curves, one atop the next, with dozens of small numbers
next to them, a planar chart in the classical form. Rush adjusted his
spectacles and motioned for me to remove the chains from my pack
and set them out. We'd rehearsed the assembly only once.

"Activate the chains," he said. "I'll do the same with the center
pole."

Hurrying, I dumped out the pile of chains, separating them
into their pairings: two full sets of copper, brass, steel, iron, gold,
pewter, and silver chains in lengths of eight feet. Once they were
laid out, I stood before them and raised my hands, speaking in a
firm voice: "*Fæge gefealleð; fehð oþer to, se þe unmurnlice madmas
dæleþ, eorles ærgestreon, egesan ne gymeð.*"

The chains vibrated in unison. Behind me, Rush spoke the
words to bring to life the glamours we'd imbued into the pole. As
he did, the frequency of the vibration of the chains increased.
The air around us crackled with untamed magic. Whorls of
bright color leapt from the sky to the ground.

"We must make sure the pole is planted firmly!" he shouted.
"One set of chains will attach to the ring on the top, the others
attach at the bottom. They must be as evenly spaced as we can get
them. Both sets of chains will then entrain and locate the most
concentrated breach of planar energies that's crossing over. By
disturbing the fields of energy in the pertinent planes and redirecting them into a parallel set of planes, we can draw the energies involved, defecting the most dangerous currents back into
the breach."

I saw the tension on his face. He returned to his diagrams and
traced his finger along notes he'd made. He straightened up,

pursing his mouth, seeming to review a mental checklist. I took the pole to a level spot.

"Not there," Rush said, motioning with his hand. "No. Farther, farther. Yes, there. Now get the chains and the pieces of the pole —and don't let the two sets of chains come into contact with each other!" Under his guidance, I positioned the metal pole, and drove the spiked end into the soil, using all of my weight. Rush hurried over and attached a length of black rope to the upraised tip, through a loop at the end. The two of us then strung the chains between the eight spikes and the center pole. Rush concentrated on the order of them, checking and re-checking the chains.

I stared at the Koeffler Tap, dread in the pit of my stomach. While it didn't look like much, I appreciated how unstable planar manipulation at this scale was. The energies could be catastrophic, and the danger was that we were blind to what we were doing. There was a reason it was one of the most dangerous techniques in magic.

Rush started a series of incantations by each radial chain, his rich voice rolling out the lengthy German words. He gestured with his free hand, holding the diagrams with the other. After the last recitation, the wind carried his final words away. He looked at the construction of spike and chains, folding the paper and pulling a quill and ink from his pocket. Just as I thought nothing had changed, I saw a slight quiver—links of iron and steel, gold and bronze oscillating at the frequency of an unseen force. Soon, all of the chains moved, some fast, some slow, as though riding on waves of warm molasses. Rush walked along the perimeter, noting the movement of the chains with quick scratches of a quill onto a paper.

"Now for the burial silver," he said.

I grabbed the glamoured box from his pack, breaking the seals on the containment magic. Sparks danced around the hinges and opening, gossamer lines of energy pulled out of the air from all around me. When I opened the box, slender lengths of lightning snapped along the length of the *argentum inferni*. I carried it to the Tap and placed it carefully around the base of the pole, seven polished discs of silver. Light ran up along the length of the pole, glowing spider silk.

"The spikes, sir," I said.

Rush turned. Small sparks of icy blue ran along the spikes that bound the chains to the ground, which now shuddered. Rush's unruly hair stood up in a corona around his head. I felt a powerful charge wash over me, crackling in my hair, setting my dress and cloak to grab at my legs. Bright lines of light darted along our equipment, and the lantern. The magic spread to the edge of the trees, a darkness that wavered, pooling, running like spilled ink. Unseen rolls of force pushed me away from the center as though I were a magnet and the Tap, a larger magnet, the similar poles repelling each other. My ears popped with a rapid shift in air pressure. The rattling of the chains against the spike grew louder.

"First Calibration!" Rush shouted. He handed me the paper to record the readings and fetched the clock-like device of brass and glass from his pack. He also pulled out his pocket watch. "Every fifteen seconds, it's vital."

He consulted one last diagram, then approached the spikes, beginning with the one that anchored the iron chain. He stepped forward and called out an incantation, lifting the device in front of him. Flashes of white light shot around the length of the chain, link to link, from the middle, in opposite directions. Where the ends linked to spike and to pole, the light met and burst into a strange floral shape that hung in the air for a moment before fading.

"Two hundred and eleven," Rush said. I wrote the figure down.

Chain by chain, we repeated the procedure, making a full circuit, each chain receiving a variant of the same spell. With the final word of the last chain, the air froze, whirling and eddying with a force strong enough to lift the bottoms of my skirts, to snatch me off my feet. Blue light broke out and crawled over every surface of the ground, our equipment, and the trees. It danced across our shoes and up into our clothing. We watched the light grow, concentrating into a complex pattern that moved and shifted, an elaborate compass rose that rotated around the center spike which lit up with a blinding glare. Overhead, the deformation in the air filled the sky with light, tracing sinuous curves—flaws within a gem—high into the sky.

"It's connecting with the breach!" Rush yelled.

I watched as a pulse of blinding blue light climbed the spike that held the first set of chains.

"The Tap is working," Rush said.

"But should it be this—"

A deafening boom erupted from the Tap, knocking both of us off our feet, resounding across the countryside, echoing out among the distant buildings and the harbor. Rush scrambled along the ground, struggling to gather his papers. I got my hands under Rush's arms and lifted him to his feet.

"I'm fine, I'm fine. Incredible," Rush said.

"Doctor," I said. I pointed at the Tap. The chains strained upward. Bright sparks flew from the center spike, racing along the links in streaks. A strange twilight rose from the center, into the sky.

"My God," Rush said. "The energies are immense—much more powerful than I'd feared."

As he stared up at the Tap, his expression turn from awe to fear. The chains grew bright with sparks and the spike flung a bolt of lightning straight up into the sky where it stretched out to the main breach. Shadows streamed from the spike, rising and gyring, lit by the glare that ran along the chains.

Rush turned. "Too much energy is coming through."

One chain snapped, and it whipped through the air with a

deep thrumming. The fear of being sliced apart drove Rush and me back. Soon, other chains snapped, two of them pulling out their spikes, until the air screamed with whirling chains. Bursts of light leapt to the sky from the spike in the center while the ground ran with shadows. The earth shook.

That's when I sensed the demon. The temperature plummeted around us. Out of the corner of my eye, I saw frost spreading on the grass, rising on the thorny stems of the rosebushes that lined the property. I had to blink away the ice crystals that sprouted on my eyelashes.

"Demon!" I called out. I wasn't sure that Rush heard me. He stood facing the Tap, hands extended, speaking the words to contain the massive energies. I turned to face the demon.

Nowhere to run now, Mistress—is there?

The consciousness of Inverressayte touched my own again. In the flashes of light and scraps of planar shadow, I saw his features revealed: round eyes ringed in pale gold; long jaws filled with fine rows of teeth; dangling lobes; claws that hooked like Barbary daggers. He rose before me.

"Get back!" I shouted. A moment later, I whispered the words to Hume's Seventh Ward. The air crackled between the demon and me.

Four revenants appeared from the trees, sprinting toward us.

Behind me, Rush—ignoring all else—attempted to complete his spell. The freed chains of the Tap had become deadly, swinging in unpredictable directions, with loud whipping sounds. More demons closed in around us. I circled behind the Doctor, keeping Inverressayte at bay, hurling wards as needed, shoving out my cloak.

I told you I wouldn't ever forget you, Mistress. Inverressayte's thoughts crawled across my awareness.

Behind me, Rush whirled the fingers of his right hand and shouted *"Mit wie getanen eren man die geste enpfie!"*

Inverressayte leapt at me, and I shouted Hume's Twelfth

Ward. The demon slid past me, only to bear into Rush, causing him to flinch and stagger forward, where one chain caught him, opening his thigh, deep into the muscle, leaving him gasping and off balance while his blood spilled out from between his fingers. I reached to grab him by the arm, but he stumbled just out of my grasp, into the deadly revolutions of the chains as they whirled and tangled. They struck him once, twice, again—drawing him into the center pole as more chains snapped across him. Blood flew out in ghastly fans. Before I could do anything, Rush disappeared into the center, chains wrapping him head to toe, binding him to the stake. Two chains tightened across his forehead, blood running down his face.

As Inverressayte spun on me, I hurled witchcraft at him. The forces in the air over the Koeffler Tap magnified my efforts, filling the air between the demon and me with colors and light. Inverressayte, unprepared for such force, spun out into the night sky, dragged into the churning breach. I didn't waste a second celebrating his demise, but staggered to Rush. He'd somehow kept one hand free, and this he lifted, then gasped, the concentration and strain apparent on his face. "*Weiter sollen sie nicht fahren.*"

The chains tightened for a moment, clumping and shifting, then falling still. My heart slammed in my chest. No more lightning exploded, no more scraps of demonic shadow floated gathered. "Doctor!" I screamed. Forgetting even the demons who gathered in around me, I ran to the pole, prying at the chains, trying to tear the old gentleman free. *No, no, no.* Sprays of blood dotted my clothes as I pried at the chains.

"Leave me—seal it." His voice was only a papery whisper. My gaze flicked to his face, grown pale.

"I won't," I said. Hard as I tried, it was little good—the chains had knotted and twisted. Three-quarters of them wouldn't even budge. "I'm getting you out. We have to heal you. Stop the bleeding."

The chains tightened as the life left him, the weight of his body dragging them downward. I smashed my palm against the chains, over, and over, and over. His eyes were still open, the strange light in the sky shining on the pale blue irises—but he was dead. A wordless cry of pain and grief built in my chest and spilled out of my mouth. I tugged the chains, rocking the pole, but even then knew he'd stepped across that threshold from which there was no returning. One step. One small step.

Leave me—seal it.

Through my tears, I heard again his final words.

A presence behind me registered in my awareness. I turned around. A line of revenants faced me, and in the center stood my master, August Swaine. His eyes glimmered.

"The betrayal never ends, it would seem."

"Let him go, demon," I spat.

"Is that what you're telling yourself, witch? That a demon has me? You're not looking with clear eyes—that's been your problem from the start."

"I know you're in there somewhere."

"I'm as fully in command of my fate as I've ever been—and you might have shared in this unfolding glory if you hadn't been such a liar. And a thief."

"It's the book, isn't it?"

"That's the wrong thing to bring up, witch."

His demons prowled the darkness behind the revenants. Swaine took a step toward me. I looked from him to the towering light that rose from the sorcerium, and over to the spot where the planar breach roared with magic. Down the hill, dark shapes—revenants—filled the lane, rushing toward the hillside. As I opened my mouth to shout a ward at the demon who possessed my master, he coiled his hand ever so slightly, and I swooned, unaware of the earth rising to smash me in the face.

22

CENTER OF THE MAELSTROM

I opened my eye with no sense of time or place. For a confused moment, I thought I was still in the demonmere, perhaps having fallen prey to exhaustion, collapsed onto a replica of my bed. I half-expected to find Doctor Rush standing nearby, hands on his cane, weighed down by the pack he bore—until I remembered the terrible chains strangling the life from him. My face swelled on one side. My limbs ached deep into the bones. From shoulders to ankle, every muscle protested, crying out as I tried to sit up.

Chains held me down, wrapped across my chest, my stomach, my ankles.

Swaine sat in a rocking chair by the cold fireplace. He stared at me unmoving, his very stillness reminding me of a serpent ready to strike. Seeing him filled me with sadness, knowing what he'd been through. He was my master, and all we shared had always been genuine—respect, affection, and, yes, love, after our own peculiar fashion.

He frowned. "You thought you might waltz in here and ruin all our fun, have you? I always knew you'd fail as my apprentice. Weak. Undisciplined. Not good enough."

"Let him go, Svaradallanave," I said calmly.

Swaine flinched, the demon reacting to his name—for that's who it was, without question. The shattering of glass that had begun when the book had appeared. Broken windows, broken glasses. The talk of songs, of lullabies, from a demon once bound within a glass music box. It all fit what I'd read of Heggen. After a moment, Swaine thrust his head forward and bared his teeth, then regained his composure and straightened, his fingers fixing the buttons on his waistcoat that had come undone. "I'd think twice about fouling my name with your mouth again, witch."

"Svaradallanave."

He roared at me and stepped over to the bed. "I'd entertained the thought of showing you mercy, witch. You just bought yourself my bad side."

"You may have caught my master unawares—but that was just luck," I said. "He bound better demons than you when he was just an apprentice, Svaradallanave. You're not worthy of a sorcerer like him. Or me, you whining *ghost*."

Oh, how demons hated to be called ghosts. There was no good explanation for it, other than poisonous pride. The demon cried out and jammed Swaine's hand onto my chin, tilting my head back as if to tear out my throat with his teeth.

"And I'm just a humble witch," I whispered, straining to croak my words out. "A delicious witch you will never, ever taste, you pathetic troll."

If I could rile the demon enough for him to forget his grip on Swaine, even for a moment, my master might have a chance. Or the demon would kill me, then and there.

I was out of options.

"You're a stubborn one," Swaine said. "Resentful."

"As a mule, sir."

He wrenched his hand from my chin and stared at me.

"But you're probably too late to save your sorcerium," I continued. "We deflected the breach. It's over. Your plans failed."

"You're lying, witch."

"See for yourself. You can't feel it? I can—but I'm no simpering ghost."

Swaine turned to the window, slouching, staring out at the washes of light that filled the sky. "Easy enough to undo your pathetic work," he muttered. "And then we'll have time to play properly, witch."

"You're too late. I told you."

"It's never too late—not with the energies of the summoning chamber. Don't you see?"

I swallowed, my throat strained. "I doubt it."

"There's no 'I' left for you, Finch. Not for much longer."

"Let's see what happens with the breach doesn't open again, Svaradallanave."

Swaine hissed and tossed his hand, sending everything across my room flying through the air, crashing to the floor. Books, papers, instruments, clothing, eye patches, shelves, candles. "When I get back, I'm going to devour you one bite at a time, witch. You'll know the meaning of suffering like few others."

I shut my eye, unsure of my next move in that most dangerous game of cat and mouse. The heart of sorcery is the domination of the will of the sorcerer over the will of the demon. A fraught endeavor under the best of circumstance. Yet the tools of sorcery —the game of names, the summonings, the glamours, wards, and bindings—rely on the irreducible nature of the demon. That was the true master, for a demon was nothing if not a slave to his own nature: strike when shown the opportunity, taunt when given the chance, hunt when given the prey. From the most inconsequential nuisance of a shadow, to an arch-fiend capable of tearing the boundaries of the planes, demons, in the end, cannot help themselves.

Had I said too much? Too little? The world spun around me, unmoored.

I opened my eye. "You talk a good game—but you've already lost," I said.

Swaine glared at me, then sprang for the door, hurrying down the hallway, down the stairs, and out the door of the manse. As soon as he was gone, I strained against the chains, trying to slide out from them. Too tight. I whispered the incantation to an old spell I'd learned as *Fey Lighte of Dawning*, which should have ignited a steady illumination across the metal, looking for the weakest point to sunder. Instead, strange little sparks flew off the links, biting miniatures of lightning that snapped and stung, only to crawl across the underside of the chains and down the sides. A deep wave of nausea rose in my throat as though the room spun sideways.

The chains were glamoured.

I'd lied to the demon, of course. The Koeffler Tap hadn't stopped the breach from widening. Deadly planar energy filled the night—I could feel it even within the manse, protected as it was by glamour after glamour.

Concentrate. Calm yourself.

I focused on my breathing. That alone. Even then, the images filled my mind of Rush, ice, narrow stairs, crashing iron, coffins, colors springing from my hands. Minutes ticked by. I stared up at the cracks in the ceiling. I'd traced them from my bed more times than I could count. Crack after crack, line after line, time itself scrawled in the plaster. The current of time carrying it—along with everything else in this world—farther from the fragile condition of order and back into its natural state of entropy.

Entropy.

I rocked side to side, as much as the chains allowed. A dull squeak sounded. It was the bedpost at the foot of the bedframe, the warped one I'd tried to fix earlier in the year. When I shifted or turned in my sleep, it always squeaked.

Entropy.

Focusing on the bedpost, I thought of the wood. I extended

my witchcraft. Around me, the wood of the frame lit up with the fine stitching of witchcraft—golden lines twined around the natural grain in the wood. Each length of wood shimmered with delicate outlines, of grain, of knots, of pitch-pockets, of joints— all of which, in time, would fall prey to entropy. Fall apart. Surrender. Witchcraft welled up inside me and flowed down my arm. The delicate lines glared as my energy flooded the heart of the wood. With a sharp crack, the warped bedpost bid farewell to the cross-pieces, falling away. The bed keeled to one side. I turned my attention to the other bedposts, letting my witchcraft spill out from my hands. The lengths of wood twisted and cracked. A cry tore from my throat. The entire bed shattered, collapsing down in a heap around me. I withdrew my senses, and the wood stilled. I untangled myself from long shards of broken board, blanket, and the chains. Once free of the chains, I gathered my energy about me.

I ignored the door—Swaine, under the thrall of the demon, had certainly set it to alert him if I passed through it, if it would even open at all—and went to the window. With a burst of witch-craft, I shattered the panes and the frame that held it. Sweeping away the clinging bits of frame and glass, I swung myself over the sill, balancing my weight at my waist. My feet hung a few yards above the ground, but I released a wave of witchcraft to the earth beneath, and when I fell, the energy grabbed at my legs and steadied me, touching me down at the moment of contact.

Strands of vile light stretched off tree, boulder, building. Worse, my witchcraft had drawn a score of demons to where I stood—but I didn't cower or crouch. I hurled a blast of energy at them, sending them scattering into the fierce currents of planar force. From the shadows of the manse stepped a pair of revenants. I lifted my hands, slamming them back against the clapboards. The force that came through me exploded, strong and unstoppable. The encroachment of the planes heightened my witchcraft, the unseen energies grown potent.

As I neared the straining revenants—both of whom snarled at me, trying to wrest themselves free—I flicked my hands, sending them careening off into the darkness, tumbling into the nearby trees. I stood before the door of the manse. The peaks of the gables glowed with fluttering swirls of greenish light, shutters banging, stretches of the roof stripped by the blast of planar winds. Creaks and groans sounded from the shaking timbers. Down the hillside, the sorcerium flared with massive columns of light extending overhead. The entire night sky shimmered with the planar breach.

Svaradallanave had Swaine, no doubt racing at that moment to check on the sorcerium—exactly where Swaine wanted him to go. Where he wanted—no, needed—*me* to go.

You're a stubborn one. Resentful.

As a mule, sir.

Swaine was in there still—and he'd let me know it, referencing the note he'd left me, the one marked with a drawing of a mule.

There's no 'I' left for you, Finch.

Again, a message to me, for the demon only ever called me *witch*, never *Finch*.

And in an instant, I knew what it meant: the levers in the sorcerium were lettered, *A* through *H*—save for the last one, which should have been *I*, but that Swaine had insisted remain unlettered. *No 'I' left for you, Finch.* That lever—what did it do? Swaine had never explained it, not plainly—though in that instant I realized he'd explained it secretly, beneath the awareness of Svallardanave, counting on me to gather the clues and make the connections. *Bending the arrow of time—to pry loose the demon. But how? By creating a Burnsian channel, one infused with such power as to magnify the power in Flüsse's phenomenon, the Spiegel Verstärkung?* That was it—it had to be. And it had to be done in the grand summoning chamber of the sorcerium: *one point of focus.*

Swaine had planned it all, keeping his work secret from Svaradallanave even as he'd felt the thorns of possession sink deeper into his will.

I needed Swaine and the demon intruder in his mind inside the sorcerium, where they were now headed.

But as the ground shook, Doctor Rush's final words came back to me: *Leave me—seal it.* The breach continued to widen, to tear apart the boundaries of the planes. Swaths of Salem flickered in and out, misshapen by the massive currents of light falling from the breach. I looked to the hillside where the Koeffler Tap still stood, the center of the maelstrom.

My gaze snapped from the hillside to the sorcerium. The sorcerium to the hillside. Doctor Rush's dying words to Swaine's desperate gambit. To do one meant to abandon the other.

All the sacrifices.

All the heroic efforts.

All hope.

I yelled in frustration, the wind shearing away my voice.

23

A CURSE OF DEMONS

I was, in the end, an apprentice.

And what was an apprentice to do but listen to her master's instruction? In this case, I summoned one of Swaine's key lessons: *Look dispassionately, see clearly.* Emotions clouded judgment. Poor judgment could mean disaster. So I tore my gaze away from the sorcerium. More than anything, I wanted to rescue Swaine—but knew that it might already be too late for him, his desperate plans notwithstanding. Rush had known, as had I, the likelihood that his condition was beyond hope. On the other hand, should the planar breach widen enough to engulf all of Salem, more lives than just my beloved master's would be at stake. Many more lives. So, heeding my master's lesson, I took off running for the hillside where the Koeffler Tap stood.

In the lane below, revenants prowled. I ignored them, keeping my gaze fixed on the Koeffler Tap. Demons swarmed me, but I held them off, hoarse from shouting wards, trembling from the massive bursts of witchcraft I launched from my hands. At the ridge leading to the Tap, a massive fiend crashed from the sky, a hulking beast of shadows eighteen feet high, riven with flashes of ill-colored light. I caught glimpses of barbed limbs, thrashing stingers. It lunged at me.

I wasn't powerful enough to face a fiend of his strength, so I turned to the contingency Rush and I had discussed of using the *occulta prolou*, the *planar eaves* he'd pioneered the study of: small overlaps in the planes to cloak and facilitate our movements. With such a massive collision of planes taking place, such eaves were legion. I slipped into the nearest planar eave, and disappeared, only to step out fifty yards up the hillside, near the Koeffler Tap. A single step carried me that far, and I stumbled, my head dizzy from the strange inversion of the planes that the eaves leveraged. I shook off the disorientation.

If I could spend over twenty hours in the demonmere, a few steps in the planar eaves was nothing.

At the top of the ridge, I leapt into the glamoured circle. As demons frenzied, I stood, wary. Turning to the Tap itself, I avoided looking at Doctor Rush's bloodless face and instead set to untangle the chains, bound and quivering as they were with the ferocious planar energy sweeping over them. Concentrating, I let my witchcraft enter the currents, suspecting I'd find a tangle of energies not dissimilar to what I'd repaired in the broken seals left by the witches. Within moments, I knew I was correct. Strand by strand, thread by thread, I unwound the massive energies coiled around the Koeffler Tap, wrenching them loose from the spike, from the chains, from the body of poor Doctor Rush. With each one I freed, the planar energy sweeping over me increased, but I blocked out all else as I worked—for the sorcerous mind has but one point of focus.

But even then, as more and more strands pulled free, I knew I wasn't doing it entirely on my own. No act is ever done on one's own, really. Swaine was there with me, in my focus. Rush, with his determination. My beloved father, with his intentions. And, more than anyone else, my mother. My memories of her were precious. Her kindness, her wit, her fragile joy always fighting with her worries. She'd never taught me a thing about witchcraft —but what I had, I'd gotten from her. My nature. That was her. I was her, still. As I bent my will into my witchcraft, I was communicating with her. Communing. As I went from one strand, to the next, to the next, pouring all that I had into freeing the Koeffler Tap, I felt her fingers within mine, her heart within my own. Perhaps also those witches who'd sacrificed all they had eighty years before, their memory stirred to life as the last witch in Salem worked to keep their promise.

When I wrenched the last strand free, the chains released. I caught the Doctor's body before he could topple to the ground. Gently as I could, I laid him out next to the Tap, pausing to straighten the spectacles on his nose before I turned back to finishing the job. The earth shook beneath me as I crouched, slamming the spikes back into their proper holes, lining the chains up in the correct arrangement. I straightened out the discs of burial silver at the base of the spike. The chains once again began their curious rippling.

From the haversack, I pulled out the remaining ingredients. A mirror, two inches by two inches. Ash from a burned coffin that twins had been buried in. A flask of magicked oil. I yanked the cork from the flask with my teeth and poured the oil over the mirror. Spitting out the cork, I said the proper incantation, a Germanic mouthful: "*Man sehe ich, spiegel oh dich, ein zwilling zu erhöhen, ein zwilling von mir, heben sie den doppel so alles sehen können, die doppelte erhöhen und ihr frei.*" I tossed the flask aside and slid open the small wooden box full of the ashes, which I sprinkled across the oily surface of the mirror. As the ashes fell, a reflection of the entire Tap including the chains rose from the tip of the original. I lowered the mirror, placing it at the base of the spike. One by one, I placed the discs of burial silver onto the oily surface of the mirror. When the last one touched the ashes and oil, a massive plume of magic erupted along the length of the center spike, blinding me. All around me, the chains strained, thrumming with the sudden winds, alive with molten light. I stumbled back to the edge of the glamour, shading my eye with my forearm. Enormous energies roared between the Koeffler Tap and the breach in the sky. I saw doubles, triples, quadruples of the chains as the Tap drew in more and more planes. From across the sky, long rivers of light bent inward, pulled into the channel of energy towering before me. Trees buckled along the hillside. Houses across Salem collapsed, shorn through with planar forces racing to the Tap. The light emanating from the top of the sorcerium flared and flickered, sending bolts into the sky.

Could I reach it in time to save my master?

Hundreds of demons rampaged between where I stood and the sorcerium. I had no time to fight them all.

But I was a witch. A witch in Salem, one versed in magic, sorcery—and demons.

And I knew the place better than anyone.

I stepped outside of the glamours. For half a moment, I let my cloak drop, drawing the attentions of a score of nearby demons, who flew at me. In a flash, I raised my cloak again, and stepped sideways, to where the next planar eave stood. Behind me, a plague of demons filled the air. I stepped into the *occulta*.

I vanished.

24

THE ART OF SORCERY

My ears filled with the roar of the planes, my progress unsteady. Everything shook around me, and instead of the graceful tunnel I should have found, I met flood and submersion, swift currents. I practically heard Doctor Rush warning me it was too unstable, that I shouldn't risk it—but I'd left safety miles behind, at that point, so I plunged ahead, straining to keep my bearings. The pressures stopped me, massive and unyielding. I cried out, shoving forward, releasing my witchcraft to find a weakness. For one grim minute, I thought I'd gotten myself stuck. The planes would devour each other, and all of my troubles would vanish along with whatever hopes still flickered in my mind. But I made it through, breathless and drained, stumbling out the other end, dragging with me a film of pale green light that clung to my limbs and clothing.

The chaos at least gave me cover. As I'd hoped, I stood not far from the sorcerium, where the worst of the disruption still raged. The observatory at the top had partially collapsed, and from within rose a massive spire of planar energy that spun, dizzying and miles high, a slender tornado of ultramarine light that crackled and hummed. Every surface of the building crawled with the spectral fire. Windows stretched, the entrance shimmered as though behind a smooth curtain of water. The ground rumbled, as did my core, to a low note of planar disturbance, a pedal that droned on beneath the unhallowed symphony that shook Salem. I shrugged my cloak up with as much strength as I could muster, and shoved my way into the energy, to the double doors of the entrance. Even with my cloak up, the planar forces battered me: my skin crawled, my muscles cramped, my face and eye twitched, my lungs struggled to bring in enough air.

Once inside, I straightened, for the wards and glamours we'd labored over had retained their integrity, keeping out the worst of the disturbance—at least on the ground floor. Others appeared neutralized. Fey light shone in through the doors and windows. Wreckage filled the sorcerium. Fury gripped me. All of the careful planning, the care that had gone into our work: defiled. Shelves smashed with an adze. Delicate rows of tincture and powder, glamoured inks and fragile springs, candles, boxes of bones and teeth, carefully copied maps—destroyed. Worse, piles of smashed planar clocks littered the floor, broken wood, sprung windings and mechanisms, shattered glass—that explained, in part, the profusion of demons. The image of Swaine himself swinging the adze, a demonic fury in his eyes, turned my stomach, knowing the wounds it caused to what remained of his awareness. Each blow might as well have struck his heart.

Worse still were the books—piles and heaps of them, opened and torn page by page apart. Paper covered everything, piled a foot high in spots. In one corner, heaps of ashes spoke to the burning. I covered my nose, for the pungent stink of feces filled the air.

Everything destroyed.

The longer I looked, the more livid I became. How long had Swaine struggled? How long had he gone before he realized that he'd lost the battle for his own volition? The beating? Earlier? And how long had he struggled with a growing doubt, questioning why his usual routines lacked focus, why his sleep vanished before burning thoughts? To then be marched up and down the hallways and rooms of his home, watching as his own hands ripped his life's work to scraps, ruining the precision and care he'd spent decades honing. Made to humiliate himself in the foulest manner. I stood at the bottom of the stairs, peering into the darkness. And what had Swaine endured—assuming he still had a level of awareness, locked deep within the coils of possession—as the fiend had begun the slow round of torture it had in mind for me? His trust and word used as malignant leverage, a prelude to whatever inhuman suffering was to be inflicted on me, the one person whom Swaine cared most about in the entire world?

Anger didn't do justice to what raged in my heart.

I ran through the darkness, up the iron stairs that curved along the right-hand walls. The railing shook, the stairs trembled. Demons lurked in the shadows, their malicious presence pressing in. At the top, I hurried to the grand summoning chamber, praying it hadn't been similarly defiled. Whereas the rest of the sorcerium was succumbing to the effects of the planar subduction, the power of the *Graves' Countervalence* still held. The glamouring and valence tuning I'd done remained in place, the strength of it clear even in the chaos. Swaine must have finished the last tunings, for I sensed the full symmetry.

But where was Swaine?

I slowed, staring at the arched ceiling. Bright lines traced the metal hexes we'd had Mr. Twelves set into the wood at the peak, molten red, yellow, and white. The towering disturbance must have been directly above that spot, turning, drilling its way through the sorcerium. Even within the protection of the *Countervalence*, the magic strained against the pressure. I cursed, reached for the nearest lantern, lighting it with a spell. Once the flame cut the darkness better, I turned to the center of the chamber, and stopped.

A thick coffin sat in the very middle of the chamber.

"August?"

I leapt, startled by the muffled voice that burst from the coffin. Rushing to it, I tried to yank the lid open, but a spell held it closed. I stood back and blasted it with witchcraft, breaking whatever magic held it closed. Pulling the lid apart, I found Mary Whitelocke inside, disheveled and terrified.

"Oh, God—Oh, God," she said in a hoarse voice. She heaved herself out of the padded interior, her eyes squinting, dress torn, hair loose, pale skin broken out into gooseflesh.

"What are you doing here?" I said.

"I couldn't just wait back there with your friend. Yes, I'm terrible. Can't keep my word. Too much faith in myself. Believe me, I've had more than enough time to realize it, trapped in this infernal coffin."

I helped steady her. "I still don't understand."

She pulled her hair back from her face. "I came to distract August. And I did—for a short while. His—those *things* of his— caught me. Dragged me to him. But I tried to charm him. Pleaded with him to calm down. Did everything I could think of to keep him from paying attention to whatever was happening anywhere else in this hellish town. So you could do what you needed."

"That was a terrible idea, Mary." I embraced her. "It may have worked, though. Just enough."

"Thank me later. Is it done? Where's the Doctor?"

"It's not done. Almost, but not. Doctor Rush—he—he didn't make it."

"Damn it all. Then it's just us, is it?" She pursed her lips. "We'll see what two determined women might do, shall we?"

"Where's my master?"

"I didn't see much, locked in that coffin—but I heard footsteps run by a short time ago."

"Where to?"

She pointed to the iron stairs leading to the observatory overhead.

"Did he say anything?" I said.

"Nothing. I, however, had plenty to say."

The floor shifted. Overhead, a large section of the ruined observatory must have broken free, crashing along the outside the chamber. I turned away from her, hurrying over to the dials. "Get the coffin off to the side."

She hauled it to the side with a grunt. "I'd like to bloody set fire to it."

I needed to tune the chamber to drive the demon from Swaine—the only place on earth where I might find such potent energy. As I ran across the chamber to the series of brass handles that controlled the flow of magic across the one hundred and eleven glamours—the grand loci, the stations, the crowns, the truss—I struggled to remember the proper combinations. There at the end was the unlettered lever. *There's no 'I' left for you, Finch.* I looked over the other dials and closed my eye, then spoke the words of activation and swung the various dials to the corresponding settings. As I did, the chamber shook and a vast magic activated across the floor. For a moment, I rested my head against the wall above the dials in thanks, then spun the dials back to their neutral settings.

Now for the next impossible step. The walls near the ceiling cracked, brick and wood pulled apart, letting in more of the fell light that engulfed the exterior. Mary hurried to the other stairs, looking down. "We're not alone—his servants are coming in," she said, her voice wavering.

I stepped to the center of the glamours within the *Counterva-lence*, the force of the glamours pressing through my cloak. I extended my senses into the roiling boundaries of the planes that battered the sorcerium. Massive. Complex. Interleaved. Folded in, over, and through each other. Yet I pried a way through their edges, the same regions as the *planar occulta*. I knew how to trace a line of force, how to sense my way forward, how to extend my magic into it. And in doing so, I created an anchor of sorts, bound to the glamoured station. Still concentrating, I stepped from the circle and ran halfway up the stairs. From there, I let my magic connect with the anchor I'd established, until it flowed back and forth. When it felt strong, I sensed the planar eave I'd just created. I stepped into it—and appeared within the glamoured station.

I had to get Swaine onto that step on the stairs, and it should send him to the station, putting him in the spot I'd need to drive Svaradallanave from his mind and body.

"They're coming!" Mary cried.

"Hold them back."

"Me? Have you lost your mind?"

"Yes, you. Anything. A fire spell. Your fists. Something. Buy me time!" I yelled.

"I'm not sure—" She got no further before a revenant crashed through the window behind her. Mary leapt out of the way, screaming. The revenant ignored her and charged toward me. I turned and let fly a massive wave of witchcraft, sending the revenant backward to the top of the stairs leading down. Mary wrenched it by the shoulder, shoved it tumbling down into the others as they tried to come up.

More windows shattered. My mind raced through the possibilities of creating more glamours to keep the revenants from overwhelming us. The doorway filled with revenants, with another half dozen already inside. I heard them smashing their way in from beneath the grand summoning chamber—tearing, clawing, wrenching at the boards. The revenants coming up the stairs staggered forward—and over the howling of the wind I heard a sudden clatter of gunshots. Moments later, a second fusillade exploded. The revenants fell. Grayson and Francis led a company of troops into the sorcerium. More troops outside fended off other revenants, firing one volley after another. Being

revenants, they would soon get up, for they couldn't be killed—
but it bought us time.

I shoved myself away from the wall and toward the stairs up
again. The floors bucked beneath me and the light outside flared.
The walls of the grand summoning chamber flickered, overlaid
with blinding curtains of golden light, glimpses of strange
spaces. As the planar breach deflected into itself, the planes
collided with a chaotic ferocity. Everything spun around me, the
air filled with detritus. Along the far wall, I saw stairs appear,
then disappear. Rooms, there and gone. The demonmere itself
smashed into the sorcerium as the planar boundaries disintegrated. The floor shifted beneath me, worse than any storm I'd
experienced on my crossing of the Atlantic. I stumbled up the
stairs, trying to reach the observatory, getting my head through
the opening into the floor above.

Swaine stood before me. "You're too late, witch."

And then he was gone. I turned. "Master?"

He stood on the other side of the chamber, smiling. "I can't
decide if I want to devour you myself, or give you to *my* master."

Hung throughout the remains of the observatory, great
sinewy tentacles, flexing and emitting a noxious corpse light.
Following them to their center, I gasped. There it stood. Open,
smug, foul, untouched: the *Occultatum Ostium*. Such trouble that
infernal volume had brought into our lives, the only book in
Salem that deserved the fate that had befallen the others. But
seeing it so, I realized how wrong we'd been. All along, it had
been an arch-fiend. Not a book. Not a relic. Not the work of some
mysterious sorcerer from the darks of history. A massively
powerful arch-fiend, bent on drawing in the darkest realms to
devour the world.

Across the chamber, glimpses of the demonmere flashed,
drawn in by this rarest of demons. Strands of energy pulled in
through the shattered roof, drawn to the open pages.

"The book. It did this," I said. "All of it."

Swaine tilted his head and gave a sinister smile. "My master draws in the darkness. That's all he's ever wanted, really. To breach the barriers in this pathetic world, to see it drown in the depths of his home. It's happening—can't you feel it?"

Other demons swarmed the edges of the chamber, nipping at me in spite of my cloak. With a yell, I threw deflection energy splashing out from my hands, sending the nearest fiends tumbling out into the encroaching planes.

Swaine disappeared again. I needed him on the stairs—there was no time to instantiate any further *planar occulta*.

"Are you going to play hide and seek with me, Svaradal-lanave?" I shouted, stepping into one of the protective glamours set into the floor of the chamber, struggling to steady myself against the tremors that shook the sorcerium. Dust and plaster fell from the ceiling, and the top of the chamber disappeared, a glaring planar incursion opening. "Are you afraid to face a true witch? Here I am."

I let my cloak fall for a heartbeat. More demons darkened the walls, but I shoved them away. Another plane crashed in from the side, and I saw myself mirrored in it, and behind me, Swaine. I spun around, raising my cloak again just as he leapt at me. With the turbid energy of the planes breaching, he hit me from multiple directions. I saw him at my back, upside down at my front. Ducking, I used my witchcraft to hurl him past me, so he crashed down the stairs. I jumped after him, hauling myself over the railing, wrapping my arm around his throat.

Swaine tried to toss me off. "You're going to suffer, witch."

"Not as much as you, Svaradallanave."

Our images flashed throughout the chamber, in different angles. One wall collapsed with shrieking timbers and nails. Swaine pulled free. Before he got up, I jumped sideways and hit him right in his left side, wrapping my arms around him and sending the two of us tumbling halfway down the stairs. We slid past ourselves, moving in the opposite direction. Swaine clawed at me in a frenzy, trying to gouge my eye, to rip at my throat, but I kept kicking, and didn't let go—even as we fell through the *occulta* I'd created, and into the glamoured circle. We crashed head-first into it. I tried to wrench myself free, but he held on with a terrible strength. I kicked him, but he didn't let go. He lifted me up, his hands around my throat, victory in his eyes—when his head snapped forward and he let go. Mary stood behind him, an iron rail from the mangled staircase in her hand. I staggered from the *Countervalence*, motioning for her to do the same. She let the iron rail fall from her hands to clang on the floor and jumped clear. Lunging for the levers on the wall, I grasped the unlettered lever and slammed it down, releasing the spells to create the Burnsian channel.

In an instant, the entirety of the *Countervalence* blazed to light. Swaine's whole body went into violent seizures and he bellowed. He shook and shook and shook, and still the demon wasn't cast out. The air rippled with potent sorcery, growing more caustic as the energies reflected back onto themselves, creating the *Spiegel Verstärkung*that Flüsse described. Mary cowered, hands over her head as the waves of energy battered the chamber. The walls screamed as peg and nail pulled free. Windows blew out. The stairs leading to the observatory shuddered, twisting.

I ran to Mary, getting her to her feet. "Run—get the others away!"

"I'm not leaving you."

"Mary—just go!"

Waves of planar force distorted the air. Hunks of the roof tore off and pale light flared bright. Mary pointed to the *Countervalence*. Swaine arched his back, rising into the air, his mouth wide in a scream. A shadow tore from him, vile and insidious, likewise arched and howling—Svaradallanave, the demon who'd once stalked me and killed my family. Svaradallanave, servant of the arch-fiend in the guise of a book. Svaradallanave, the fiend who'd possessed my beloved master. The demon lifted, turning to me. I didn't balk. I walked to the near edge of the countervalence, my feet on the inscriptions. From the corner of the chamber, the adze that had caused so much destruction screamed through the air, spinning end over cruel end toward my head. I held still. The handle of the adze thrummed as it came to a dead stop a foot from my face. I released the witchcraft, and as the tool fell to the floor, I stepped into the circle, right in front of Svaradallanave. He lunged. I didn't dive out of the way. Instead, I used all the force of my witchcraft to drive him upward, using his own strength against him, pivoting him into the peak of the *Spiegel Verstärkung*. As he fought me, I screamed and filled the chamber with every ounce of energy I had, hammering him upward—where he burst into inky shadow, foul filaments immediately sucked up into the raging tower of planar energy reaching into the breach.

Wind and heat wrapped me as the *Countervalence* and the grand summoning chamber crumbled under the immense energies. Mary rushed across the way to the wall and grabbed the unmarked lever. "This one?" she shouted.

"Yes!"

She heaved the lever upward and the Burnsian channel began to dissipate. I rushed to Swaine. His eyes were open, but I feared him dead, he lay so motionless. "Master!"

He rose to one elbow. "Up. The. Stairs," he gasped.

"It's really you?"

He nodded weakly. "Finch, it's me."

"How do I know?"

"Intention. The intention. Do you remember what you told me about a glamour? What your father said? The intention within the metal?"

His words struck at my memory of the first night I'd been in Salem, when he'd quizzed me about a glamour in the barn. Svaradallanave couldn't know it. I yanked Swaine by the arm, helping him free of the glamoured circle.

"The book, sir—it's the book."

"It's holding the breach from closing," he said, getting to his feet. "Struggling to drag its world into this one. We have to stop it."

"But I closed the breach—with a Koeffler Tap."

"The book won't let it shut all the way—a catastrophic planar collapse is imminent—come!" He turned and limped up the stairs, which even then were displaced and skewed as the walls came apart. I followed. At the top, I skidded to a halt.

Swaine waded through the tentacles and glaring light, his hair wild, his clothes fluttering. Tentacles whipped him. "Finch! Hold it back!"

I flooded the tentacles with witchcraft, putting all I had left into it. In the center, Swaine reached the book itself. He leapt on top of it. Tentacles whipped the air, infernal energy battering the collapsing observatory. In the mayhem, Swaine turned to me. "Run!"

"Not without you, sir!"

"Go!"

The remaining walls and roof gave way, sending everything upward into the roaring maw of the planar breach. Swaine lifted along with the wreckage, the book locked his arms. He rotated. I reached for him, but missed him by a yard as the floor let go, crumbling beneath the massive planar energy. The air ignited with colors and force. I fell to my backside and rode the floor into the gaping hole that opened underneath us. A massive whirlpool of energy roared into the sky, and Swaine spun as though caught in a tornado, crashing against the walls that still stood. I saw doubles of him, triples. Fractured reflections of myself, refracted in the planar collision. A massive burst of magic exploded, sending me reeling, my witch senses overwhelmed. Demons howled and shrieked. The floor burst into hundreds of jagged lengths of wood, splintering and flying off in every direction. A chunk of it scraped the side of my head.

"Finch!"

I looked behind me. Mary Whitelocke stood in the doorway, holding a hand up to shade her eyes from the blinding glare, her dress fluttering, sparks of magic dancing around her in silver embers. She ran over and pulled me back by the collar of my dress. I scrambled to my feet even as the wall next to us crumbled, sucked into the void, taking the iron stairway with it with a deafening ruckus. The entire sorcerium tore apart.

"Go!" I yelled. We ran down the stairs together, diving out through the collapsing doorway just in time. Looking up, I saw Swaine, tumbling through the air, higher, higher, a faint shape against the roiling magic. I cried out and reached my hands overhead—but Mary grabbed me by the arm and pulled me away from the disintegrating building. Pale light engulfed what remained of the foundation as the final wall collapsed. We both watched the towering rotation lift the timbers and stones up into the closing breach. The sky flared with unearthly light. From all across Salem, magic rose to the sky—and then with a massive boom, vanished.

In the sudden darkness, I could barely stand. Mary held me up. Scraps of paper fell from the sky, along with bits of leaf, of branch, of shingle. All around, soldiers gathered. Mist pooled in the low spots. Broken branches littered the ground as far as I could see, the path of a storm to remember. Trunks with white blazes. Fallen houses, reduced finally to rubble.

"By God, Finch," Grayson said, hurrying over to us. "Sackville and his men raced us here—and they nearly beat us to you—until demons got them. Took his head clean off. We only had to round up the few survivors before we saw what was happening here. We were rounding up the survivors when your clockmaker friend here found us and warned what was happening here. But look at you—you bloody did it."

Robert Twelves rested against a musket, winded. We shared a glance and he nodded. Francis handed me a water pouch, and I took a long, cool pull from it. As I looked around, soldiers doffed their hats in salute. Rattlesnakes, as well. They may not have known the full meaning of what they'd seen—but they knew enough.

"You helped," I said, giving Mary a squeeze. "All of you."

Grayson shrugged. "Notice you didn't even need to ask."

"I'm fairly certain I asked."

"No point rehashing the particulars," he said, waving my comment away. "Francis here—the man ought to be a general, by the way—he was the one who realized what Sackville was trying to do. As for me, it was about bloody time my family made up for certain failings. Let's leave it at that."

"Speak for yourself," Mary said. She tightened her arm around me, looking over the wreckage. "Is it safe?"

"It won't be safe for a long while. Maybe not ever." I scanned the darkened countryside. The sky, clear now of magic, glittered with stars. "But I think it will hold, for now."

My gaze searched the heavens for any sign of the breach. Tears rolled down my cheeks, fell from my chin.

Beyond all that I've described to you lies one thing, Finch, Swaine told me the first night I met him. *And that one thing is the art—and I mean* art *in the highest sense—of sorcery. That is my calling, and what I've pursued since I knew east from north. Do you understand?*

Even though all before me appeared to be in ruins, I believe in that moment I did.

I understood.

25

YOUR HUMBLE SERVANT

There are still demons. There will always be demons.

Many still prowl Salem. A few venture beyond, into the vales and forests that border that quiet and abandoned corner of this otherwise fair province.

Yet His Majesty no longer commissions the services of a Royal Doctor of Magickal Sciences here. After the chaotic events of the late spring in 1736, there were council hearings. Investigations. Politics. Accusations. Posturing. Still, the dead remained dead, and the living carried on without them. Doctor Ephraim Rush was buried in a small ceremony, his heroism largely untold. Governor Lionel Sackville—shadowed by various tales of scandalous debauchery and madness carefully spread through the circles of proper society—was given a larger funeral. A new governor, selected from yet another powerful Boston family, assumed office, his steady hand ready to guide the province past its recent troubles.

To most eyes, the colony gets along just fine. Any problems of an infernal nature are soon taken care of—as if on their own. No one questions a well-dressed young woman with an eye-patch in the company of this or that handsome man of influence. Boston is a vibrant city, after all. There is talk, to be sure—there will always be talk. Rumors make the rounds, passed around with a delicious thrill: tales of the well-dressed young woman with the eye-patch rooting out cruel voices heard from abandoned wells, unpleasant shadows beneath bridge or pier, silencing clanging grave bells in the midnight. I may not bear the title of Royal Doctor of Magickal Sciences—and an appointment such as *Royal Sorceress* or even *Royal Witch* would be absurd—but I'm afforded respect by those who understand.

As for myself, I make sure to have more than one thing in my life. Work, and pleasure. Duty, and laughter. I do all I can for my dear companions, every last one of them, which is all anyone could ever hope for in the end. They've become family to me— though I remain unmarried, much to the frustration of the many gossiping jays in the small town north of Boston where I reside, near the edges of the forest that borders Salem.

Swaine left me a small fortune, which I used to establish a bookshop. I often travel the colony buying various tomes and printings, repairing bindings of special collections. The owners of taverns and inns throughout the province always have a tale for me as I make my frequent rounds. Furthermore, I maintain a steady correspondence with a score of specialized book merchants throughout the Colonies, in England, and in Europe, always making known my interest in any volumes pertaining to the unseen arts, a battered and curious tome of changing weight and uneasy appearance in particular.

Demons of another sort haunt my sleep to this day. Regrets. Choices not made. Words not spoken. Friends lost. Not that I'm surprised, for we each bear our own share of such demons, do we not?

Several times each year, under the cover of night, I ride deep along the forest roads heading east, until I pass the new signs forbidding trespass past the borders of Salem. Soldiers stationed at small buildings half a mile beyond the signs know me and only need to see my cloak to wave me on. I ride until I can smell the Atlantic on the breeze. Salem reminds me, as ever, of its silence just beneath the curl of the waves of the harbor and the wind sighing amongst the ruined buildings. Sometimes I look up at the manse where I apprenticed. Sometimes I find it too painful.

I check the seals. Mending. Reinforcing. Crafting. Expanding them in the hopes that one day, even this haunted stretch of rocky coast might return to something closer to life.

Over the years, I've developed a habit of visiting the spot where the sorcerium once stood. Little in the way of grass or shrub grows there. The scorch marks and magic have faded with the seasons. There are several boulders I put in place to mark it, and to dissuade any future builders for seeing it as suitable for any new dwelling. Between the stones, a small door is set into the ground, one built by Robert Twelves to my peculiar specifications. It opens easily enough from the inside, but not at all from the outside, thanks to his design and my spells. Beneath the door is a curious set of stone stairs, leading down, and down, and down. I'd found them while investigating the ashes months after the catastrophe.

I haven't explored them. Not yet, and probably I never will. Still, I visit them, and sometimes release the magic to open the door so I might leave a folded letter on the top step. I've always found all my previous letters—until one day earlier this very autumn, when on an afternoon beneath a sharp blue sky broken up by orange and red leaves taking flight from the nearby maples, a cool breeze tugging at the hems of my dress, I'd discovered the entire collection missing.

Perhaps I'm just a romantic, letting my emotions obscure reason (I won't plead innocent to such a charge), but the sight of that empty step filled my heart with hope. For days afterwards, I found myself thinking back to when I'd first arrived in Salem. That perilous night, my first in the Colonies, when I'd had no one left in my life. No family, no friends, no hopes—yet Swaine had given me those and more, in time. He'd shown me respect and allowed me to nurture my own. Knowledge. Confidence. Skills. Expertise. A way of looking at the world. At life. I remember still the very first words Swaine ever spoke to me: *Alive the whole time, were you?* Recalling them does me good, for I know that I shall be, yes—for the rest of my days.

And as for August Swaine, my beloved master, I confess to taking comfort in the belief that he's out there somewhere, even now, exploring the vast rooms within the heavenly mansion. I nurture a small, wavering flame of hope I'll see him again. I'd dearly love to. Perhaps one day, year, or decade from now he'll be weary of unlocking the secrets of the universe, and return.

But knowing my master as I do—which is to say as well as anyone—I rather doubt he'll ever tire of it.

Your humble servant, &c.,
K. Finch

A WORD FROM KEVAN

You're the best—thanks for reading *The Halls of Midnight*! I'm with Finch: Swaine lives, out there somewhere. I genuinely hope you had as much fun reading the trilogy as I had writing it.

Keep up to date on my upcoming books, novellas, and exclusives by joining my private newsletter.

As a welcome, I'll send you a free ebook of *Sorcery of the Stony Heart* (the prequel novella to *The Books of Conjury*), along with *A Spark of Will: The Trans-Atlantic Diary of August Swaine*, an exclusive novelette you can't get anywhere else.

It's easy, just sign up here: **Join Newsletter**

ALSO BY KEVAN DALE

The Books of Conjury Series:

The Magic of Unkindness

The Grave Raven

Sorcery of the Stony Heart

The Books of Conjury: The Complete Trilogy

Horror:

Revolutionary Dead

The Devil's Key

Ghost at Dusk

Horror Box Set:

The Demons of New England: A Horror Collection

Find out more at www.kevandale.com